J.B. was far from happy

He could see that Correll's strategy was already falling to pieces, and he and Mildred were a long way from where they wanted to be—at the side of Ryan and the rest of their companions. The only way to get out of this situation was to be back-to-back with people they could trust. At least that way they all had a chance.

The Armorer straightened his wag and headed toward the gap between the rocks that formed the entrance to the arena. Ahead of him he could see the Summerfield convoy from the rear, but the front was lost in the swirl of the dust storm. Sec men were racing back to their wags, and those who were already mounted turned, blasters at the ready. He could also see sec men standing guard on the top of the supply wags, with homemade flamethrowers. They bore little resemblance to anything the Armorer had ever seen, but he recognized the danger with an unerring instinct.

"Get into position and hold on," he yelled. "This is going to be a little tricky."

JAMES AXLER

DEATH LANDS®

Hellbenders

A GOLD EAGLE BOOK FROM

W RLDWIDE®

TORONTO • NEW YORK • LONDON
AMSTERDAM • PARIS • SYDNEY • HAMBURG
STOCKHOLM • ATHENS • TOKYO • MILAN
MADRID • WARSAW • BUDAPEST • AUCKLAND

First edition March 2004

ISBN 0-373-62575-8

HELLBENDERS

Copyright © 2004 by Worldwide Library.

Printed in U.S.A.

If you prick us, do we not bleed? if you tickle us, do we not laugh? if you poison us, do we not die? and if you wrong us, shall we not revenge?

—William Shakespeare
The Merchant of Venice

THE DEATHLANDS SAGA

This world is their legacy, a world born in the violent nuclear spasm of 2001 that was the bitter outcome of a struggle for global dominance.

There is no real escape from this shockscape where life always hangs in the balance, vulnerable to newly demonic nature, barbarism, lawlessness.

But they are the warrior survivalists, and they endure—in the way of the lion, the hawk and the tiger, true to nature's heart despite its ruination.

Ryan Cawdor: The privileged son of an East Coast baron. Acquainted with betrayal from a tender age, he is a master of the hard realities.

Krysty Wroth: Harmony ville's own Titian-haired beauty, a woman with the strength of tempered steel. Her premonitions and Gaia powers have been fostered by her Mother Sonja.

J. B. Dix, the Armorer: Weapons master and Ryan's close ally, he, too, honed his skills traversing the Deathlands with the legendary Trader.

Doctor Theophilus Tanner: Torn from his family and a gentler life in 1896, Doc has been thrown into a future he couldn't have imagined.

Dr. Mildred Wyeth: Her father was killed by the Ku Klux Klan, but her fate is not much lighter. Restored from predark cryogenic suspension, she brings twentieth-century healing skills to a nightmare.

Jak Lauren: A true child of the wastelands, reared on adversity, loss and danger, the albino teenager is a fierce fighter and loyal friend.

Dean Cawdor: Ryan's young son by Sharona accepts the only world he knows, and yet he is the seedling bearing the promise of tomorrow.

In a world where all was lost, they are humanity's last hope....

Chapter One

The swallowing mire of darkness began to clear. To Dean, it seemed as though the swamp mist on the blackest of moon-clouded nights had begun to lift. The darkness that was all around him began slowly to loosen. He felt life return to his leaden limbs, and most importantly, it seemed to him that his brain began to work properly, bringing him back from the strange worlds of unconsciousness and the deep, dark fears that surfaced during every mat-trans jump.

Feeling a well of nausea in the pit of his stomach, Dean rose slowly on one elbow, moving with care and allowing his tortured frame to adjust to the new equilibrium.

Dean Cawdor was the youngest of the band of seven people gathered in the mat-trans chamber. Sitting upright and risking opening an eye when he felt the spinning in his head begin to recede, the youth looked at his companions. His father, Ryan, was already on his feet, although still looking a little groggy. Dean resembled a younger, leaner version of the man, with only time and harsh experience telling in the few inches of height between them and the older man's more strongly developed musculature.

Dean risked rising to his feet on muscles still a little shaky. He was trembling slightly as he looked around the chamber. They'd obviously all been unconscious for some time, as the disks that usually glowed before and after every jump were flat and colorless. He reached down and grasped his Browning Hi-Power, the blaster that felt so comfortable in his grip it was like an extension of his hand.

"You okay, son?" Ryan asked, the ghost of a smile crossing his face. The curling, dark hair and serious countenance were mirrored in Dean, but the jagged scar that ran the length of the left side of Ryan's face, broken by the eye patch that covered the empty eye socket was courtesy of his brother Harvey, the now deceased former baron of Front Royal.

Dean nodded, then grimaced as the nausea returned at his sudden head movement.

"Take some time—who knows what's out there?" Ryan said, casting a glance at the door of the chamber, which would open out onto...who knew what? Some redoubts they had landed in had been occupied, some deserted, some providing food and shelter, some leaving them almost completely blocked off from the outside world. Beyond the sealed door of the chamber—automatically locked once the old comp terminals put the mat-trans programs into operation—could be anything, and they needed to be fully alert before they could risk taking a look.

Beside Ryan, at his feet and beginning to regain consciousness as he spoke, was Krysty Wroth, Ryan's lover, fellow fighter and friend. A tall, Amazonian woman, she opened startling green eyes on the world, still fogged slightly by the jump.

"That was a bad one, lover," she whispered to Ryan as she began to slowly rise. "It feels like we almost didn't make it." She winced as every muscle in her body protested at her ascent. Her long, flowing red hair hung freely over her shoulders. Ryan noted this, and had a notion that outside the chamber held little in immediate danger: Krysty's hair was sentient, a result of her mutie genes, and could foretell danger ahead. It would curl in tightly to her neck and scalp and warn of any approaching enemies, be they natural or the result of human activity.

"We're here, and we're in one piece," Ryan replied, glancing across again at Dean, who agreed.

"Just about," the younger Cawdor replied.

Looking about, Dean could see that the other four members of the close-knit group that traversed the Deathlands were beginning to come around.

J. B. Dix grunted and stirred, shifting from his slumped position until he was sitting with his back against the wall of the chamber. He reached out for the battered fedora that had slipped from his head and placed it firmly on his crown. Then he reached into one of the capacious pockets of his jacket and withdrew the wire-framed spectacles, without which his vision was dangerously poor. He placed them on the bridge of his nose and pushed them up until they were in place, and he looked around at the chamber.

"Mauve?" he muttered, almost to himself. "Haven't

been many chambers with this color. Mebbe this is a new one."

"Good Lord! Mauve?" muttered a voice beside the Armorer, as Mildred Wyeth began to return to consciousness. J.B., who had replaced his hat and spectacles one-handed, disentangled the fingers of his other hand from Mildred's and began to replace his weapons in their holsters: the Uzi on his back, the Smith & Wesson M-4000 shotgun with its deadly load of barbed metal fléchettes on one thigh and the Tekna knife in the scabbard at his waist. Ryan, who had a SIG-Sauer pistol and Steyr rifle, as well as a razor-sharp panga, already had his weapons ready. Krysty, like Dean, had checked and holstered her .38-caliber Smith & Wesson 640 as a reflex, without even thinking about it.

"How you feelin', Millie?" J.B. asked.

"What sort of an answer you want—the truth, or one where I don't cuss every word?" Mildred replied, her brown eyes showing the humor coming through the agony of awakening. She stretched, the gray pallor of postjump trauma showing through even on her dark skin. Her long beaded plaits shook as she trembled, stretching every muscle that she could persuade to work. "I swear," she said, straining through the effort, "even getting thawed was better than this."

Dr. Mildred Wyeth was one of only two members of the group that had firsthand knowledge of the world before skydark. In the late twentieth century she, as a working doctor herself, had accepted that she would have to have a minor operation. There was no real risk, except that she developed a severe allergic reaction to the anesthetic, and she was cryogenically frozen until the problem could be sorted out. Then there came a bigger problem: the nukecaust. And so Mildred lay frozen for more than a hundred years until she was discovered by Ryan and his companions, who managed to revive her. Waking up into an alien world, Mildred's mental toughness had enabled her to cope with the sudden change, and her old life had also equipped her to cope with the dangers, as she was a crack shot who had been an Olympic medalist for target shooting before the world had been nuked. She soon found that moving, breathing targets were as easy to hit when your life depended on it, and her Czech-made ZKR pistol had become a part of her persona.

Mildred clambered to her feet, swaying slightly as she adjusted to having all her atoms in one piece once more. The part of her that had been a doctor still wondered what the constant tearing apart and reassembling of their constituent atoms was doing to them, but the part of her that had adjusted to the new world figured it was a problem that had, of necessity, to be low on the list of priorities.

Except when she looked across at the two remaining members of the group, and the two who always had the most problems regaining their consciousness and equilibrium after a jump. For different reasons, Jak Lauren and Dr. Theophilus Tanner were at their most physically vulnerable during the period of a mat-trans jump.

Jak moaned, curled up in a fetal position on the floor. Tendrils of his thin, stringy white hair were caked in vomit as it lay across his face, and when he opened his red, albino eyes they were sightless at first. His whipcord-thin body seemed dwarfed by the camou trousers, heavy boots and patched jacket that appeared to swallow up his small frame.

Yet this was deceptive; Jak Lauren was a child of the bayous, whose hunting instincts and ability to chill in a multiplicity of manners had been honed by his early life in the swamplands. He had proved his strength, speed and cunning many times after joining Ryan's band, and his loyalty was beyond question.

Mildred hurried over to Jak, bending to check his pulse. It was strong but erratic. She stepped back as another stream of bile shot from his mouth, and his body convulsed in a spasm of retching.

"Dammit, you nearly got me, Jak," she whispered as she avoided the vomit.

"Sorry," he replied weakly, his eyes coming into focus, "try harder next time."

"You're feeling better, then," she said simply, helping him to sit upright, careful to avoid the hidden jagged metal and pieces of glass sewn into his jacket.

As he adjusted himself into a sitting position, Jak took in his surroundings. "Made it," he said softly.

"Looks like it," Mildred replied, adding, "at least, I think so." She glanced over to where Doc Tanner lay. Beside him lay his weapons: the silver-tipped lion's-head cane with a hidden blade, rapier thin, made of the finest tempered Toledo steel. Next to it sat the ancient LeMat percussion pistol, with its double barrels, one of which was primed for a charge of shot, the other for a ball that was of an incredible diameter and density for such a pistol. They were old weapons, but ones that, in the hands of the skilled Doc Tanner, were deadly.

Theophilus Tanner was, like Mildred, one of the few people in the Deathlands with any firsthand knowledge of the world before skydark. Except that his story was more incredible than anything that any of the companions could have dreamed, and hadn't even come out of the mouth of Tanner himself. Some of the things they had learned about the man had come through chance discoveries in files and records left behind in some of the places they had visited.

Lying on the floor of the chamber with his frock coat wrapped around him and his white mane of hair obscuring his features, Doc could be mistaken—on glimpsing his weathered and lined features—for a man in his sixties. And yet he was only in his late thirties. Doc had been the subject of an experiment by Operation Chronos, a part of the Totality Concept, a U.S. Government project that had been partly responsible for the war that led to the devastation of skydark, and that had bequeathed the redoubts and the mat-trans units to those who came after.

Doc had been born in the late 1860s in a rural part of Vermont, and was a doctor both of science and of philosophy. A happily married man, he had been snatched away from his beloved wife, Emily, and his children, Rachel and Jolyon, by a random time trawl operated by the whitecoat scientists of Operation Chronos. He had fought and struggled, both mentally and physically, with his captors. Doc had become a problem, and the solution was to send him forward in time. Doc had been shot a hundred years into the future, ironically saving him from the fate that soon caught up with his tormentors, but leaving him adrift in a world completely unlike anything he could ever have imagined.

Doc's physical frame showed signs of the stresses of such time travel, but it was his mind that was much more of a concern to those he traveled with. In flashes, Doc was erudite and sharp, but at other times he was in a different world than those around him, and his grasp on reality could be dangerously thin, the silken thread of his psyche perilously close to snapping.

As Mildred attended to him, he mumbled incoherently, his pulse fading in and out with his consciousness, as though he were actually close to just fading away in front of them. Without saying anything, Mildred knew that the others mirrored her thoughts: how many more of these jumps could Doc's mind and body take?

And then, just when she thought that he was about to fade again, his eyes snapped open, the clear blue orbs immediately focused on her.

"By the Three Kennedys," he whispered hoarsely, "I do believe we've arrived safely once more. Perhaps we should stick around, see what's happening."

Ryan looked at Krysty. The ends of her hair were wispy tendrils that began to flutter, as though from the slightest breeze.

There was no movement in the air.

Her green eyes caught his and fixed them with an intent stare. "I don't know," she said hesitantly, with an almost unconscious shake of her head. "I just can't tell right now. I think there's something. It's not danger exactly, more a kind of...distant threat."

The one-eyed man nodded crisply. He trusted Krysty's almost doomielike feelings, and particularly the early-warning system of her hair, which he had come to know over their time together to be an arbiter of threats that she herself may have little idea of.

"Triple red, friends," he cautioned, inclining his head to J.B. The Armorer nodded in return, moving toward the back of the group. They would follow their usual formation: Ryan would lead from the front, followed by Krysty and Jak. Doc, as the most immediately vulnerable, would be kept in the middle, followed by Dean and Mildred. J.B. brought up the rear, and was skilled in the art of keeping their asses covered. Nothing had gotten past the man.

And it seemed as though there would be little to trouble that reputation in this redoubt. Ryan opened the door and stood back. Exiting a chamber into an unknown environment could always be a risk. He lowered his breathing so that the very sound of his central nervous system seemed to deaden within, allowing him to better detect any noises that might come from outside the chamber. His eye flickered across the narrow scope of fire afforded by the door. He could hear or see nothing. Turning his head, he could see Krysty. Her sentient hair hadn't moved, and her steady gaze told him of no danger. He raised an eyebrow as he looked at Jak. The albino hunter had also stilled his breathing, his every sense concentrated on detecting signs of life.

Jak suddenly opened his blood-red orbs, the fire in them burning strong now that he had recovered from the effects of the jump. He shook his head almost imperceptibly.

Ryan, satisfied that there was little danger, but still prepared for any action, tensed his steel-coiled muscles and eased through the door. He had the Steyr up and searching, but the area appeared to be clean. At Ryan's command, his companions left the chamber and filed through the anteroom and into the comp control room.

"No signs of life in here," Ryan began, "but what about outside, lover?"

Krysty pursed her lips. "Something, but not right around here. We need to keep it triple red, though."

J.B. and Jak both looked up at the ceiling together.

"Sec cameras?" the Armorer asked.

"Uh-huh," Jak grunted in reply. "Never know."

As they both looked around, they could see the old vid cameras, but noticed that the winking red lights that usually indicated a working camera were extinguished on all.

"That's good," J.B. commented. "No one's gonna be expecting us."

"I wouldn't bet on that," Dean said softly.

"Why?" J.B. asked, looking over to where Dean had wandered. The youth was near the exit door to the unit, hunkered down and examining something on the floor.

"Take a look at this," Dean said, picking an object off the floor and carrying it over to the rest of the group.

"A self-heat," Mildred said as she got a better glimpse of the object.

It was, indeed, a self-heat. Most redoubts had large supplies of these vacuum-packed foods, sealed in such a way that unwrapping them triggered a reaction in the packaging that heated the food within. They usually tasted terrible, but were always good to plunder from the redoubts as they were manufactured with the preDark sec forces in mind, and so had an emphasis on nutritional and energy value over actual taste. They were invaluable. During their time together, the companions had become all too familiar with the self-heats.

"More than just that," Dean replied. "Take a look at it...a close look."

Doc leaned forward, squinting as he tried to focus hard on the crumpled package. He extended a finger and prodded delicately at the package. He then withdrew his hand and rubbed ruminatively at his fingertip with his other hand.

"Now, that is interesting," he mused softly. "I would not say that it was as recent as today or yesterday, but the remains of that self-heat are dryish but still with a residue of moisture. Enough to put it, in these hermetic conditions, as recently as a week."

"Company, then," Ryan said simply. "They may not be around now, but they aren't going to be far away. Form up and we'll move out. Hopefully they'll have scavenged and then gone, leaving us with at least the chance to take a shower, mebbe some fresh clothes and grab some sleep."

"When was the last time we got that lucky?" Mildred commented wryly.

Ryan allowed himself the briefest flash of humor before shouldering the Steyr and unholstering his pistol.

"Okay, people, you know the drill," he said firmly as they fell into line behind him.

Ryan punched in the 3-5-7 sec code, waiting as the door lifted. Behind him, the others readied themselves for action at any second.

But the corridor beyond the door was still and empty. Ryan stepped out, covering both sides with the SIG-Sauer. He could see nothing along the hundred-yard stretch of corridor in each direction, one end terminating in an elevator, the other in a gently curving bend. He moved into a defensive position behind one of the concrete support pillars that helped to shore up the deep earthworks of the redoubt against the vast pressure of the earth above that bore down on the honeycombed structure.

"Seems quiet," he said softly, beckoning the others to join him. "Reckon we'll be better off taking the tunnel and working our way up rather than try the elevator. Safer."

"Yeah, if there is anyone around, they'll soon be on to us if we get it creaking into action," Mildred concurred, looking at the elevator doors. "At least this way we can keep quiet."

"I don't think we'll need to," Krysty said. "Whatever the problem is, it's not people."

"Somehow, my dear Krysty, I find that not in the slight-est whit reassuring," Doc remarked as he peered toward the curve in the tunnel.

"Stay close on triple-red, people."

They walked carefully along the corridor, rounding the bend in a formation that hugged the wall to keep as much cover as possible. As they did so, they all noticed the un-earthly quiet of the redoubt.

"Something's not right," Ryan said as they paused. "Look at this..." he continued, indicating a part of the wall that seemed to have been recently—and clumsily—re-paired. It was a large, irregular circle, and seemed to have been filled in and then not finished properly. There was also an old girder, salvaged from some other part of the redoubt, used farther along their route to shore up yet an-other section of the wall. And on the floor, surrounding the rough work, were signs of recent habitation—a water canteen left behind, some self-heats and a pool of con-gealed oil that hadn't yet fully soaked into the concrete floor.

"Gotta be some people around to have done this—and fairly recently," J.B. added. "So where are they?"

As if in mocking answer to his question, the tunnel around them seemed to vibrate through its very center, growing more intense in a matter of seconds until the floor was shaking beneath their feet.

"Dark night!" J.B. shouted as the wall of the tunnel in front of him began to disintegrate in a shower of powdered concrete.

Chapter Two

"Fireblast! What the hell is happening?" Ryan yelled as he tried to keep his feet. The vibration in the tunnel continued to shake the floors and walls, crumbling concrete dust and flaking plaster, a light rain of those materials making visibility suddenly difficult and even painful as the abrasive mist scratched at their eyes.

In the confusion it was almost impossible for anyone in the group to tell exactly what was happening. One thing was for sure—they needed to regroup and stick close together. Without Ryan even having to give the command, Dean and J.B., who had wandered farthest from the formation, began to make their unsteady way back toward the others.

"Surely we have not come this far to fall prey to something as simple and neutral as an earthquake," Doc said, almost to himself.

"Could have been worse—could have been floods," Ryan replied, although Doc's exclamation had required no answer.

But it was Mildred who, in the flash of a second, knew what Doc meant. It crossed her mind, as it always did when they faced such problems, that they had taken and fought their way past so many man-made obstructions on their path, so many who would wish to chill them for no good reason, that it seemed as though the scales of justice were unfairly tipped for them to take their last bow at the mercy of the earth itself. Yet, given their location and the factors that had made the earth itself so unstable, was that not a man-made obstruction?

This crossed her mind in the time it took her to move closer to the pack, finding herself beside Jak as J.B. and Dean closed in. Doc, Ryan and Krysty stood a few yards away.

A crucial few yards.

The earth rumbled around them. The stressed steel girders supporting the concrete pillars that had stood firm for so long against the outside pressure of rock began to sing and screech with the torsion that made them begin to bend within the concrete itself. The large gaps in the surrounding walls that had seemed hairline cracks a few minutes earlier began to assume the proportions of gaping maws. The hurried repair to the walls that they had passed a few yards back fell out with a loud bang, tumbling to the shaking floor and breaking into a myriad of pieces that danced across the unsteady surface.

"Try to stay on your feet," Ryan yelled above the noise. "Move toward the next level—mebbe it's localized."

As an option, all the companions knew that it was grasping at nonexistent straws. The intensity of the vibration here was such that it was highly unlikely to have abated if they could make their way up the sloping tunnel to an upper level. The earth shifts, they knew from experience, were stronger the deeper you went, but this was too harsh to suddenly drop away in an ascent of less than a hundred feet.

That was always assuming they could make any progress at all before the pressure of the shifting rocks caved in the redoubt tunnel. Every step forward seemed to take them three steps back as they tried to move on the unstable floor.

J.B. led the way as he was nearest the ascending path. The inclines in the tunnel slopes were always relatively gentle, to allow the internal use of some maintenance vehicles, so the ascent by slope would be of necessity slower than by the elevator—useless in the current circumstances—or by the emergency stairwell, which they didn't have time to find.

Jak and Dean were at J.B.'s heels. Mildred hung back and stopped for a second to look behind, a vague awareness hitting her that she could hear or feel no one immediately to her rear. Krysty and Ryan were some way behind, helping Doc, who had lost his balance and crashed to the tunnel floor. Hoisting him with a hand under each of his arms, Ryan and Krysty had propelled him forward as he hit the upright, hoping to give him some impetus. Thus, Doc was coming toward Mildred at some speed. His balance still looked precarious, and Mildred took another step toward him in order to try to steady and assist him. Although she called him a mad old buzzard, and could be exasperated by his wandering mind at times, Mildred had a grudging liking for the older man—perhaps because he, like herself, represented an earlier age set adrift, and they were both strangers in this strange land.

It was a step that was to prove decisive. Doc was a few yards from her, keeping his balance well, the intense concentration showing on his face. Mildred was focused on him, which may explain why neither of them noticed that the wall of the tunnel to one side was suddenly beginning to break up with a spiderweb pattern that resembled a cracking glass.

Mildred felt a sudden rush of air almost simultaneously with the hail of tiny concrete shards that sailed across the breadth of the tunnel, completely obscuring Doc from view. Where a moment before she had a clear view of the old man as he ran stumblingly toward her, she now saw nothing but gray and darkness. Some of the shards that flew out from the main cluster hit her on the head and upper body. She felt a numbing blow on her face and stinging on her hands. There was no pain, but her eyes filled with blood from what she figured was a superficial scalp wound. The problem was, with the dust and concrete rain, the blood was now making it almost impossible for her to see. Her torso had been protected by her fatigue jacket, for which she was grateful. She had felt the concrete chips rip at her clothing, but they had caused no pain.

At least she was still conscious. She moved her arm to wipe the blood from her eyes and realized that everything seemed to be moving in slow motion. Hell, she was even thinking in slow motion...a cold wave of nausea and fear swept through her gut as she realized that the blow to her head had affected her more than she had thought, and that she was now lying on the floor of the tunnel, mildly concussed but enough to slow her actions to a possibly fatal degree. The tunnel was vibrating much less, as though the pressure had been released by the sudden explosion.

And then the mist cleared for a moment as she wiped her eyes, and she thought that the blow had to have rendered her mad, as well as concussed.

For Doc Tanner, too, the sudden hail of concrete had come as something of a shock. One moment he had been moving toward the good Dr. Wyeth, who was holding out a hand to help him maintain his equilibrium, as well as his momentum; the next moment a force much greater than his own had hit him full in the body, arresting his forward motion and flinging him back, as though he had run straight into a wall. He felt rather than saw the hail of concrete that passed before him, stray shards like an abrasive rain that showered over his face and body, plucking at his clothes and breaking the skin of his face and hands in several places. The wind knocked solidly from his body, Doc collapsed to the ground. He hadn't been quite as near the point of impact as Mildred, and so wasn't as concussed. Nonetheless, time did seem to run a little slower than he had expected as he tried to gather his thoughts and marshal his actions. For instance, he had noticed that the tunnel had ceased to shake.

When he looked up and saw what had made the impact, and what had caused the cessation of the vibrations, he truly believed for one second that he had lost all possession of his senses.

For the thing that both Mildred and Doc saw from their prone positions was quite unlike anything that either of them had seen during their travels—or hoped that they would ever see.

It was moving quite slowly, which was hardly surprising given the size and construction of the creature. It was immense in size, possibly fifteen feet in diameter, and with a pale and almost translucent flesh that seemed to move independently in every part. The smell of the oozing mucus that covered and moisturized every part of the flesh was intense within the tunnel, filling their nostrils with its stench even though one breath had made both, independently, decide to try to breathe as little as possible while it was crossing the floor.

The giant mutie creature, from the shape that was just about discernible, and from the length that could only be estimated, as part of it was still concealed in the wall, seemed to be some kind of earth- or sandworm. In the glistening ooze that covered the pale flesh, large ring segments could just about be distinguished, and it had no features at the front of its body, just an open maw with teeth that were double rowed around the almost perfect circle of its mouth, seemingly made of matter little harder than the flesh.

Not that either Mildred or Doc wished to discover the

truth of this. Both were still, partly from shock and their injuries, and partly from the sudden numbing fear of encountering something so alien.

The mutie creature had obviously been burrowing through the earth, and the tunnel of the redoubt was just a tunnel that crossed its path at one point. Now the huge hole that had been badly repaired back along the tunnel was explained. The casts of the giant worm also accounted for some of the material used to block the hole that had seemed to be unidentifiable: whoever had repaired the hole had used some of the cast to help block the gap and seal it. Who that could be was a question for another time. For now, the only thing that mattered was the giant worm before them.

The sudden and violent vibration of the tunnel was now explained—a localized disturbance caused by the approach and passing of the worm as it ate its way through the earth and rock. That would explain why the tunnel and the mat-trans chamber were still in one piece, and it would account for why this level was deserted even though there were general signs of habitation. If the appearances by the worms were of any frequency, it would perhaps be much safer to stay at a higher level of the redoubt.

And no surprise. As the worm turned its front end, showing its teeth and maw, it was an awesome and appalling sight. It seemed to have no eyes, but had to surely have some kind of sensory equipment. If so, could it detect their presence, and did it see them as a threat?

Standing back behind Doc, Ryan and Krysty had instinctively raised the blasters they held. On the other side, Dean, Jak and J.B. had done likewise. It was a tense waiting game. Would the worm attack, or would it just move on, sensing no threat to itself?

The stench grew overpowering in the suddenly cramped confines of the tunnel. The odor also carried with it the heat of the giant, elongated body. The worm was partially in the tunnel and partially in the hole in the wall, leaving them with little idea as to its actual length. The flabby, pulpy body had just flopped down from the hole in the wall as the burrowing creature had hit empty air, the flesh plopping heavily to the concrete floor. The oozing mucus would leave a trail in the creature's wake, and as it was currently static, the clear, viscous fluid spread out from beneath it toward Mildred on one side and Doc on the other.

J.B. and Jak held their fire, the Armorer drawing in his breath as he watched the creature turn what had to pass for its head, eerily soundless for something of that size. C'mon, move, you bastard, he urged silently, hoping that it wouldn't notice Mildred as she lay there, still a little dazed.

Seeing the creature move its front end her way, and still not being fully in control of her faculties, Mildred did the one thing that, under any other circumstance, she wouldn't: she scrabbled backward, trying to escape from the mutie's maw. If she had been one hundred percent her usual self, Mildred would have figured that to move would draw attention to herself, whereas to stay still would hopefully mean that the sightless creature wouldn't notice her presence.

But Mildred was still dazed and concussed, and a deep-rooted fear instinct took over. She didn't even scramble to her feet. Lifting herself on her arms from behind, and taking purchase on the floor with her heels, she scuttled backward crablike.

The noise and movement seemed to attract the attention of the giant mutie, even though it was impossible to tell how it could have noticed. The front end and maw moved downward and toward Mildred. With no eyes, it was impossible to tell whether this was a threatening, or merely a curious, gesture. But one thing was for sure—it was too close to be comfortable with it.

Instinct took over in Dean. He raised his Browning Hi-Power blaster and snapped off two shots toward the mutie's maw. The slugs hit home, thudding into the viscous mass of the creature with a sickeningly slushy sound that was audible after the crack of the blaster shots. The creature obviously felt the impact in some way, however its central nervous system—assuming it actually had one—worked. It reared into the air so that it took up the whole of the tunnel, its foremost extremity brushing against the roof of the concrete construction.

"Hot pipe," Dean breathed, "that should have taken out its brain."

"Who says it has one?" J.B. replied sharply. "We need to hold it back while Millie gets away."

Even as he spoke, the Armorer raised the barrel of his

Uzi, flicking to rapid fire and bracing the stock against his body, his legs spread to anchor himself to the floor. He sent a stream of hot metal into the body of the beast, spraying it so that it rippled with the wave of impact. It thrashed its head, moving slightly backward and enabling Mildred, still scrambling toward them, to get some distance between her and the giant mutie.

Jak and Dean, equipped with handblasters that would need reloading more quickly than J.B.'s Uzi, took their shots with more care. Dean aimed for the end of the creature with the open maw, looking to place more shots within the beast. Jak took the end that disappeared into the tunnel wall, looking to rip holes in it with the slugs from the .357 Magnum Colt Python, the shots roaring from his revolver.

The creature showed no sign of emotion, made no sound, but was clearly enraged by this attack as it reared back under the initial impact, then ignored the repeated hits about its body and began to slither toward the group of four, Mildred now joining them on her feet, directing shots from the ZKR toward the beast.

J.B. wondered if a gren tossed into the maw would disable the creature, but had no idea where Ryan, Krysty and Doc were on the other side of the beast. The last thing he wanted was to bring down part of the corridor along with the mutie, thus blocking them off.

On the other side of the creature, Doc had regained his feet and had retreated a few steps to be nearer to Ryan and Krysty as the mutie moved in the opposite direction. Although it blocked all view of anything on its far side, the noise of the blasterfire and the direction of its movement made it totally clear what was happening.

"I fear that the creature will be impervious to bullets," Doc said quickly, "and if it is a mutation of the species I believe it to be, then the worst thing John Barrymore could do would be to use a gren."

"Why?" Ryan queried.

Doc looked astonished. "But my dear boy, a whole host of worms rather than one?"

"But smaller, Doc," Ryan replied. "Easier to chill and drive off. Anyway, too risky to use a gren. Could bring down the corridor."

"Then what?" Krysty exclaimed. "We can't leave them."

"No, but we can distract that bastard, mebbe drive it back into its hole if it doesn't know where to turn," the one-eyed warrior said, holstering the SIG-Sauer and un-slinging his Steyr.

Krysty and Doc both agreed, and as Ryan loosed a round from the rifle, Krysty began to fire steadily with her Smith & Wesson revolver, while Doc gave the creature a charge of shot.

Attacked on both sides, its flesh irritated and torn, the confused giant mutie worm began to turn toward the group headed by Ryan, before another wave of fire from the other side made it swing around again.

Each side poured round after round into the creature, cursing it for the waste of every precious shell, but knowing that there was no other way to defeat it.

Still turning from side to side, the creature began to slither back into its hole, its maw the last thing to disappear. Its speed was the greater for it only having to slide back through the empty rock, its last cast some distance back.

The companions ceased fire as the corridor gave a little shudder and tremor at the passing of the creature back into the rock from whence it had come. Finally, both sides could see each other once more.

"Shit, don't want that sort of trouble too often," Mildred said, still shaking her head to clear it. "Bet you're pissed at losing all those rounds, John."

The Armorer gave her a grim smile. "We're not too bad. I kinda hope whoever's been here hasn't cleaned out the armory, though."

Jak inclined his head. He spoke softly after a few seconds. "Mebbe know sooner than want—hear someone on move."

Chapter Three

"How far?" Ryan asked of the albino.

"Two levels up—coming fast now," Jak replied, his eyes shut tight as he listened carefully for noises that the others couldn't detect.

"And I don't think they're particularly friendly, lover," Krysty added softly. A swift glance from Ryan to the woman confirmed this, as her sentient hair was closing to her neck and scalp, detectable even as he watched.

J.B. had been pondering as this exchange took place, and turned to Ryan. "If this redoubt is like the others, then the armory and dispensary are two floors up, and the next level is where the dorms and showers are."

"And the kitchens," Ryan added, nodding his agreement.

"Great." Mildred grimaced, allowing a shaft of blackened humor to penetrate the conversation, "at least we can try to beat them to death with a cooking pot."

Ryan snorted. "Yeah, great option. How much ammo we got, J.B.?"

The Armorer looked into the canvas and leather bag he had habitually slung over his back. The bag contained the companions' spare ammo and grens.

Ryan knew what the set look on the Armorer's face meant before the man even mouthed the words.

"I'd say we've got enough, in a decent firefight, to last us about five minutes before it's all used. We need to find an armory of some kind...or else chill those coldhearts up there with every shot counting."

"But we've still got the grens," Dean said. "What d'you reckon?"

J.B. looked up at the ceiling of the tunnel, turning his head with a slowness that seemed somehow overly luxurious when an enemy was so near.

"Can't risk the grens down here," he said decisively. "There's too many cracks already in the walls, and if there have been a shitload of those worms crawling through here, then the whole area could be shot through like wormwood. One gren in the wrong place and the only chilling there'll be will be our own."

"Guess that settles that," Ryan said. "The amount of firefighting we did with that mutie worm bastard, they're gonna know we're down here. This has got no cover at all, so let's get going. Shape up, people."

Blasters ready, they fell into formation and moved forward. Ryan took the lead, with Jak moving up to join him and keep his senses alert for the location of the enemy. Krysty came next, with Doc just behind, reloading the LeMat as they moved. Dean and Mildred followed, with J.B. bringing up the rear, switching from the Uzi to the M-4000. He had more cartridges packed with the deadly barbed-metal fléchettes, and figured that they could inflict more confusion and damage at close range than Uzi fire. Besides, in such a situation he would have to switch the Uzi to single shot rather than rapid fire.

The curving corridor was doglegged as it moved upward, enabling the incline to be relatively gentle and for the slope to need less space underground, allowing rooms and units to lead off it. It was good for the companions, as it didn't make great demands on their calf muscles, sapping strength. But the downside was that it had more than its fair share of blind corners, and Ryan kept the pace slow as they moved up. He kept his eye firmly on Jak, who would indicate with the briefest shake of his white mane that the enemy was still on the descent, and not around the corner.

It was a race against time. Ryan wanted to find a position that provided cover before the descending enemy came either head-on into them or was able to establish a position of cover first, and be able to pick off the approaching companions.

At each corner, the sinews and cords in the one-eyed man's neck tightened and bulged as he concentrated every muscle, every instinct, every reaction to be ready for the onslaught. But the expected attack didn't come. Ryan's gut feeling was that whoever was in charge of the approaching force was of the same opinions as himself, and was playing odds on whether the oncoming companions were to rush straight in, or establish cover.

"Slowed down," Jak whispered hoarsely to Ryan. "Not far."

The one-eyed warrior assented. They had reached the next level of the redoubt, the incline on the slope leveling out onto a flat floor. Ahead of them a sec door was open, its red coloring just showing at the side of the wall, disappearing into a concrete pillar that also contained the housing for the sec door release mechanism.

On this side of the door, to their right, lay a dormitory, a shower room to the left. Both doors were closed.

Ryan signaled for the companions to slow, indicating the concrete support that arched across the circumference of the tunnel. They were to split into two groups. Ryan took himself, Krysty, Jak and Doc to the left, while Dean, Mildred and J.B. split off to the right, assuming positions that kept them close to the wall, taking advantage of the scant cover provided by the concrete pillar.

"Jak, think you can take out that room, see if we're alone here—and quick?" Ryan asked.

Jak nodded, a grin splitting his scarred and pitted white visage.

On the other side, J.B. had guessed exactly what Ryan was telling the albino, even though the one-eyed man had deliberately kept his voice low, in case the rooms were, in fact, occupied. The Armorer turned to Dean and Mildred.

"We need to see if those rooms are free. Ryan's sending Jak into the shower room. I'll take the dorm."

"I'll do it. I may be quicker," Dean said, his dark eyes glittering with the fire of battle. It took the Armorer less than a fraction of a second to decide. With a nod, he indicated to Dean that he could take on the task.

Dean and Jak glanced at each other across the breadth of the tunnel. Jak held up a white hand, skin almost pearlescent in the fluorescent overhead lighting. Three fingers were erect. Jak curled one, then two, and then the third, bunching them into a fist.

Dean caught the count immediately: three...two... one...and now.

As one, the two young men sprang from their stations behind the pillar, their companions ready to cover them should any fire be drawn by their sudden action.

There was none. Within seconds, each youth was in front of the room he had to recce and secure.

It was bizarre that many rooms in redoubts that didn't house comp equipment or supplies like the armory or the dispensary hadn't been fitted with sec doors. Perhaps, in the distant days before skydark, this was the result of a bureaucrat penny-pinching on the black budget of the Totality Concept. But all that it meant for Jak and Dean was that they didn't have to punch in a sec code and wait for the door to creep open at the slow speed usually favored by the creaking and worn-out systems.

Jak didn't bother with the smooth knob of the door in front of him. Raising one combat-booted foot, he used every ounce of strength in the wiry muscles of his calf and thigh to crash his foot into the area of the door just below the chromium. The thin metal of the door crumpled, the fragile lock, which was a simple Yale in design—giving under the sudden stress. The door flew back, slamming hard against the wall with a crash. If anyone had been waiting behind it for Jak to enter, then the force of it would have stunned them.

Not that the albino cared about that at this precise moment. Even before the door had reached the wall, he had adjusted his balance and taken a flying leap into the darkened shower room, somersaulting in the air and making himself a hard target to hit.

The fact that there was no light within the room was of no hindrance to Jak. In dim or darkened conditions his pigmentless red eyes were better adjusted to the gloom. He had spent much of his early youth in the bayou hunting by night, and his instincts had evolved to the point where it was possible for him to become almost at one with the shadows.

The shower room itself resembled a locker room, where it was possible to dry off and change clothes, the towels and soap being kept in freestanding metal cabinets. Through a narrow channel was the tiled shower area, where the actual showers were a series of self-contained cubicles.

Plenty of places for an enemy to hide, but also plenty of places for Jak to take cover.

The .357 Magnum Colt Python blaster was in his fist as he emerged upright from the somersault, his trigger finger resting lightly on the guard. He adjusted it without thinking, so that he was ready to squeeze off a shot if necessary. In his other hand, which he held palm up, lay one of his razor-sharp leaf-bladed throwing knives. As he shifted, weight forward on the balls of his feet to facilitate rapid motion, a shaft of light from the corridor outside caught the blade, its edges glittering. Without even registering that he had noticed this, Jak shifted the angle of his hand so that the light no longer caught on the blade.

The room was silent, and Jak couldn't detect any sign of an enemy, not even the merest whisper of breath. He scanned the room, his eyes taking in the shadows. They were constant; nothing was moving in here. Satisfied that the room was empty, but still keeping triple alert lest the opposition be as skillful in the art of hunting as himself, Jak moved lightly and quickly to the shower cubicles themselves.

Normally he would have taken each in turn, opening the doors and investigating each. But time was of the essence, and at this juncture he had to marry speed with stealth, a marriage that was not always satisfactory to the equal use of both.

With a yelping screech that he knew, from past experience, would both frighten and surprise anyone lurking in the shower cubicles, Jak threw himself forward into a series of rolls, straining every thigh and calf muscle on the upward thrust in order to propel himself forward without losing impetus, and also to throw out one combat-booted foot and crash open the door to each shower stall as he passed it. All the while his Colt Python stayed focused and aimed at the stalls and cubicles as he passed them, finger loose on the trigger to prevent accidents, but the tendons like coiled springs that would squeeze on instinct within a fraction of a second.

If intruders were hiding in any of the cubicles, the force of the door being kicked back in their face, and the sudden appearance and noise that Jak had caused, would have been enough to cause them to attack.

Jak came up against the wall, landing in a squatting position with his back to the wall, his blaster and knife swiveling toward any point of attack.

There was nothing. It would seem that the stalls were empty. Rising swiftly and easily to his feet, Jak skipped back past the stalls, turning to face each as he passed, the Colt Python trained on the empty space, lest there was a lurking enemy with the patience and cunning that he possessed. But there was nothing except empty space.

Jak ran from the cubicle, sidling up against the wall until he reached the concrete pillar that provided shelter for Ryan and Krysty.

"Clear," he said simply.

Meanwhile, Dean had been tackling the dormitories.

The younger Cawdor didn't have Jak's speed and sharpened hunting instincts, but he did have the quickness of youth and a sense of battle that he had inherited from his father, which had been sharpened by the time he had spent with the companions.

Dean's approach to the closed door was more subtle than Jak's. He didn't have the acrobatic skill to attempt a similar kind of entry, so he opted for a different approach. Flattening himself against the wall to one side of the door, Dean closed his hand around the chromium doorknob and twisted it, flicking his powerful wrist so that the door was also propelled backward. Before the lock had even clicked, his hand was back across his chest, safe from any fire that may have greeted the first movement of the door.

Nothing came forth, and the door opened on a darkened room—not that he was aware of this. He hadn't, as yet, taken a look. Instead, he took three deep breaths, concentrating his attention on the task ahead. He knew the layouts of these dorm rooms from previous redoubts. If the room had been changed by the inhabitants, then he had a problem. That was just a chance he would have to take.

Dean swooped low, turning and throwing himself into the room at an angle, his body crouched low. The trajectory would make him difficult to hit, and he knew where he was headed.

Luck was with him. Whoever inhabited the redoubt either hadn't moved anything in the dorms, or never used them. Because the metal storage locker—in which spare bedding was usually stored—was exactly where he had guessed it would be, offering him some degree of cover as it rested almost snug to two walls. Almost. The gap was enough for him to squeeze into, covering him on three sides and enabling him to take in the rest of the room.

The dormitory was a large space with beds running in rows, small lockers between each bed. The beds themselves were high, with narrow metal shafts for legs that gave plenty of room underneath for any enemy to use as a crawl space. The room was rectangular, with no other nooks or crannies for anyone to secrete themselves.

From his position, Dean was able to take in the room

at a glance. It seemed to be empty, and where the open door let a shaft of light pour into the room, there was an illumination that aided him immensely, casting a light over any enemy position while keeping him still in shadow.

Though it seemed empty, there were still a few pools of shadow where the light had failed to penetrate. These would have to be dealt with.

Dean left his position and dropped to his belly, the Browning Hi-Power blaster held in front of him. Using his feet, he pushed off from the wall and started to crawl under the beds, using his shadow cover to surprise anyone he might come across. Despite every sense telling him that the dorm was empty, he had to make certain.

It was a swift process. Dean moved through the shadows and light with ease, encountering no obstacles. The dorm, like the shower room, was empty.

As Dean reached the last of the beds, he rose fluidly to his feet and slipped out of the room, staying close to the wall as he moved back to where J.B., Doc and Mildred were waiting.

"It's empty," he breathed as he moved back into cover behind the pillar and indicated the same to his father, standing opposite, with a gesture.

The one-eyed man nodded curtly. It was time to put his plan into action. Gesturing to J.B., he indicated that they should move out from behind the pillar and take the empty rooms to establish a base of operations. And there was little time. The approaching enemy was now audible to all the companions, not just Jak. The advancing force seemed to be small, and was moving slowly. It wasn't hard to guess that they were taking the corridor section by section, as well, not underestimating how difficult and smart their enemy may be. This gave the companions enough time to move, but suggested to them that they may be in for a small war of attrition rather than a straightforward fire-fight.

Looking ahead, both Ryan and J.B. could see that the corridor was clear at present, but about a hundred yards ahead of the sec door was a sharp bend that presented them with a blind spot. The sec door itself was about twenty yards distant, giving them a total of about 120 yards between themselves and any enemy sighting.

It wasn't a lot of distance, and it didn't buy them a lot of time.

Ryan and J.B. swung out from their cover in unison, J.B. clutching the M-4000 and Ryan holding the Steyr SSG-70. They would provide covering fire as Jak and Dean, followed by Mildred and Krysty, and finally Doc moved around them and into the empty rooms. Jak and Dean provided cover while Ryan and J.B. moved forward to join them.

The unseen enemy force was stealthy, but was gaining ground. The first group tentatively rounded the bend, risking the blind corner.

J.B. raised the M-4000 and fired into the middle of the group of three. They consisted of two men and a woman, all of whom were moving low, trying to present as small a target as possible. Two of them had blasters that looked from this distance to be Heckler & Koch G-12 caseless rifles, of the type that were sometimes found in the redoubts. The woman was carrying a 12-gauge, double-barreled shotgun. The Armorer took it in at a glance and wondered, at the back of his mind, how she had come across what appeared to be a Purdey, a rare and beautiful thing to J.B., and something that he had thought never to see, though he had read of them.

This thought stayed in his mind as the approaching enemy raised their blasters. He let fly with a cartridge from the M-4000, the explosion of the scattergun sounding large off the low ceiling of the redoubt tunnel. The air was filled with the heat and smell of the charge, and the load of barbed metal fléchettes found its target with ease, spreading out over the hundred or so yards to the target.

The three approaching people were hit by hot, barbed metal that tore into exposed flesh and ripped through the motley collection of clothing they wore. The man in the center took the majority of the charge. His scream of agony as the metal hit his face and chest was choked off by the blood that flooded into his throat and lungs as arteries were ripped and torn by the metallic onslaught. The force of the impact threw him backward, the H&K flying away from him.

Instinctively, the woman threw up her arms to protect her face, the Purdey raised above her head as she did so. Fléchettes bit into the area of her chest and stomach exposed by the movement, the thin material of her shirt and undershirt providing no protection as they were shredded to ribbons by the hot metal, ripping into her flesh and scoring the breastbone and ribs beneath. She crumpled, gasping for breath in lungs that had been lacerated by the barbs, unable to draw any air into her shattered rib cage.

The man on the far side was slightly quicker. He managed to loose off one shot from the H&K that hit the ceiling above J.B.'s head, dislodging chips of concrete and making the Armorer duck his head as the concrete dust rained down. But there was no chance for a second chance, as the fléchettes again found their target, taking out the man at the shoulder, ripping into flesh and severing tendons, causing him to drop the H&K and stumble in agony into the wall. Sliding down, he used his free arm to try to staunch the flow of blood from his shattered arm and shoulder.

J.B. pulled back into the cover of the dorm as the next wave followed. The enemy had dropped lower, using their fallen comrades as cover, loosing off shots that were intended to drive J.B. back rather than hit him.

Looking ahead, Ryan squinted, trying to count the number of the opposition. Three were down, and four had come into play behind them. He caught the glimpse of movement from the angle of the tunnel and felt sure there were at least two more in reserve.

So they had been outnumbered to begin with. J.B.'s opening volley had leveled the field a little, but the number of people lurking around the corner was an unknown quantity.

With ammunition running low and the possible numbers unknown, there was only one move that Ryan could see as viable at this point. He turned to Jak and Krysty.

"I'm going to try and close the sec door," he said softly. "It leaves us trapped behind here, but at least those coldhearts will have to be the ones opening the door again, making them vulnerable."

"We'll cover you," Krysty replied in an equally low tone. "But what about the others? We can't tell them without making those bastards out there aware of what we're doing."

Ryan grinned. It was mirthless and almost vulpine. "Just cover me, lover. J.B.'ll soon pick up on it."

With that, Ryan shouldered the Steyr and unleathered the SIG-Sauer. He would need a blaster for his own cover and safety while he was out there, and as he planned to punch in the sec code, a handblaster represented the best option.

"Okay?" Jak said, standing ready at the doorway. Across the hall, through the open door of the dorms, Ryan could see J.B. and Dean. He gestured with his blaster, and the Armorer gave him the briefest nod of understanding.

In the corridor, all was quiet. Uncannily so, given that there were seven people in the two side rooms, and at least nine people at the bend of the tunnel—although two of those were chilled, and the only sound that broke the silence was the low moan from the survivor of the first wave, now almost delirious and drifting close to unconsciousness from loss of blood.

The silence was about to be broken. Ryan, standing where he could be seen from the opposing door, indicated with a slight inclination of his head that he was about to leave the shower room.

J.B. and Jak swung into place at the edge of the door, and on a mental count of three both men swung out and laid down a covering fire as the one-eyed man darted from the doorway, under Jak, and headed for the sec door panel.

The sudden movement caught the opposition off guard, and there was a second of silence before the opening fire was returned. The enemy was torn between firing at Jak and J.B., or trying to pick off Ryan as he moved rapidly along the wall. He had twenty yards to make, and only a couple of seconds in which to do it.

"Dammit, he's going for the door. Concentrate on One-eye!"

The voice had been low and drawling, but had carried a steely authority that cut through the noise of the blaster-fire. Ryan mentally marked that down as the voice of the opposition leader as he reached the panel.

"Try to take out the panel," the voice called over the fire, and suddenly Ryan found that the only threat he faced was that of ricochets and flying concrete chips as the fire became less heavy, and concentrated solely on taking out the panel on the other side of the sec door.

Fireblast, the one-eyed warrior thought, the man's smarter than I thought. For Ryan knew that the closed door put the opposition at a disadvantage, and the best way to stop the door closing, at that distance, was to try to disable the mechanism rather than chill him. If the panel on the other side was shot up, then the door's closing mechanism would jam.

By this time, Ryan had reached the panel and was tapping in the sec code, hoping that his luck would hold and that some sharpshooter on the opposing side wouldn't get lucky. J.B. and Jak were doing their best to tilt the odds by laying down a covering fire that was preventing the opposing marksmen from being able to take full aim.

Sweat dripped down the one-eyed man's forehead as he punched the last digit of the code, stinging his good eye and running into the empty socket behind the eye patch.

"Work, dammit, work," he gritted as the last digit was entered, and the door began to creak into action, moving from its housing in the wall. Ryan flattened himself against the wall, sheltered from any real danger by the pillar housing the control panel. He had the SIG-Sauer leveled, barrel pointing slightly downward, ready to blast anyone who may be so foolish as to try to spring into action before the door closed. He just hoped it would close fully; otherwise it would leave a gap someone could fire through, and would make it difficult for him to retreat back to cover.

Jak and J.B. had ceased firing once the door reached halfway closed, unwilling to waste any more ammo than was necessary. The opposition obviously felt the same, as the blasterfire from their side decreased to the odd shot.

The door creaked the last few inches and came to rest on the wall, effectively sealing them off from their enemy.

Tentatively, the companions emerged from the two rooms to join Ryan, who was now standing before the door, able at last to relax the muscles that ached with the tension of battle.

"So what now?" Mildred asked.

"Ah, now that is the question, is it not?" Doc said, leaning on his sword stick. "I believe we are in what is commonly referred to as stalemate."

"What?" Dean asked with a puzzled expression.

Doc favored the youth with an indulgent look. "Ah, my dear boy, it is something that comes from a time before this. Once, when men could afford to take time out from the affairs of the world, there was a game of skill and tactics called chess. The object, as in all games, was for one of the competitors to win. But—and here's the rub—if both players were equally matched, then often the game would end with neither in a position to win."

"Sorry, Doc, but I don't see what that's got to do with a stale mate...." Dean pronounced it as two separate words, and looked to the others for assistance.

"The old game survived some," Krysty said quietly. "Mother Sonja and Uncle Tyas McCann would play for days back in Harmony. You see, Dean, to get in a winning position would be mate. To win totally would be checkmate. But to be stuck in a position where it was impossible for either to win would be stalemate."

"And that's just where we are," Ryan added. "Stuck."

The one-eyed man took a step back and surveyed the sec door. There was nothing else they could do now except wait. If their enemies on the other side wanted to attack them, they would have to operate the door and so give the companions the opportunity to take their covering positions and pick them off as the door opened. But they couldn't go forward without risking the same. Their defensive position was secured, but at the expense of moving farther up the redoubt. Their only option would be retreat to the mat-trans.

An uneasy few minutes ensued on both sides of the sec door, as the leader of the opposing force was having similar thoughts to those of Ryan. Except for one extra fact that was bothering him intensely. How the hell had these people gotten into the old place that was his camp? For his people occupied the upper levels and didn't risk coming too far down because of the giant worms and the damage they caused. It made the lower levels too unstable to live in safely. So mebbe there was some other way into the tunnels from the outside that they didn't know about.

"Hey! You on the other side! Only one of you I've seen is One-eye, but I guess from the blasterfire that there's more of you back there—you wanna talk?"

Ryan exchanged glances with the other companions. J.B. shrugged. Krysty gave a noncommittal shrug, but her hair hadn't tensed any more. Dean and Jak wore skeptical expressions. Mildred shook her head gently, muttering, "See what the guy has to say. We don't have to open the door to hear it, right?"

Doc smiled broadly. "I would say it was an excellent sign, my dear Ryan," he whispered urgently. "After all, the fact that the gentleman is willing to exchange in dialogue suggests a certain intelligence, does it not?"

"Guess so," the one-eyed warrior said quietly. Then, more loudly, "Okay, what you got to say? You started, so you go first."

"Strikes me that we've got ourselves in a stupid situation," the drawling, low voice said. "See, we live here, and when we hear a firefight going on, we've got to look after our territory, see that we're safe. And you? Well, way I see it is that you don't know who the hell we are and you've gotta see you're safe. So we had a firefight and you chilled Janny and Ken. Cy, he's probably gonna be okay eventually...time'll tell. But that don't mean we need to chill you to get our pride back, y'see that?"

"Fine words, but how can we trust you? How can you trust us?" Ryan queried.

"Fair point, my friend," the voice said.

"I'm not your friend yet," Ryan countered. "I don't like shouting through this bastard thick door, so let's get to it."

"Okay," came the response. Yet, despite the thickness of the metal sec door, the man on the other side didn't seem to have to shout for his voice to be heard clearly. "Let me ask you something, stranger. I don't think you came in through some tunnel that we don't know about."

"That's not a question," Ryan countered.

"No. So how about if I ask you if you got into the tunnels through that place where all the colored lights flicker and change all the time?"

Ryan was momentarily stunned to silence. Had this man guessed the secret of the mat-trans that they were among the few to know?

"Why do you say that?" Ryan asked slowly.

"Because it's old tech and it still works...must, otherwise the lights wouldn't be working. We've got some idea of how bits work, but the rest of it is still a mystery."

Ryan paused before answering. A lot would hinge on his next few words. He obviously paused a little too long, as his opposing number was spurred to speech, perhaps making Ryan's decision easier.

"Hell, don't clam up on me now," the low drawl said with a vaguely sardonic undercurrent. "Listen, I'm kind of like the baron around here, though we're too small to be a ville. The name's Joe Correll, and I'll tell you as much as this. We know all this stuff comes from before skydark, and we can tell that a lot of it here still works...but how to work it, and what it does? Well, we sure as shit don't know that. But we know where we can get what we need to know, and I'm figuring that mebbe you know something, if you came here by using some of it. But mebbe you need to know more. See, I can't see any reason you'd come to this shithole unless it was an accident. So mebbe we can help each other. Sure gotta be better than this or a chilling, and it'll come to that if we go on this way."

Ryan bit the skin on the end of his thumb in concentration. "Okay, listen up," he finally said. "We know a little—enough to travel using some old tech, and mebbe to use some of the old comps. But there's a lot we half know, and mebbe if we join you and find out some more, then we can get to use a lot of the old tech to our advantage. So I guess I'm saying yes, Joe Correll." He looked at his people as he spoke. They all assented.

"Okay, then," Correll drawled. "I'm gonna open the door. We all keep our blasters to hand, but we hold fire. Yeah?"

"Yeah," the one-eyed man agreed, glancing at his companions.

"Okay... I'm hitting the numbers now," Correll said. "Get ready."

The door began to move, and in their state of tension it seemed to take an eternity to open.

Chapter Four

The door had reached three-quarters of the way to the tunnel ceiling, pulled three-quarters of the way across the breadth, before their opposition became fully visible, and Ryan and Joe Correll came face-to-face.

Correll stood about the same height as Ryan, but was rangy and lean, with the appearance of one who had, at one point, been malnourished and had found it hard to build up his muscles once more. This impression was born out by his face: it was long, with gaunt, high cheekbones that only accentuated the sallow skin stretched tight. His eyes were deep-set, with a darkness underneath them that made his steady, staring gaze seem all the more intent. His nose was scarred and had been broken several times, and the long, thin blond hair that he wore tied back into a ponytail was an ash blond, flecked with more gray than should have been evident in a man of his years. He wore old, tattered fatigues that hung on his lean frame, and a Heckler & Koch was hanging by his side, still grasped in his hand but with the barrel pointing downward.

His eyes met Ryan's gaze, and locked there. The one-eyed man knew immediately that Correll would tear them apart if they crossed him, but would play by agreed rules if they were going his way. He would be a good ally, but a dangerous enemy.

Correll was thinking much the same thing as he sized up Ryan. He was impressed by the obvious strength of the man, and the fact that he had lost an eye, had a jagged scar to prove it had been a tough fight. That he had obviously chilled the opponent and was still here was proof of his abilities. Correll's gaze flickered over the rest of the companions. Mildred fascinated him, as he hadn't seen a black woman for many a year; Krysty was an obvious beauty, and looked strong; the white one showed the signs of many battles, and from his size Correll would have expected him to have been chilled long ago—obviously a good fighter; the old man seemed crazy, smiling to himself as he stood there with an ancient blaster in his fist— yet he had to be able to look after himself. Likewise the boy, who was barely in his teens, yet had to be a good fighter, as this group was far too small to carry any passengers. Besides, he looked like One-eye, mebbe a son, so he probably learned to fight from his father.

They were a small group, and looked too odd to have taken on and outsmarted his people. So mebbe they could help after all in the task ahead.

Ryan noticed the movement of Correll's gaze, and wondered what was going on behind the impassive countenance. He heard a small grunt in the back of Correll's throat, the slightest nod, as if to himself, and then Correll spoke.

"So what do I call you, One-eye? You know me, after all."

Ryan answered simply with his name, taking the opportunity to look over the rest of the company who were behind Correll. There had been a party of ten after all, then, as there were six people lining up behind the leader. Five of them were men, all looking lean and ready to fight. The sole woman was stouter, with a better developed musculature. She looked to be of Native American heritage, as her skin had a darker tint, and her hair was black, like her glittering eyes. All of them were dressed in better fatigues, camou and old military clothes than their leader, which made a part of Ryan wonder why Correll still wore his old rags. They all had the wariness that Ryan could feel in his own people, yet they had all relaxed the instant Correll had spoken, as though they trusted his every word, as well as following it. They carried Uzis, H&Ks, and one had an M-4000 like the one J.B. carried. Their clothes and blasters suggested that they had been in this redoubt for some time, and had made full use of what had been left behind after skydark.

In the distance, back at the bend of the tunnel, Ryan could see the two chilled corpses, and the wounded man, now semiconscious.

"Let Mildred go and see to your man," Ryan added after he had spoken his name, indicating the woman with an inclination of his head. "She knows a lot of healing skills and understands some of the old medicines. Let her take him to the med lab here, she may be able to help him."

Correll furrowed his brow. "Med lab?" He pronounced the words as though they were completely foreign, rolling them around his tongue.

Mildred spoke for the first time. "Med lab—it's usually on the same level as the armory. Look, a couple of your people carry him, and I'll see if I can help him."

Correll gave Mildred a penetrating stare that, for one moment, completely fazed her. She felt a shudder run down her spine as those deep-set eyes seemed to search into her. Then he nodded, turning his head to two of the men behind.

"Lonnie, Travis—help this here lady to take Cy to the med lab, see if she can help him. Let her lead."

He had, once again, pronounced the words "med lab"as though they were something strange and freakish, but his voice still carried authority. Two of the men—a tall, crop-haired guy and a slightly shorter guy with longer, red hair—nodded, shouldered their blasters and moved back to where Cy was lying. Mildred, with the briefest of glances at Ryan and J.B., holstered her ZKR, which had been in her hand, pointing down, as were all the blasters, and hurried past the one-eyed man and his counterpart, moving through the other people to reach the injured man.

The two men assigned to assist her were about to lift him, but she stayed them with a simple "Wait, please," and examined the prone body as they hovered over her. It was a bad injury, and she couldn't guarantee saving the use of the arm, but as long as the refrigeration on the blood-and-plasma bank in the redoubt was still working, she may be able to keep him alive. "Okay, let's go," she said firmly, establishing her authority and leading Lonnie and Travis, carrying the prone Cy, out of sight around the tunnel bend and in search of the med lab.

Correll had turned to watch them go, and now he returned his gaze to Ryan.

"So, Ryan Cawdor, we know who we are. Introduce me to the rest of your people, and then we can go back to the living quarters and you can meet my people."

Correll slowly shouldered his H&K and extended his hand in a gesture. Ryan holstered the SIG-Sauer and grasped Correll's hand. The grip was firm and dry.

"That's a deal," Ryan said.

After the introductions had been made, the two forces joined up and moved out of the lower tunnel, walking up toward where the redoubt dwellers had made their home. Correll explained on the way that his people had learned early on that the worms liked to dig deep in these parts, and apart from one or two isolated incidents they had never experienced any problems with the giant muties on the upper levels. They rarely used the lower levels, just venturing down when necessary to use the shower room, or take supplies, or effect repairs.

Jak and Dean volunteered themselves to help the woman and one of the other men carry the corpses of those they had chilled up to the higher levels, where they would be disposed of. The man and woman still seemed to have a degree of hostility over the chilling, even though they abided by their leader's word, and seemed uneasy at

Jak and Dean assisting. But both felt it was a necessary gesture and carried on regardless.

They passed the med lab, and Correll stopped to see what was going on.

Mildred turned as the door opened. Travis was assisting her, his red hair pushed back from his face as he leaned over the prone Cy, but Lonnie had been overcome by seeing the state of Cy's wound closeup, and was standing some distance away.

"What's going on?" Correll asked.

Mildred, bent over the recumbent man's shoulder, spared Correll the briefest of looks. "Hard to say at the moment," she replied as she returned to her work. "There was some superficial flesh wounding from the fléchettes, but the real damage is around the joint itself. I've cleaned up the rest of his arm, and I'm looking at the tendons and muscle damage, see what I can do. Thing is, I'm no surgeon. I can patch him up, but he may not be able to use the arm too well."

Correll nodded, as much to himself as anyone else. "That is as may be, and there is nothing we can do about it. I thank you for your help. We'll leave you to your task."

They left the med lab and rejoined the rest of the party, waiting outside.

"Tell me, my dear sir," Doc asked, taking advantage of this unexpected break, "how did you come to be living here?"

"In good time, Dr. Tanner, in good time," Correll said. "First we must do what is necessary."

They reached the upper level of the redoubt, and went past an area that was obviously where the inhabitants had made their home. There were several people about, and they stopped to stare as Correll led the party past them. No one spoke, and a hush descended on the level.

"It's not exactly the best way for them to get acquainted with us, is it?" Krysty whispered to Ryan. "They're really going to love us for this."

Correll looked back at her. "They'll know the truth soon enough. First we do this."

There was an edge to his voice that brooked no argument, and Ryan felt a nagging doubt begin to creep at the back of his mind. The low drawl in which Correll spoke barely changed in pitch or volume, yet was stopped from being a monotone by an underlying edge. Ryan had the vaguest notion that the edge in the man's voice was that of madness. He was driven by something, but the one-eyed warrior had yet to find out exactly what that something was.

They walked on, past the area of habitation and up toward the main ramp and double set of sec doors leading to the outside. Correll punched in a code and opened the first set, leading them through. He paused before the second set, which opened onto the outside.

"Blasters ready," he intoned. "That means you, as well, Ryan Cawdor, and your people. Every time that we go outside, we need to be triple-red aware."

"Your enemies, or just muties and wildlife?" Ryan asked.

The ghost of a smile flickered across Correll's face. "It's all wildlife out there, friend, and they're all our enemies."

He punched in the final code and pressed a lever, the outer sec doors lifting to reveal to Ryan and the companions the world outside this particular redoubt.

In truth, it was hard to tell what the outside was like, as the fluorescent lighting inside made it hard for their eyes to adjust to the gloom outside. Although both J.B. and Ryan had wrist chrons, it was useless for them to use those as they had no idea whereabouts in the Deathlands they had landed. The Armorer had hoped that a look at the terrain would give him an idea, as he was usually accurate at judging their general location by the topography of the land. But wherever they were, it seemed to be late evening, and in the cloudless sky overhead there were stars beginning to show through the twilight.

"We must hurry," Correll said, breaking into their respective thoughts. "The open door will be visible for some way. Come..."

He led most of the party outside and onto the bare rock around. Two of his sec people stayed within the boundary of the redoubt, and at a nod from their leader, closed the sec door.

"I don't want the inside visible any longer than necessary when it's dark," he offered by way of explanation before leading them across the rock floor to an incline.

Looking around, the companions could tell that the redoubt was recessed into the side of a mountain that had a series of graded ridges running up the side. These had been fashioned into a road at one time, as there were still traces of blacktop material, but an earth movement—either the earth itself or possibly even the activities of the mutie worms—had caused much of the rock to fall away.

Correll stopped and pointed over the incline. It began gently, then after a few yards fell away into nothing. He said, "See, everyone who comes near figures that there was something leading up here, and then it all went. But that ain't true. We only discovered this place by chance and fate, and then because there's another road that moves from the other side of the hill and goes up then down before it gets to here. See, you take the long route and sometimes you get what you want, whereas you always want the quickest, then you get fucked off."

Ryan looked at the road that ran in the opposite direction from the sheltered entrance to the redoubt. It certainly ran up, and then out of sight around the side of the mountain. But it was obvious to the one-eyed man that Correll was talking about something else when he mouthed the last sentence. Something that had to do with the secrets of the old tech that he believed they could find.

J.B., meanwhile, was taking a good look around, his eyes adjusting to the gloom, trying to work out where they could be in the Deathlands. The mountain on which they stood was one of a few scattered for as far as he could see. He could turn 180 degrees and get a good view of what the terrain was like. It seemed to be scattered mountains, with desert in between. Although the air was cold now, he guessed that it could be mighty hot at the peak of the day. Enough that there was little scrub and vegetation around.

Correll disturbed his musings.

"Time to consign these friends to the past," he said sadly. "Fate said their time had come, and you can't argue with that."

The man and woman carrying one end each of the chilled corpses moved toward the incline where Correll was standing. Jak and Dean, each grasping the other end of a corpse, followed, not knowing what was expected of them. In turn, each of the corpses was tossed over the side of the incline. Dean lingered to take a look below. It was impossible to see what was at the bottom of the mountain, as the darkness and shadow closed in. He looked back toward Correll, an unspoken question forming.

"There's mutie dogs and jackals down there, other kinds of rodent. They pick the bones clean. Ain't much clue left of us being here, ain't no chance of any illness spreading, and you feed the fuckers and they don't bother us much. Serves a lot of purposes."

Correll shrugged and turned back to the sec door, walking rapidly up the rock floor to where the metal door, its camou paint barely touched by the rad-blasted years, was silent and still. The rest of his party followed, with Ryan and his companions following a fraction of a second later.

Correll rapped on the door with his knuckles. It barely sounded on the thick metal, but the pair on the other side of the door had to have been listening for his return and signal, as the door immediately began to rise. Correll entered while it was still rising to its full height, and was greeted by Lonnie, who had joined the others at the sec door. The crop-haired man seemed relieved to have left the med lab.

"Well?" Correll asked simply.

"He's getting something called plasma, and the doctor did something to his shoulder, gave him some of the drugs. Travis is with him now, but he's asleep and seems to be out of pain. Travis could learn a lot from her."

"Good." Correll nodded.

Then, turning to Ryan and his companions as they approached, he continued, "Your friend Mildred seems to be extremely knowledgeable. Cy sounds like he's in good hands."

"It is only fair, as we were responsible," Doc murmured. The silence that greeted his remark made him feel uncomfortable.

"Really don't think you should have pointed that out," Krysty muttered, looking at their erstwhile opponents.

"No, the old man is right," Correll interjected. "But that was appropriate for all, then. Perhaps it gave us a chance to learn something about the other. The past is another land."

"Let's hope we've sailed away from it, then," J.B. whispered to Ryan as Correll led them all back down the corridor.

"Yeah, and the tide doesn't wash us back," the one-eyed man replied thoughtfully.

They were led into the section of the redoubt that was now used as living quarters by Correll's people. Because of the problems caused by the giant worms and the manner in which they caused damage and possible death on the lower levels of the redoubt, it had been necessary for the community to base all their living operations around the upper two levels, rather than spread themselves across the whole base. Therefore, although they used the shower room with caution, they had taken most of the bedding from the dorms and used what had been offices and sec command posts and surveillance rooms to make new sleeping areas. They seemed to have either paired off, or slept and lived in small groups in what had once been military offices. The kitchens, which were also on one of the lower levels, had also been plundered, and the ovens and microwaves that had been previously installed in those areas had been taken out and reinstalled in an upper level area that had once, in the days before skydark, been used as an area for briefing the redoubt personnel. Thus, it was a long room that had plenty of space in which to deploy the ovens and also store much of the supplies from the kitchen areas.

J.B. and Ryan both observed this with interest, but kept their peace. Dean, however, wasn't so silent, and as they passed this area he noted to Krysty, "If they've got those working, then they must have a pretty good idea of how a lot of this works."

Correll stopped and turned to the younger Cawdor. "Son, I wish I could say you were right, but I don't think any of us can claim that great a knowledge. Thing is, we've lived down here a while, and when the muties got too keen on using this place as a shortcut to wherever the hell they're headed, then we all kinda figured that we needed to use that as little as possible. Which meant taking all the ovens out and getting them here, where it was safe. Only thing we had to leave was the really cold place—couldn't figure a way of getting the food from that room and keeping it cold, so we had to leave that there and kinda take our chances like with the showers. But the other stuff... See, we took them apart kinda slow, so we could make out where everything went. Then we pulled them up here and figured out which bits of cable looked the same. But as to how it all actually works?"

"Have you tried anything else?" Dean persisted.

Correll allowed himself a ghostly smile that seemed unnatural on his grim visage. "Son, we live among this stuff, now. Where we eat and sleep, there's flickering lights and old tech all around. Sometimes some of it gives out, sometimes we try to fix it. I don't know if we do any good. I don't even know if we really learn anything from it, but sometimes the lights start again, and sometimes you can still see the outside and some parts of in here on the screens."

Doc looked around him. "I think you do yourself a disservice, my dear sir. The air-conditioning is still working, there is still water filtered through the plant, you have nearly all the facilities up and running. You should be congratulated."

"I thank you kindly," Correll replied graciously, "but the truth of the matter is that fate has been kind to us since our arrival here. We know how to keep things running, but if we had a real problem, then our feeble knowledge would be sorely stretched. Which is why, my friend, we wish to discover some more secrets of the old tech, and so unlock the way this place runs."

Ryan interrupted. "Which is exactly what we'd like to do."

Correll nodded. "Yes, we will talk more of this, but first we should eat. Your friend Mildred will be joining us. She has done a very fine job."

Turning on his heel in a manner that suggested conversation was now over, Correll moved off, trailing his party and the companions in his wake.

As they walked on, J.B. turned it over in his mind. Correll and his people had the knowledge to keep some of the plant working, and working well. They would also, presumably, be able to maintain the wags that were stored on the second level. J.B. hadn't noticed any on their way up, but then the wag bays were always kept apart from the rest of the redoubt because of the hazards of fuel storage. If the wags had been in as good a condition as the rest of the redoubt seemed to be, then they would have good transport, and plenty of fuel. From the way in which the party initially opposing them had been armed, it was an obvious conclusion that the armory had been well-equipped, and—taking a surreptitious glance at the party around him—they knew well enough how to look after their blasters. He had no doubt that the med lab was well equipped, as Millie would have made her feelings known on the matter to the man Lonnie, and Correll would have felt the rough edge of Millie's tongue secondhand.

All in all, they had a good base from which to wage a war, and the equipment with which to win it. Redoubts this well equipped and maintained were rare, and anyone who stumbled across them had just gotten lucky.

Thing was, what did Correll and his people want to do with it? J.B. had a creeping feeling, tingling at the back of his neck, that Correll was spoiling for a fight with someone, and the companions had just stumbled into the beginnings of a private war, with the search for old tech and the arrival of an outside interest just the excuse and impetus he needed.

Coincidentally, much the same set of thoughts were running through Ryan's head as they walked on.

Mebbe, the one-eyed man mused, they would learn something later that night.

THE COMPANIONS WERE given their own sleeping and living space, with bedding and a change of clothes taken from the supplies that still existed. The space was an old office that had just had the office furniture removed, and was noticeably free from much in the way of old tech.

"You can shower if you're willing to take a chance," Correll said as his parting shot. "Ain't usually a problem, just be ready to move fast if you feel those tremors."

When he and the accompanying party had left them

alone, Krysty said, "I don't know about you, lover, but it doesn't all add up yet."

Ryan shook his head. "Mebbe we'll discover more when we eat—mebbe get to meet the rest properly."

"Yeah, I don't think this is that big a community," added Mildred, who had joined them when Correll had shown them their quarters. "Should be fairly easy to keep tabs on them all, get the feel of what's going on."

"Should be..." J.B. said quietly. "Reckon they've got enough here to start a small war, and that's what they're after."

Ryan agreed. "But why?"

"Dunno yet, but I guess we can't hurry it up—so if it's okay with everyone, I'll take my chances with the showers," Dean interjected. "May as well face it clean and fresh." He grinned.

"Sound good," Jak added, running a hand through his stringy white hair. "Good cold water make sharper."

"Yeah, I could go for that," Ryan agreed. "We'll take it in shifts, stand lookout for any mutie trouble."

They started to go, but Ryan noticed that Doc was still standing against the wall, looking pensive. As the others left, Ryan broke away and went over to Doc.

"What is it?"

Doc, lost in reverie, grunted and looked up at Ryan. For a moment, it seemed as though the old man's eyes were a million miles and thousand of years from that room. The distance and desolation in them was enough to make Ryan—for all that he had seen—start back. Then the mists cleared for Doc, and he was once again back with the one-eyed warrior.

"I'm sorry, my dear boy, but for a moment I felt as though I was standing outside of myself, outside of everything."

"You okay, Doc?"

"By the Three Kennedys, what a ridiculous question." Doc laughed bitterly. "You of all people should know that the last thing I really am is okay. But for a second, I was reminded of something that I seem to remember from what seems many years ago. I suppose it is many years," he added, surprise entering his tone, "but that is by the by. It is our host. There is something about the gentleman that haunts me. I feel he is a lost soul."

"I think it's me you've lost there, Doc," Ryan said softly. He felt Doc was trying to tell him something important, but he couldn't quite grasp it.

"He is driven by an inner demon that has taken over everything that he is or was. It is a demon that is part of him, and yet is apart. It has control of him to such an extent that it will care not for anyone or anything around. We should be wary of him, my dear Ryan, very wary. He means us no harm, I am sure, but we are the catalyst for him to put his own plans for vengeance into operation. And he will be merciless."

Ryan chewed his lip, trying to unravel Doc's language, the likes of which was no longer heard in the Deathlands. Finally, he nodded. "I understand. I figured along the same lines, I guess. But it's a matter of playing the odds, Doc, and I figure that we should go with it. If we pay heed, and keep our backs covered—"

"Then that is all we can do," Doc finished.

WITHIN A FEW HOURS, the companions, refreshed by their showers, were visited by Lonnie and Travis, who informed them that they would be eating shortly in the large room where the ovens were now installed. Travis also informed Mildred that Cy was sleeping, and that his condition was stable.

"But I'd be grateful if you could take a look at him later," he added.

Mildred agreed, and waited until Lonnie and Travis had left before murmuring, "Considering we injured him, they're being too damn nice about it."

J.B. shrugged. "That's life—and chilling—Millie. Most places they'd have chilled us straight away, but..."

"But we'll find out soon enough," Ryan finished.

The companions made their way to the eating room. The rest of the redoubt was empty except for one man, who sat alone in one of the living quarters. Doc looked in, and observed that it was a room that housed the monitors for all the sec cameras in the redoubt. To his surprise, none of the monitors were dark.

"Good heavens, that is most unusual!" he exclaimed.

The man on duty turned to him and shrugged. "Hell, if any of these go down, we probably couldn't fix 'em. Have to start posting guards. Still, our luck's holding so far. Guess Papa Joe's right—mebbe it is our fate to be here and get even."

Doc nodded and smiled. "Guess so, friend," he said cheerily before slipping out of the room, adding to himself, "Now, that really is interesting."

As they reached the eating room, they could see that the whole community was gathered together. There were about thirty in all, with only one-third of those being female. They were eating in relative silence, with only a very low hum of conversation taking place. Looking around, Dean could see that there were no children—no one, in fact, who seemed to be under the age of sixteen. The youngest-looking man in the room was a whip-thin boy who had the beginning of a beard, and was hunched over his food, as though wanting to appear invisible. Yet this had the opposite effect, as his intensity was such that he appeared to radiate a nervous energy that drew your eyes to him. Bizarrely, it was almost as though he could feel Dean looking at him. He turned to face the younger Cawdor, his eyes burning bright through his spectacles, a keen intelligence showing through. His eyes locked on Dean's, as though he were assessing him. Then he gave the faintest of grins, and the briefest of nods, before turning back to his food.

Unusual for a community setup, there seemed to be no table and privileges reserved for the baron—although it had been noticeable that Correll hadn't referred to himself as such—and the man who was leader was seated to one side of the room, with a group of people among whom were Travis and the Native American woman who had been in the defense party they had faced earlier. Correll stood when he noticed the companions enter, and beckoned them to him. They seated themselves at his table, some of the redoubt community moving to make room, and were served food by those who acted as cooks. Even these seemed to be on a par with everyone else, as there was no sign of a pecking order, and the cooks were as lean and fit as the people they had faced earlier.

In fact, this was one thing that all seemed to share. They seemed trained and fit, ready for combat at any time. This was a community that was carrying no passengers.

While they ate, they made small talk, and it wasn't until the meal was nearly over that Ryan judged it time to broach the subject that had, sooner or later, to be talked about.

The one-eyed man downed some of the brew that had been supplied with the meal, then took a breath. "I guess it's about time we all leveled. You know we came here using old tech. It was something we stumbled on, and we can't control it although we know how to trigger it. It's some kind of system for transporting people and objects across vast distances by breaking it all up into atoms and shooting it across from one comp to another."

Correll nodded slowly, sucking in his breath. "That'd be crazy talk if I hadn't known there was no other way to get into this place. So you can work it, but not control it?"

Ryan shook his head. "Guess it's like you in that sense. You know something about the old tech, enough to use some and keep some going, but not enough to really make it work for you."

Correll nodded. "That's what we can find out. It'll be sweet, and we can settle a few old scores. But to get at that knowledge, I need to know you'll join us in a firefight."

"Never shirked one yet," Ryan said levelly. "Just tell us what it's about."

Correll sat back in his seat and looked up at the ceiling. "We've been here for about ten years now, just getting ourselves ready for when fate decrees we can rise again. See, I used to be sec chief for Charity—" he spit the name of the ville with an undisguised venom "—which is just about the stupidest name you can think of for a ville run by such a coldheart son of a gaudy like Baron Al 'Red' Jourgensen. Got run out of town because I was heading sec on a convoy headed for a trade rendezvous. We got raided by a party from Summerfield—they're the ones who know something about the old ways, 'cause they had blasters and shit like you ain't seen before. We didn't stand a chance. All the things we were trading, all the jack we carried, it all went. Red wanted to chill me and the rest of the party who survived, so we had to run. Dammit, there was shit all we could do...."

"Anyway, we found this place, and over the years there were others who Red was a shit to.... See, we lost the trade and jack 'cause Red didn't let me take enough blasters or men. Always frightened he was gonna be overthrown if he let that happen. Stupe bastard deserves what he'll get. We all come from Charity, but we won't show none to old Red."

"So why is it right now?" Krysty asked.

Correll raised an eyebrow. "Fate works in strange ways. It's hard desert land out there, and that rad-blasting sun means jackshit grows that well. Summerfield may have old tech, but they ain't got shit to protect their water, and they lost a whole heap of women 'cause of rad sickness. While Red— Well, that stupe fucker has screwed up his whole farming scheme, and there ain't jackshit to eat. He needs jack for food and seed crop to start over."

J.B. nodded to himself. From the description of the land, and what he'd seen earlier on the outside, he was now sure that he had been correct in his guess that they had landed somewhere in New Mex. That knowledge may be useful.

Correll was in full flow. "So Charity and Summerfield have a little deal going down. Red is selling them some women for breeding stock, and in return he gets jack to buy food and seed crop to start over. Thing is, we know the route they gonna have to take, and we're gonna take them out. Get the jack and the women, then in the confusion when they think they're double-crossing each other, we take out Summerfield, get their secrets, then wipe that bastard Red off the face of the earth."

Correll's speech had been listened to by all in silence, the hush spreading as he talked longer. Now he was cheered by the assembled throng.

"We've trained hard, denied ourselves families, denied ourselves rest, and now fate has delivered vengeance to us," he yelled, to be greeted by whoops and hollers.

"They call us the Hellbenders out there," one of the

group screamed. "I know, I ain't been here long. But they're right—we're sure as hell bent on vengeance."

Ryan touched Correll on the arm, and the leader looked down at him, his eyes wild and gleaming, for a moment not seeing the one-eyed man.

"So when the hell does this begin?" Ryan queried.

"Seven days, friend, as long as it took to create this dust bowl before skydark. If that can happen, we can sure as hell get it together to whip some ass."

Chapter Five

"It is not very long," Doc mused. "Not very long at all."

It was the morning after their first meal with the people they now knew were called the Hellbenders, and while Mildred went with Travis to check on Cy's condition, the rest of the companions were taking a few moments to assess, through headaches caused by the previous night's strong brew, what they had learned.

As the evening had worn on, and the redoubt dwellers had become intoxicated, so the rowdiness had increased. People were singing and shouting at one another, and Correll had tried to make himself heard to Ryan. But the volume from the assembled throng was too great, and the gaunt man's voice strained to be heard.

It was then that he gave a demonstration of his authority that made the one-eyed man assess the power that he held, and conclude that it was very great. Frustrated at not being able to make himself heard, a cloud of fury crossing his brow, Correll rose to his feet and then climbed onto the table. This movement immediately caught the eye of J.B., who rose an eyebrow at Ryan, receiving a similar gesture from his friend. This would be a telling moment.

Correll drew a long knife from a scabbard attached to his thigh. It was similar to Ryan's panga, but with a more curved blade that caught light from the candles that were augmenting the now dimmed fluorescent tubes, reflecting it in glittering patterns. Correll tossed the knife in the air so that it spun, and as it came back down he caught it by the point and, in one fluid motion, threw it so that it described a parabola around the circumference of the room. It skidded low across the tops of heads, its passing marked by a rush of air that breathed on the people, making them stop and turn. If someone had been standing higher than head height—on a chair, or on a table—then the knife would have sliced into them. As it was, Correll had judged the height to perfection, leaving nothing in the wake of the flight but a series of turned heads and a growing silence around the room.

The knife returned to him, its speed still strong. Correll leaned back without moving either of his feet and plucked the knife out of the air by its point as it passed him, killing the momentum dead with a downward flick of his wrist.

The room was now silent, all eyes on their leader.

"Good. I hate it when you all get too rowdy and I'm trying to talk. I was about to explain to our friends here that the mission on which they will join us is fast approaching. I have had intelligence reports that the trade-off is to be in seven days' time. So we go on triple red and train hard. The countdown begins here. Enjoy tonight, but wake up tomorrow to work hard. Vengeance will soon be ours."

With which he stood down from the table to a moment's silence before the assembled throng, having been given the countdown to that which they desired, erupted into cheering and whooping before resuming their festivities—this time with a renewed sense of purpose.

THE FOLLOWING MORNING, Krysty remembered the conversation with an appalling clarity, just as she remembered the expression on Correll's face as he spoke. His eyes glittered, his skin drew tight as the veins on his temples throbbed and the sinews stood out on his neck.

"It could never be too long, Doc," she said. "I don't think I could ever wait too long to go into a firefight with him."

"Fight whether want or not," Jak said with a shrug. "Fight him, fight Charity...fight someone."

"Jak's right," Ryan agreed. "We're caught between that rock and that hard place here. If we try to pull out on Correll, we'll buy the farm right now. But—"

"But seeing the way he is, what kind of suicidal strategies does he have planned?" J.B. finished. Like Ryan, the Armorer had an uneasy feeling that Correll would stop at nothing to achieve his aim, not caring for the lives of his people—or, for that matter, his own.

"Right now we've got to go with it," Ryan stated simply. "We've got no option here. But mebbe we can find a way to fill any holes in his plans and get nearer that old tech knowledge."

"It sure would help," Dean said, almost to himself. He had learned a few things at the Brody school, from the limited knowledge that was available. Like Mildred, he had an interest in the old comp tech that had led to them investigating the machines in redoubts whenever they had the chance, but those chances didn't come too often.

Doc eyed Krysty shrewdly. "I fear you are not happy with such a plan," he murmured to her. "In truth, neither am I. But Ryan is correct. In terms of options, we are severely limited."

"I know it, Doc," Krysty answered, "but it doesn't mean I have to like it."

Mildred returned with Travis and entered on these words, the redoubt dweller behind her. She took in the situation at a glance, and immediately launched into a detailed report on her patient's condition, along with praise for Travis's skills, in order to deflect her companion from asking questions about, or dwelling on, anything he may have overheard as they entered.

Travis was unassuming about the praise he received. "I was only doing what you said," he said to Mildred before, obviously uncomfortable at being lauded, changing the subject. "Look, we should be getting down to the meeting room. There's a briefing, and I can't believe Mr. C. doesn't want you there. Not after last night."

So saying, he led them from their room through the corridors to the room where they had eaten the previous evening.

"Nicely done, Millie," J.B. whispered as they went.

"No more than you should expect, John," she returned.

When they reached the meeting room, it was to find that the rest of the community was gathered, with Correll at the head, waiting for their arrival. After asking briefly how Cy was doing, Correll turned his attention to a crudely drawn map that was pinned to the wall.

"Now, most of the next six days we're going to spend shaping up, sharpening those reflexes. There'll be a training regime and combat tactics to learn. You're good and sharp, but I want you sharper still. Ryan," he said, turning to the one-eyed man, "I want you in on this with me. I figure an outside view from someone with your experience could be kinda interesting. And I want J.B. around, as well, 'cause we got to get that armory in the best shape it's ever been, and you're the man for that."

The Armorer nodded, not letting his feelings show. It was in the companions' best interests to have the armory in A1 condition, but it would also be good to know exactly what Correll had in his armory in case they had to stand against him.

Correll continued, pointing at the map. "I figure that the route will take both convoys around the really arid areas here—" he pointed at a spot toward the center of the distance between the two villes "—but they'll still want to meet as near to the center as possible. I know Jourgensen, and so does Hutter, the baron in Summerfield," he added for the benefit of the companions. "Any kind of advantage Jourgensen could get, he'd take with both greedy hands, so Hutter'll want to keep things as neutral as possible. And guess what, people? It just so happens that brings them nice and near to us.

"While most of us train, there's going to have to be volunteers for a recce party to scout Charity. I managed to get word from our spy in Charity about the meet, but Jourgensen has got the shape and size of the party well and truly sewn up. We need to get someone close enough to the ville to see what's going on."

There was a moment's silence, then Lonnie rose to his feet. "I'll go," he said simply. The Native American woman rose to her feet, casting a hostile and suspicious look at the companions as she did.

"Count me in," she muttered.

Correll shook his head. "No way, Jenny. You've got to oversee the armory, and I'll need you to work with J.B."

"Shit, Joe, can't someone else do that? I don't want to work with them," she added, spitting out the last word as she glared at the companions.

Correll's face hardened—if that was possible in a visage that was so gaunt to begin with. "I know how you feel. Lance was a good man, and it was sad to see him pass. But that's fate. These people were defending themselves as we were. There was no malice, and we hold none against them."

Jenny turned and looked directly at Correll, her eyes meeting his with a blaze of defiance and anger. She matched him for a few moments, then looked down. "Okay," she mumbled, "if that's the way it's got to be."

"It is," Correll said softly. "Sit down and let's see someone else."

She reluctantly sat, and others rose to take her place. The recce party would consist of the lean, crop-haired Lonnie; Mik, a small, lean-faced man with several piercings and sardonic gaze; Tilly, a woman with large brown eyes and mouth set in determination, and the whip-thin boy in spectacles who had caught Dean's gaze the evening before. His name was Danny, and it seemed that he was the youngest member of the community.

"I think we shouldn't forget our friends," Correll said when he had approved the volunteers. "It would only be reasonable to send someone from your group on the recce," he added directly to Ryan.

The one-eyed man wasn't keen on the idea. He would have preferred to keep his people together at this time. He didn't believe that Correll had any notions of chilling the group, but he figured that the man was unpredictable and possibly insane, driven beyond reason by his cause. But what could Ryan do? To dissent would be to cause a problem that was, at this stage, unnecessary and undesirable.

"Mebbe," he said slowly. "You want me, J.B. and Mildred here, right?" Correll nodded. Ryan continued, "So you take your pick out of the rest."

Correll eyed Ryan, the sunken orbs boring into the one-eyed man.

"Okay," he said finally, "I'm reckoning that Jak is the best tracker and hunter you've got, and I'm also reckoning that your boy Dean—if he's anything like you—will be good to have in a firefight. I'll pick them."

Ryan nodded agreement, looking to Dean and Jak. Both assented, and seemed happy enough.

"I'd like to go, as well," Doc said suddenly.

"Why?" Correll asked. "No offence intended, but you don't seem the most physically able to undertake such a mission."

Doc gave a sly grin. "That's precisely why. You see, my dear sir, I would consider that you are, quite reasonably, testing us in some manner. If that is so, then the onus is on me, as the most physically frail seeming of the group, to prove that we will—every last one of us—be able to pull our weight when the time comes for action. Therefore, what better way to do this than to take part in such a mission."

Correll said nothing for a moment, instead levelly gazing at Doc. Finally, he spoke. "You use a lot of words to say something, but when you get there it makes sense. Okay, Dr. Tanner, you can join the recce party."

It was a two-day trek from the redoubt to Charity, and as soon as the meeting was concluded, the party began to prepare. To get there, scout and return would take a total of five days, leaving them with only the sixth day to rest, recuperate and report before the attack.

It would take two days to make the trek as they would be going by foot to avoid detection by any sec patrols or passing wags on their way to either of the villes. Even in the wastelands they would traverse, it would be easier to hide on foot than if they were in a wag. The objective was to avoid attracting attention, either by being noticed or by having to chill any passing wag, which may then be missed and spark an alarm.

So it was that the three companions who joined with the four Hellbenders found themselves being kitted out for desert survival by Jenny, the Native American who was in charge of both the armory and stores. She gave them self-heats and water canteens, and each had an individual tent made of a lightweight material with a thin, tubular metal frame that folded up into a light backpack.

"This is a most splendid thing," Doc commented as he unraveled and examined the tent, pointedly ignoring the hostile stare he received from the Native American woman. "I must admit, I've never come across anything like this in any of the other stores."

Jenny gave him a quizzical look, the hostility momentarily dissipating. "You've seen other places like this?" she asked.

Remembering that Ryan had said nothing of the other bases, allowing Correll to draw his own conclusions about where they came from, Doc refused to be drawn. "We've seen many places," he commented elliptically, "and perhaps if you had seen what we have, then you may have a more tolerant attitude to what happens," he chided.

The Native American stopped for a moment, considering what Doc had said, before nodding to herself. "Okay," she murmured to the older man, "you and me can talk more about this when you get back. Mebbe you can make me see your point of view."

Doc joined the others in the party, who had already been kitted out by the redoubt's quartermaster. Jak and Dean weren't surprised by what Doc had achieved, but the four Hellbenders were amazed.

"Tell you something," commented the wiry and small Mik, sniffing as he spoke, "that's a rarity, that is, getting her to crack her face and stop being so sour."

Lonnie pulled an amused face. "Yeah, but you only say that 'cause she won't let you fuck her."

"That's got nothing to do with it," Mik retorted with a dirty laugh.

"Yeah, laugh now, 'cause this ain't gonna be much fun," interjected the nervous, wiry teenager Danny.

The conversation died, and the other three Hellbenders stared at the youth.

"Well, it's true, ain't it?" he said defensively. "This is not going to be fun, y'know?"

"We know, but you don't have to make a big deal of it," Tilly said, her dark eyes flashing anger. "You're always on such a down, boy."

"Never mind that now," Lonnie said calmly. "We need to get going." He turned to the three companions. "We'll take a route that leads us down the far side of the rock, and then circle the hot spots."

"Hot spots?" Dean queried.

"There's two kinds out there. Some of them are still holding a lot of rad blasting in there, and there ain't shit that lives in those. And the others are sun hot spots, where it just gets too hot to move, and there's no cover. Ain't no way that we could even carry enough water to make up for the amount of dehydration we'd get there. It makes it a kinda roundabout route, but it's got less danger attached."

"But always danger," Jak added. It was a statement rather than a question.

Lonnie made no comment, but led the party up to the

top level and then through to the sec doors leading out to the rock face in which the entry door to the redoubt was housed. After punching in the code and pressing the lever, he led the seven-strong party out into the harsh glare of the late morning. Jak shielded his pink albino eyes from the brightness, while the others took in the vista that lay beyond the ridge on which they stood. The door closed ponderously behind them.

The cloudless blue sky was tinged with a pink that bespoke of high chem residue that floated in the upper atmosphere. Below, the two stark blocks of plateaued rock that they had seen the previous night while disposing of the chilled bodies stood a rich red stone against the pale, sandy soil that stood at their respective bases. Some sparse scrub and a few Joshua trees stood weakly, attesting to the lack of moisture in the soil. Beyond the barely nurturing shadow around the rock, out into the relentless sun, little was visible but a semi-dust-bowl desert.

Lonnie led them up the rough road, with its few surviving traces of blacktop, that seemed to take them away from their intended direction and up around to the rear of the small mountain.

The air was dry and rasped at their lungs, the prickling heat making them break into a sweat before they had even reached the apex of the road and rounded the rock.

"This is a trifle ominous," Doc remarked, gasping in breath.

"Don't worry too much," Tilly replied in between gasps

of her own, "this is deceptive...wrong time of day for this height, this heat..."

"Don't talk, save it," Lonnie snapped.

He was right. They needed to conserve and work on their breathing, pacing themselves to make the top of the road without losing too much water.

The road leveled out and bent around the side of the mountain. They were able to ease their effort, knowing that they would soon be into the descent around the far side. The curving surface of the road was shadowed by a sheer ascent of rock wall, shielding their view of the far side until they actually turned into the first dip downward. When they did, the companions understood why the redoubt had been safe.

Coming around the side of the mountain, there was almost a compulsion to huddle against the sheer rock wall beside them to fight off the feelings of emptiness that the facing landscape engendered. Where, on the side of the mountain facing the redoubt, there was at least some kind of scrub, or some rock formations to break up the endless emptiness, on this side there was nothing. The mountain on which they stood fell away, the rock plunging down, taking the remains of the blacktop on a steep ascent that— it immediately occurred to Jak—would make a descent by wag difficult to control. Perhaps, he thought, this was part of the reason why the Hellbenders disdained wags so much, and yet also why they had been so secure in their position.

But this was only a passing thought. What really occupied the minds of the three who hadn't seen this view before was how desolate and dead it seemed. For miles, stretching to a horizon tinged pink by the distant reflection of chem deposits in the equally empty sky, there was nothing except flat, dull dust bowl and sand. No lichens or scrub broke the emptiness, no creatures moved—even the slightest movement would have been detectable against the deadness that surrounded—and there were no other outcrops to break up the unremitting, bland sameness of the land.

"By the Three Kennedys," Doc gasped, "this is surely hell. I have seen many things across this land, but the unrelenting tedium and lack of any life..."

"Yeah, this is basically where the real shit rad-blasting begins," Mik replied, even though Doc had made more of a statement than a query. The small, rat-featured man flashed Doc a wry grin. "One of the reasons this is such a good place to have base, ain't it? We're on the edge of total extinction—who'd ever look for us there?"

Doc conceded the point with an inclination of his head, and the party responded to Lonnie's gesture to move on down by beginning their descent.

As they stumbled down the rocky road, Dean, Doc and Jak were all thinking along similar lines. The remaining blacktop surface under their feet was crumbling as they touched it. Given that wags very rarely ventured around this side of the mountain, and it was only the Hellbenders themselves who used to it to access their base in the redoubt, the road was extremely unsafe. It was perfect for keeping out strangers. No one even having the misfortune to stumble around the dead side of the mountain would have the seeming idiocy to take a crumbling road to nowhere, but it didn't bode well for when the assault parties left the redoubt to mount the attack on the trade convoys in a few short days.

Stray rocks and stones gave way under them, gravel and dirt making the surface unsteady. The road down the mountain was only just wide enough for most wags, being about twelve feet from the sheer rock wall on one side to the sheer drop on the other. They had kept close to the wall as the uneven surface tended to pitch and yawl underfoot, causing them to stumble.

They descended with Lonnie and Mik in the lead, as surefooted as it was possible to get on this surface, with Jak and Doc following, sandwiching Tilly between them. Danny, who traveled as nervously as his mannerisms would suggest, hung back and took the descent with a nervous care. Dean also hung back, fascinated by the teenager.

"You okay there?" Dean asked as Danny stumbled on yet another decaying stretch of road and pitched forward onto his knees. Dean took him under the arm and lifted, assisting him back to his feet.

"Yeah, guess so," Danny mumbled. "This ain't my idea of fun, though."

"So why did you volunteer for it?" Dean asked.

Danny shrugged, pushing his spectacles back onto his nose. "Don't know, really. I'm not cut out for all this, I should have stayed back at base, fiddling with the old tech and trying to make some sense of it."

"You use the comps?" Dean said, wondering if he had found someone from the Hellbenders whose interest would mirror his own.

"I try," Danny replied with a shrug. "When I was a little kid, I lived in Charity. My dad was on sec there, and where Baron Al had some of the old stuff, then I'd get to mess around on it. I suppose it was all the pretty lights when I was small," he added in a sardonic tone, with a grin that Dean echoed.

"You mean to say that the baron actually had some of the old comps up and working?"

Danny waved his hand in a dismissive gesture. "I wouldn't exactly say that. See, as much as I can remember it—and I've been here for what seems like years—part of Charity is built on what used to be some kind of place where they made stuff like that. So they had generators of their own, and lots of the old stuff in different stages, like different parts of the process of putting it together, y'know? Sometimes Baron Al'd fuel up the generator and run some of them, try to make sense of them. There were still papers in all the old offices that probably tell you how it all works, but the dumb fuck couldn't read at all and didn't trust anyone else."

"So how come you got to use them?" Dean asked, wondering what, then, had caused Danny and his father to leave Charity.

"Wasn't supposed to, but my dad had to look after me

and work for the baron on sec. He was a really good sec man at one time, and then when my mom died there was no one else to look after me, so he got detailed on all the jobs where he didn't have to go so far. Then he could take me with him. It wasn't s'posed to be that way, and Baron Al didn't know shit about it, but Joe was chief sec then, and he and my dad got on. It was harder once he got banished, and Dad had to sneak me in.

"He got to be sec on all the things that Baron Al thought were important, but weren't under direct threat from outside—which, I guess, more or less meant all the old tech he'd got and was hoping to use. I'd be in there sometimes looking at stuff and he'd turn up with some other guys, and then I'd have to hide. That was easy, 'cause it was always Dad that did the search. But I'd hear Baron Al talking about the stuff to these other guys, and he figured that he could make himself ruler of all the Deathlands if he could figure out how to use it."

Dean took all of this in as they neared the bottom of the mountain road. It seemed to him that Danny knew more about the old tech than he perhaps even realized, and if together they could find some way into Charity and get to see, or mebbe steal, some of those papers, then that could be even better than getting the old tech itself. Dean figured that it was the paperwork that held the key to how the tech operated, and that was the real secret, the real treasure.

"So how did it all come to an end?" Dean asked as they leveled out from the steep descent and hit the soft desert soil at ground level.

Danny shrugged. "I got too involved in the comps one day, didn't hear anyone coming until it was too late."

"How come the baron didn't chill you?"

Danny grimaced. "It was kinda more complicated than that. The baron was with someone—I think it was some trader who claimed he knew something about the old tech. They were right on me before I heard them, and although I hid, I guess the trader heard or saw me just getting out of sight. Dad did the search and left me alone, but just as Baron Al was about to start talking about his plans, coming on like he always did, the trader stopped him and came right over to where I was hiding.

"Course, that really fucked things over. Baron Al didn't recognize me, but he was really pissed at Dad for not finding a kid, and real pissed at being shown up like that. He had a blaster on Dad and was about to chill him and me on the spot. Dad went for his, and I guess he wanted to end Baron Al's reign and worry about shit afterwards. But it didn't go that way 'cause the trader thought it would be a good opportunity to try and steal some of the old tech stuff. Stupe bastard actually tried to palm some radio stuff that didn't work—I know 'cause I'd tried it out before— and Baron Al caught sight of him.

"It was chaos. Baron Al chilled the trader, and as he moved he put himself just out of line for Dad's shot, which took him down but left him alive. Course, all that noise brought all the sec out of the woodwork, and Dad had to steal a wag and head out to the desert with me. He knew Joe was out here somewhere, and just had to trust to us finding him, or him finding us, before Baron Al caught up with us or we ran out of water or food—what little we were able to grab."

Danny's tone suddenly changed. Up to this point, he had been matter-of-fact about his tale, as though he was distantly recalling it from memory. But now the memory became crystal clear, and his tone dropped down to a hush, a sadness invading the very timbre of his voice.

"Thing is, it was too late for Dad. There was a firefight as we got out of Charity, and he caught a couple of slugs. It didn't seem too bad, but I guess he was bleeding a lot inside, and he got less and less strong the more hours we were in the wag. It was evening when we broke out of Charity. By morning he'd bought the farm. I managed to keep driving, even though I'd never actually driven a wag before. I guess I must have nearly bought that farm by the time some of Joe's people found me. They must have seen the wag on a patrol or something. Shit, I don't know how else they could have come across us, as I don't think Dad knew where he was heading, and I sure as shit didn't. It was fate. As Joe says. He recognized my dad when they brought the wag in, and I guess I've been there ever since."

Danny shrugged, his story over.

"So you wanna get even with that scumbag Baron Al?" Dean said.

Danny nodded. "Guess we all do, but yeah."

"Have to see what we can do, right, you guys?" Dean added, addressing Jak and Doc.

"Fight is fight," Jak said noncommittally.

They were rounding the base of the mountain, coming around to the direction in which they had first faced, and the direction in which their objective lay. Now the mission was about to begin.

Lonnie turned to them as they reached the last point of shadow, with only the blazing heat of the day ahead. "Cut the crap," he said simply. "We need to preserve our strength and breath for this."

"Yeah, and that means you especially," Mik added, giving Danny a beady-eyed stare. "You talk far too much, kid."

BACK IN THE REDOUBT, Correll was dividing the remaining people into groups to take turns at training, target practice and maintenance of equipment.

One thing that all the companions had noted in their brief time at the redoubt was that the only Hellbenders to carry blasters had been those that had formed the defensive party that had met them a few levels down. The rest of the redoubt dwellers were unarmed.

Ryan raised the matter with Correll, who told him, "We don't have to among ourselves. Fate has brought us all together for a reason, and when you're united in that purpose, then there's no need for blasters. Sure, the sec that met you have their blasters still—it's a precaution till we get to know you, especially as we didn't ask for yours."

"Why not?" Ryan asked.

To which Correll shrugged. "You wanted to keep blasting, you wouldn't have agreed to a truce down on the lower level. It's fate."

The one-eyed man was, in truth, a little baffled by the reasoning of the Hellbenders' leader, but decided the best course of action was to say nothing. When both parties could benefit from the action on Charity and Summerfield, it didn't make sense to rock the boat.

Krysty and Mildred were among the first to be sent to target practice, while Ryan was deputed to be on the first training party, honing reflexes and fitness in the gym section of the old redoubt. J.B., as he'd suspected, was sent along to assist Jenny at the armory, making sure that blasters were oiled, cleaned and supplied with spare clips and belts of ammo for those who would be assigned them, and that all grens were primed and ready for action.

But as soon as he arrived at the armory, he knew he was going to have problems. The Native American woman had just dispatched the recce party, and so was still in the quartermaster's stores when the Armorer arrived at the empty room. He punched the sec code into the panel, and as the door swept back with a low hiss, he echoed this with a low whistle at the sight within.

Stepping into the dim room, he turned to the panel on the wall beside the interior sec door switch, and lighted the room.

Like all redoubt armories, it was large warehouse of a room, with a low ceiling but a deep set, going back some twenty-five feet into the rock. The walls were lined with racks on which were boxes of rifles, pistols and ammunition, boxes of grens and plas-ex, and racks in which rifles and machine pistols with extensions were stored upright.

There were Uzis, Heckler & Kochs, Steyrs, Smith & Wesson M-4000s, and a couple of antitank rifles and bazookas that were stored upright to one side of the armory.

J.B. stepped farther into the room and examined the markings on the sides of the boxes. There was also a variety of Smith & Wesson and Glock handblasters, as well as the relevant ammo. The plas-ex was of the expected variety, and the grens came in both shrapnel, stun and gas varieties, giving the attack party an extensive choice of weaponry from which to arm themselves.

J.B. had very rarely seen a redoubt—even the one that had been inhabited by the descendants of the original soldiery where they had encountered the Rat King comp— in which the armory had been so beautifully maintained. The air-conditioning system, which in most redoubts had an automatic dust removal filter, had obviously been kept in working order, and whoever had been put in charge of the armory here had been true to their job in keeping the weapons on view oiled and maintained. He opened a couple of the cases at random, and under the oilskin cloths that protected the different blasters he found that time had been put into keeping the weapons in combat-ready condition.

The Armorer replaced the lid on the last crate he had checked, and sat back on his haunches in front of the black metal racks that housed the crated weapons. He pushed his fedora back on his head and scratched at his hairline. Behind the glass of his spectacles, his eyes glittered with thoughts and ideas that shot across his brain:

given the combination of weapons, he was already trying to work out the allocation and placing of certain weaponry in order to maximize the potential for winning.

J.B. was lost in a world of strategies and alternative planning, and so didn't consciously hear Jenny outside the closed sec door. But at the first whirr of the door as it began to move, he whirled around, and was ready for her as she entered the room. He was glad, as from her expression she wasn't pleased to see him.

"You couldn't wait for me?" It was phrased as a question but contained more than a hint of suspicion.

J.B. shrugged. "Correll asked me to come down here and take a look around. There was no one about when I got here, so I was just taking an inventory."

"Trying to find fault?"

"No, you keep a good armory. Everything's in excellent condition. It's rare to see that."

Her attitude softened slightly. "I'll take that as a compliment."

"One thing, though."

"Yeah?" Her attitude hardened immediately.

"Don't be defensive. I just want to know if any of these weapons have ever been used."

Confusion clouded her brow. "I don't know. I've been doing this a few years, but before that..." She paused, thinking back. "I don't recall any ever being used on an attack. We keep ourselves to ourselves and don't get many intruders."

J.B. ignored the way in which the last remark had been

pointed and concentrated on the important point. "Okay, so if these are well kept but unused, there's a few tests we should run."

"Such as?"

He allowed the briefest of smiles to ghost across his lips at her attitude. "Well, if you'll stop hitting out every time I say something, then mebbe I'll get a chance to show you."

Chapter Six

The trip across the wastelands that lay between the redoubt and the ville of Charity was uneventful for most of the first day. Not uneventful in the sense of nothing happening and it being an easy trek, but rather in the sense of it being a seemingly unending slog of relentless tedium, with nothing to break up the monotony and put marker points or breathing spaces in the day.

There was no other way to tackle the trek on foot than like this. Lonnie, who was leading the expedition, had a chart that had been drawn up from the knowledge of the terrain gleaned by years of patrolling the area, and he also had a portable sextant that Dean recognized immediately as being similar to the one the J.B. used to chart their position in the Deathlands whenever they arrived at a new destination and exited a redoubt.

There was little in the way of shelter and respite along the route, which had to be as straight a line as possible. It was a heel of a distance to Charity, and the only way to do it on foot in the time they had been allocated was to head straight for it. Unfortunately for the party, this meant a day's long slog across the desert wastes under the harsh and pitiless glare of the rad-blasted sun, walking at a steady pace that was slow enough to preserve some of their precious water by not perspiring too freely with the effort, but quick enough to maintain a steady rate at covering the distance.

They walked mostly in silence, each individual counting his or her steps and keeping time to a steady beat to maintain the pace. It was strange how, after a short while, time began to mean little, and distance even less. All that mattered was the relentless tyranny of the beat, as they kept time with an almost metronomic regularity.

As they traveled, Danny began to lag. Oddly, Doc kept pace well. If anything, the Hellbenders in the party had expected the seemingly old man to be the one who would hold them up. But Jak and Dean knew well enough that Doc knew his limitations, and would cut his cloth accordingly. Doc hadn't kept himself alive for so long without knowing how to cope with the stresses and weaknesses that time trawling had put on his prematurely aged body. The grim set of his mouth and the dull, lifeless eyes staring ahead, seeing something that was only in his own head, bespoke of the effort he was putting in to the trek.

Lonnie, Mik and Tilly were well used to the physical demands of the desert, but Danny had spent most of his short life with his head buried in pieces of old tech, and so was unprepared for the rigors of walking in the desert. Dean dropped back when the youngster began to flag, lending him an arm and walking him into step so that he established a better rhythm to his walk, maximizing the efficiency of his stride. He even whispered "One-two-three-four-one-two-three-four" in time with their walk, urging Danny to repeat it as a mantra and so work himself into the pace better.

It worked, and every time the youngster started to fall behind, Dean was able to ease him into step easily.

Which left Jak, who was adaptable and hardened to almost every kind of environment, to take in the harsh and unwelcoming landscape around them as they traveled. The albino took the pace with ease, and had a loping stride that almost seemed to propel him forward of its own accord as his heavy combat boots appeared to bounce off the dusty surface with each footfall.

In truth, there was little to see. They walked miles between pitifully small patches of scrub, a few sickly trees and patches of crabgrass all that marked the passing of another oasis. But Jak was still pleased to see them, as it boded well for there being some sort of moisture present in the dusty soil, an opportunity of having some plant life from which to glean some moisture if their own canteens ran low.

And where there was scrub, there was also bound to be some kind of animal or reptile life. Certainly there were insects, as they had found themselves attacked individually and as a group by a few stray mutie insects that were derived from mosquitoes but had larger bodies and fibrous wings that beat with a loud hum in the still desert air. They seemed to hunt individually or in pairs, not in swarms, and although they were large and irritating, they were easily frightened away by a wave of the arm and the use of the insect repellent that had been handed to them from the redoubt stores. It was over a hundred years old, and developed for insects that hadn't been genetically mutated by radiation, but it was obviously still extremely potent.

As they passed the oases, Jak caught sight of small, meerkat creatures diving for cover into their burrows. They seemed small and harmless enough, but Jak knew from long experience that you don't know the dangers a new animal holds until you have to come up against it.

Likewise the lizard life that he observed, poking their heads above ground from their holes in the dry and dusty earth, cold and expressionless eyes observing the strangers who passed their territory. They seemed to be Gilas, but small and perhaps harmless. One thing for sure—Jak didn't particularly want to come up against their claws and perhaps venomous tongues.

Also, in the distance and possibly beyond the senses of the others, not as finely honed as Jak's in the first instance, and dulled further by the monotony of their march, he was sure that there were some packs of either cat or dog type creatures—possibly wild coyote. There were either several packs, or they were being tracked from a distance.

Jak noted this at the back of his mind. It was a good reason to be even more triple alert than the others, who had seemed to notice nothing this far.

But there was to be a more immediate problem, and from a most unexpected quarter.

The sun had long since traveled past its peak, and the setting of the angry red orb and a cessation of the heat weren't far away. The light began to fade as the night fell, and the recce party was able to slacken its pace.

"Another couple of miles and we should be able to camp for the night," Lonnie croaked in a harsh whisper, the arid air and necessary conservation of their water leaving him with a parched and aching throat.

"Good," Jak replied. "Make camp before too cold."

"Yeah," Lonnie agreed, looking up at the twilight sky, which was clear of any cloud cover. "Gonna be a cold one. Next patch of scrub is about two miles ahead. Should be able to get there and make the camp before it gets too cold."

"About fucking time," Mik moaned, "I need to eat and rest."

"That's all you ever do anyway," Tilly retorted.

"Children, children," Doc chided, chuckling, "please let's save the arguments until we are safely home."

But Jak wasn't listening to the easy banter of the tired people who had rest within sight. His attention was taken by something that was just to the right of the course they were taking.

"Look," he said, indicating the object, "what that?"

Lonnie followed the line of the albino's arm to where the object lay on the desert floor.

"Fucked if I know," he murmured. "It's not in our path, though, so why bother?"

"Because whatever make it mebbe is," Jak answered.

Lonnie indicated his grudging agreement with a shrug. "Mebbe take a look, then," he grunted, leading the party off their chosen course.

"Aw, c'mon, is this really necessary?" Mik moaned, his ratlike features contorted into mock agony. "We really need to make camp."

"I don't want to detour any more than you do," Lonnie retorted hotly, "but Jak's right, dammit. We can't take risks out here."

He led the group toward the object that Jak had questioned. It would waste little time and effort, in truth, as the object was only a short detour from their objective, and so would still enable them to make camp before the rapidly cooling night became too cold.

As they approached the object, they realized that it was much taller than it at first appeared. It was about ten feet in height, and seemed to be made of a spiral of round earth, damp and somehow molded together, that wound its way up from a broad base to a point that seemed to end arbitrarily.

They gathered around the bottom of it, and at a gesture from Lonnie spread out so that they encircled it.

"What you reckon?" Lonnie rasped. "How far around does this damn thing go?"

"Got to be twenty-five, thirty feet," Dean answered.

"Shit, what makes something this big? And how?" Tilly asked tremulously.

"That ain't difficult to answer," Danny said with a sad shake of his head. "Think about it, Tilly. What do we know that's this big?"

"You have got to be kidding me," she replied. "Not all the way out here?"

"My dear girl," Doc chided softly, "just because you think of those rather large worms as always burrowing through the depths of what you have taken as your home, it doesn't mean that they exist purely within the confines of that area alone. Good Lord, they are, after all, in transit. Where, pray tell, do you think they have come from, or indeed where they are going?"

"Yeah," Mik interjected, "but you never see anything like that down in the tunnels, for Chrissakes...just what the fuck is it, exactly?"

"A cast," Dean answered him in a matter-of-fact tone. "It's what the worm shits out after it's eaten its way through the earth."

Mik stepped back. "So this is worm shit?" he screeched.

Dean allowed himself a laugh. "Yeah, good as."

Mik spit on the ground, and was about to say something when Lonnie cut him short.

"If it's leaving this here," the recce leader stated flatly, "then it means that it must have surfaced near here."

Jak nodded. "Wonder how long that take you," he muttered. "Check it long gone, yeah?"

Lonnie restrained himself from attacking Jak for what he saw as the latter's insolence in the face of his position as recce leader, and nodded briefly. "Fan out and search," he said sharply.

"What the fuck are we looking for?" Mik whined. "And will it take long?"

"Look burrow," Jak stated, breaking across Lonnie.

"Yeah, and it shouldn't be hard to miss," Dean added.

The party spread out, fanning backward around the cast, which stood like some mute monument to mutie nature.

It was Doc who found the hole, following a trail in the dust.

"This way," he called. "The desert wind has covered the impression, but if the light was better I think you might notice that it has left a trail. It must be remarkably light for its size, as it has not impressed much, but I fear it has left its burrow here."

Doc prodded around with his foot as the others all turned toward him. He seemed to be probing the earth with his toes and the end of his cane, as though something didn't make sense.

Jak quickened his pace, breaking into a run. Dean did likewise when he saw the albino increase his speed, but he didn't realize why Jak had taken such action. Seeing Doc's apparently aimless motions, Jak had realized that the giant mutie worm had left some cast behind it to cover the hole it had made at the entry to the burrow. But this was just to cover its tracks—the majority of the cast was aboveground, as they had seen. On the assumption that the worm couldn't produce more than it had ingested from the earth, that meant that there wasn't enough cast left for the hole to be covered deeply.

With a sudden cry of surprise, Doc found the boundary of the wormhole as his cane and left leg plunged through the thin crust of the cast, and he began to fall through into the hole beneath, which could extend into the earth to any depth before the cast deposits began again.

Within a matter of seconds, Jak had reached Doc. He slowed when he was a few feet from the older man, scanning the earth around for signs of where the wormhole began. Doc's descent had been slowed by the fact that he was relatively light, and although the cast couldn't support his weight, particularly after his prodding had broken through it in one spot, it was still porous and damp enough for the earth to hold together, and thick enough to stop him falling straight through.

The line delineating where the hole ended was indicated by the damper earth of the cast, which had begun to be sucked in at the sides. So it was easy for Jak to pick out—even in the fading light—just where the solid ground ended and the thin crust of earth cast began.

Dean came up beside the albino, and following his line of view, took in what Jak could see.

"Hang on, Doc," he called. "Don't move too much, it'll disturb the surface."

"While I thank you for your sage and timely advice, I think I may just have been able to work that out for myself," Doc returned with more than a hint of sarcasm. "However, I fear that before too long I may not be able to help moving, particularly in a downward direction at a rapid rate."

"Okay, Doc—just hang on," Dean repeated as he turned to Jak. "Well?"

The albino looked from the old man to the edge of the circle, sizing it up rapidly. "Follow," he snapped, running around the hole until he came to the point where the prone Doc was nearest to the edge of the cast circle.

The other members of the recce party had by now joined them, but stood back to let Jak take control.

Pointing across and gesturing, Jak told Dean, "Crawl across, spread weight. Take Doc then try pull back. Take my legs and pull fucking hard."

Dean nodded shortly, and Jak dropped to his belly, edging across the cast surface toward Doc, using his arms and legs to spread his weight over as much of the surface as possible and not disturb the crust any more than was necessary.

"Jak, dear boy, so glad to see you," Doc breathed as the albino approached.

"Take each hand, try come with me," Jak said by way of acknowledgment, offering his outstretched hands to Doc, who gladly took them, placing his sword stick—extracted from the cast during his initial struggles—between his teeth. It had been with him throughout his dangers, and he was damned if he would yield it so easily.

Jak felt Doc's grip on his wrist clamp into place, the older man's fingers like iron, despite his apparent frailties. In return, the albino closed his hands around Doc's forearms, his own grip tightening and digging into the stringy sinews of the older man. Jak began to shuffle backward, using his feet to try to gain purchase without digging too far into the crust and breaking it any more than it had been broken already.

On the edge of the circle, Dean also dropped to his belly and reached out to grab Jak's ankles as they came within range. He steeled himself, knowing that once he grabbed hold he had to cling on for dear life and be prepared for the sudden shock and pull downward should the crust give way beneath Jak and Doc.

Jak's ankles met with Dean's hands, and the young Cawdor grasped tightly, beginning to flex his biceps and pull backward, adding his own momentum to the backward motion of the albino.

Doc felt the crust yield around him, its spongy grip giving way as he wriggled and tried to haul himself forward with the help of the pull that Jak was exerting. Slowly, with an almost infinite care that had to be balanced with the inevitable moment when time would give out and the crust would just collapse from its own decay, the albino hunter and Doc began to move across the surface of the cast, Jak's ankles and half of his calves now over the edge of the cast and back on solid ground.

Doc's leg came free, and he was just edging his way out of the hole when he felt the cast begin to give way around him. By unplugging the gap he had caused, he had freed the vacuum and allowed the hole beneath to suck in the rest of the cast.

"It is going!" he yelled as the earth fell away beneath him, dragging him with it until he fell free with a sudden jolt that made his shoulders lurch sickeningly. In turn, Jak felt the sudden pull of gravity on Doc's weight shoot through his own shoulders before he, too, was rendered defenseless by the loss of the cast surface beneath him. Agony shot through him as his knees buckled the wrong way, his legs kept rigid by that part of them anchored to the solid earth by Dean.

"Quick, help him," Danny yelled, seeing the agony on Dean's face as he tried to cling to Jak and Doc, and attempt to pull them out of the hole, which had now fully opened.

The other three members of the recce party were quick to move to Dean's aid, helping Danny to secure Dean and take some of the strain by grabbing at Jak's legs.

Pulling back, Mik and Tilly had hold of Dean, while Lonnie and Danny reached out over the hole to grasp Jak and haul him in, Lonnie grabbing hold of Doc as he came into view.

Before too long, Jak and Doc were on solid ground, the older man lying on his back, gasping for breath and feeling the burning agony of stretched muscle and tendons, while Jak lay facedown, gathering himself. Dean rolled over onto his back, breathing heavily, and spoke to the sky.

"Thanks" was all he could utter.

Lonnie was about to say something when a distant rumble stopped him dead. Jak looked up sharply, his senses instinctively placing the sound as under the earth.

"Big trouble," he said.

Chapter Seven

Mildred lined up the target, drawing a bead with her ZKR. The Czech-made target pistol sat lightly in her hand, palm firm around the grip, finger coiled around the trigger, squeezing with an infinite gentleness and care. Her free hand was cupped lightly beneath, supporting but not pressuring. She could feel the eyes of the Hellbenders she had joined at the target range bore into her back, willing her to screw up.

No way. In the days before skydark, when she had won a silver medal at the last Olympiad before the nukecaust, she had felt eyes boring into her many times. Then it was idle competition; this time it was deciding whether she could hack it in a life-or-death situation. In many ways the pressure was equal. It all came down to whether Mildred could shut herself off, focus on the task in hand and score on the target.

No problem.

She squeezed her trigger finger and let loose a cluster of four shots, two to the center of the target that circled the mannequin's chest, and two to the target that was—of necessity—much smaller and situated in its head.

"Check that out," she said clearly as the deafening noise of the cordite explosions began to subside in the enclosed target room.

A lean black man with a shorn crop of black-and-gray hair that was receding took hurried strides toward the target mannequin. He was shorter than Mildred—about five feet four—and was composed almost entirely of muscle. He was the only black man in the entire redoubt, and had been eyeing her since she had arrived in the shooting gallery. The fact that she was the only black woman may have had something to do with it, but Mildred wasn't too keen to address this fact. She wanted to get in the shooting practice that Correll had ordered and get back to her patient. Cy had come around shortly before she had left the med lab, and she wanted to run a couple of tests.

"Hey, sister, that was pretty fine shooting," the man at the target yelled back over the length of the room. "Two clean shots in the center of each area. That's a good eye."

"A still target isn't a problem," she replied with a dismissive wave. "A moving one is much more of a challenge—and much more realistic."

"She's got a point, Rudi," agreed another of the Hellbenders clustered in the gallery. Besides Mildred and Rudi, who was now making his way back toward the group, there were four others, none of whom she particularly recognized. A small, sturdy woman with short blond hair and green eyes looked at Mildred askance.

"You always like to play hunter, do ya?" she asked. Mildred thought she caught an edge in the woman's voice. She wasn't the only one. Rudi gave the woman a sharp stare.

"Leave it, Cath," he snapped.

"I was only saying," the blonde replied. "Papa Joe sent her here to get some practice in, right? Only she ain't really doing that if she just shoots at a standing target, is she?"

It seemed reasonable enough, but there was an edge to the woman's voice that the other three Hellbenders in the room picked up on. There were two men and a woman, all dressed in camou and showing the muscularity that suggested Correll liked to train his people hard. Other than that, Mildred couldn't yet identify them. They exchanged glances that Mildred read as meaning that the blonde could be trouble. Without meaning to, Mildred had walked into a situation.

There was only one way out.

"She's right," Mildred said with mock sadness, shaking her head so that her plaits swung about her. "I really need to take the more difficult option here."

The blonde grinned with a lopsided expression that made her look sinister, an impression reinforced by her tone of voice as she said, "That can be arranged."

She walked over to a panel on the wall, where Rudi joined her. While they argued in whispers that Mildred couldn't quite catch, one of the others came across to her.

"Cath thinks everyone is after Rudi," he said simply, "and she's a possessive bitch. But harsh. You know how this works?" he asked, indicating the range. Mildred shook her head, so he outlined the course briefly, and had just finished when Cath and Rudi came over to Mildred.

"You ready to show how good you are?" the blonde said, sneering. When Mildred nodded, she added, "I've set the fucker on the highest level, just to give you a good workout."

"Thanks," Mildred said, trying to keep the sarcasm from her voice.

She took her mark at the beginning of the course, and waited.

The lights dimmed, and Cath screamed "Go!" as she triggered the course.

Mildred had to take the course at top speed, running down the middle of the concourse from one end to the other. Along the way she had to fire at opposition targets as they sprang up, avoid firing at figures without targets that were sprung as decoys, and also avoid being hit by opposition fire, which was indicated by paint bombs.

It was a test of her reflexes, her flexibility and her sure eye. The targets were to each side and in front, causing her to change direction and pull back at speed as they sometimes sprang up to her rear, or right in front of her. And all the time she was acutely aware of the paint bombs that were fired from oblique positions.

The two-hundred-yard course was littered with targets and decoys, and Mildred had to pitch and roll to avoid the paint bombs, snapping off shots as she rolled or came to her feet, twisting around the targets and decoys that hurled upward into her path, giving her little time to catch her breath, let alone reload the ZKR.

She acted completely on instinct, letting it wash over

her conscious mind and take control, and before she knew it, she was at the end of the course, back against the wall, panting heavily.

The lights came up. She looked down, there was no paint anywhere on her body. She turned and tried to look over her shoulder, but the whoops of the other Hellbenders told her that she had made it through unscathed. Rudi was walking the length of the course, whistling softly to himself. When he reached Mildred he looked at her, shook his head in disbelief and turned to the others.

"She hit all the bastard targets and didn't chill a decoy," he yelled, unable to keep the amazement from his voice.

Mildred was also unable to contain herself. Not only was she pleased that her senses and instinct were still sharp, but she also couldn't resist a wry grin at the expression of frustration and displeasure on Cath's face.

"Now, if you'll excuse me, I have work to do." Despite herself, she was unable to prevent a little smugness from intruding on her tone as she left the Hellbenders to their target practice and returned to the med lab.

TRAINING TOOK PLACE in the gym that was on the third level of the redoubt. It was still fully equipped from beyond skydark, with a variety of gym equipment both manual and electronic. In the center of the room, a space was cleared for a gym mat that delineated an area where unarmed combat could take place.

Ryan and Krysty were training along with several of the Hellbenders. Many of them were using the old treadmills to work on their muscle strength and stamina, walking long distances at a fast pace with full backpack and weaponry to simulate marching conditions. Ryan was among those who were using the wall bars to climb, hauling themselves up by their arms alone in order to increase arm strength.

Krysty was standing with a small group that was training in unarmed combat, perfecting methods of hand-to-hand fighting.

Training in hand-to-hand was always tricky. There was no way that any of them could pull punches, as that would be almost to defeat the point of playing. However, to seriously damage one of your colleagues with the planned attack so close wasn't a good thing. So the only option was for both opponents in the ring at any time to concentrate on defense.

A short, stocky man with Hispanic coloring and flowing black hair tied back in a ponytail was in combat with Travis. They were evenly matched in terms of physique, but Travis moved more quickly, jerkily, and with a sense of nervousness that the other man didn't possess.

One of the spectators leaned across to Krysty. "See Juan," he whispered from the corner of his mouth, "he's just about the best fighter we've got in here. Guy's so good that he doesn't need a blaster."

"Everyone need a blaster, no matter how good," the Titian-haired beauty replied, "because if your opponent has one, then you're fucked if you can't fight from a distance of more than a few feet."

"Guess you're right there." The Hellbender chuckled, stroking the short, stubbly beard that decorated his pointed chin.

Whether Juan heard this exchange, Krysty couldn't tell. She just knew that suddenly he increased the intensity of his attack, and from making purely defensive moves to block Travis's assault, he upped a gear and moved onto the offensive. Blocking a forearm punch from his opponent, Juan followed through smoothly to drive Travis's arm back, leaving the area of his chest exposed. Travis moved his other arm across to block the expected blow that Juan shaped to make, but instead of making the chop that his flattened hand suggested, the Hispanic shuffled to move his weight and brought up one foot to drive it into the now exposed and turned groin of his opponent. Caught out completely, the sharp blow drove the breath from Travis's body as a lightning pain shot through his groin, the trapped nerve deadening all sensation in his leg and making it buckle while his genitals and lower gut felt as though a red-hot knife had been slicing through them.

Stunned by the pain and loss of balance, Travis fell forward, stumbling and throwing his arms open to try to regain his balance. Juan took full advantage of this defenseless position by driving home a one-two fisted attack, the right hand taking the prone man in the chest and driving him back, his head snapping up in shock and pain and coming into the perfect position for the second blow to slam into his mouth and nose, the hard knuckles of the Hispanic shattering two of his teeth and causing others to drive into the soft pulp flesh of his mouth while his nose exploded in a shower of blood, the tender skin and cartilage of the septum rupturing.

Travis's eyes turned up in his head, and he toppled backward, unconscious before he hit the mat, his head bouncing hard, twice, before he came to rest.

"I need nothing," Juan said in a low growl, turning to where Krysty stood. His eyes were dulled by blood lust, and they bore into her with a stony expression. "So what do you need?" he added coldly.

"Nothing," the woman replied, her own eyes equally cold, the hair about her face and neck fluttering wildly as the prehensile tissue within it responded to the sudden danger. "And that really wasn't necessary. If you have something you want to prove, then prove it."

"I just have," Juan said.

Krysty raised an eyebrow. "Really? I didn't notice you tell Travis you'd changed the rules."

"There are no rules."

"Yeah? You gonna tell Correll that if Travis can't take part in the attack—if anyone else you mess up can't take part in the attack?" She waited, but the Hispanic refused to answer.

Krysty continued, "Thought not. If you have something to say to me—something to prove to me—then you deal with it with me. Understand?"

Still keeping her eyes on him, Krysty moved onto the mat. She removed the blaster that was holstered in the small of her back and placed it at the side of the mat, her eyes still fixed on the Hispanic. Juan moved back and thumbed his cheek, wiping sweat from it. His eyes were like steel as he returned her stare.

"So you want to go the whole way?"

"Yeah," she replied. "If that's what it takes."

"What about your boyfriend?" Juan asked her, gesturing to where Ryan was positioned, his forearms and calves entwined on a rope dangling from the ceiling. The one-eyed man was observing, but made no effort to move for any of his blasters or for his panga. Indeed, he kept his face set and hard, betraying no emotions of any kind.

Krysty didn't look over her shoulder. She knew how Ryan would react. It was imperative that she fight this battle herself, and that he be seen openly to give her no support. All the companions had to prove to the Hellbenders that they stood by themselves, and that although they were together there were no free rides. They also had to show—if possible—that they were better fighters, and stronger.

"He's got nothing to do with this," Krysty replied calmly. "This is you and me. I win, you stop playing the fool and work toward winning the real battle, not showing off like a triple-stupe kid."

"And if I win—which I will?"

"Then you can chill me if you like. No one, and I mean no one, will stop you," Krysty answered.

"Then it begins," Juan said simply.

He moved forward, crouched low, his gaze needle sharp to spot the slightest movement of muscle that would betray her intentions in terms of direction and action. Sensing this, Krysty stayed still, the only thing that moved being her hair.

"Ya know," Juan muttered in a menacing undertone, "the only thing I hate more than a smart-mouth is a mutie. And you're nothing more than a smart-mouth mutie bitch, which puts you lower 'n the lowest gaudy slut."

"You'll have to do better than that if you want to rile me," she replied.

Now! Before she even had a chance to finish the sentence, Juan had made his move, stepping forward on his right foot and feinting a chop with his right hand. Her speech should have been enough to slow her defenses for that vital second for him to break through, especially as he wished to deceive her over the actual direction of the blow. In theory, she should have moved late to stop a right-hand blow and left herself open to a left-hand attack.

At least, that was what Juan expected. What he got was an entirely different matter, as Krysty moved in the opposite direction and then bent into the now misplaced left-hand punch, grabbing his wrist and using the momentum to throw the Hispanic off balance. Juan was thrown forward, and as his rib cage passed her, she brought her foot up in a vicious kick, the pointed silver toe of her boot catching him beneath the last rib and driving the breath from his body. He screamed with the pain and tried to turn and fall well as she released him, her parting gesture being to viciously twist and sprain his wrist as she let go.

The Hispanic was unable to fall correctly from this hold, and his shoulder jarred painfully as he hit the mat.

"Shit, the mutie bitch is hot to trot," said an unidentified voice in the gathering crowd.

"Fuck it, can't trust them," breathed another.

Ryan had stayed up on the rope, believing it best to stay well away and let Krysty win this one on her own—as he was sure she could. But he scanned the crowd gathered around the mat, trying to identify who had uttered the last sentences. The last thing he wanted was for there to be problems because the Hellbenders were suspicious of Krysty's mutie genes.

Krysty, for her part, heard the comments and saw red. Mebbe that was Juan's problem. The Hispanic was trying desperately to scramble to his feet, but he was badly winded, and his wrist let him down when he tried to put weight on it, causing him to collapse again.

She took another step over to him and lifted him by the hair, slamming her fist into his cheekbone as she did so, then letting him fall before he had a chance to flail back at her. He slammed back onto the gym mat, blood pouring from the shattered inside of his mouth.

"Is that it?" she asked, breathing heavily and yet speaking with an ominous calm. "Is that why you felt the need to prove yourself? Because I'm just a mutie to you and therefore inferior? You stupe bastard, we're all the same here, even those of us who've just joined you. We are one because we have one target. It's Charity that's the enemy, not me. I ought to really finish you off, in case you get any bright ideas about settling scores later."

Juan had struggled onto his elbows while she said this,

and she took advantage of that to take a kick at him, placing her foot under his rising body so that her toes connected with his breastbone, jolting his heart and making him yelp with intense pain. The momentum of her kick drove him farther upward, and she grabbed him by the hair, pulling him to his feet with one hand while she drove a succession of jabs into his face with the other. By the time she stopped, he was nearly unconscious, and his face was a mess of bruised and swollen flesh.

She let him fall to the mat and then looked at the gathered Hellbenders, her eyes flashing defiance.

"He's not worth chilling. Neither am I. Save that for the attack. Nothing is stronger than a blaster at a distance, but remember I know that, too, if you think about settling his score for him."

With which she pushed her way through the crowd and stormed out of the gym room.

Ryan slid down the rope. He observed the stunned crowd and smiled with a vulpine lack of humor.

"Think about what she said...and just be glad she's on your side when the attack comes."

Chapter Eight

"By the Three Kennedys!" Doc breathed, "surely not..."

The old man lay a few feet from the giant wormhole, gathering his thoughts and regaining what breath he could. Dean was on his haunches, breathing heavily, while Jak still lay facedown, frozen by his close attention to the rumbling, which grew louder by the second.

Mik, Danny, Lonnie and Tilly stood close by, also frozen as they listened.

"What...is that?" Danny asked slowly, in the tones of one who actually knew the answer but didn't wish to make an acknowledgment of that knowledge.

"Mutie worm," Jak barked, jumping to his feet. "Disturbed burrow, made fear danger."

"So it's coming to investigate?" Mik yelled in disbelief. "Why doesn't the stupe fucker just run away, like any other intelligent dumb creature would?"

"Apart from the inherent contradiction in that last statement, I would say it was a pointless question. Better just to get the hell away from here ourselves," Doc answered him, scrambling to his feet and making tracks to run away from the hole.

"Doc's right," Dean cried. "That thing's going to make a bigger hole when it comes out than when it went in, and what's more it has all that disturbed cast to push out of the way."

"Great, a worm-shit shower," Mik said.

They were all on their feet now and running in the same direction. They were headed back toward the path they had been taking, bringing them back on course for Charity and away from the giant cast that had attracted their attention in the first instance.

"How do we know that this isn't where the worm is going to surface and we're running right into it?" Danny yelled breathlessly as they ran.

Dean would have yelled back that the creature was most likely to come back up its own tunnel rather than create a new one, but was stayed from this by a gigantic shudder that rippled through the earth and threw them from their feet.

"Fuck-fuck-fuck-fuck—"

Dean could hear Mik swear over and over like a mantra, forming an undertone to the rumble and then explosion as the worm surfaced, throwing the dry desert earth into the air with an explosive force, showering them with dry dust and particles of hard-packed earth. It was fortunate that most of the topsoil in this region was so devoid of moisture, that the dry earth scattered and parted so easily, with only the densely packed pieces being hard but small enough not to cause anything other than the slightest abrasions and discomfort.

The rain of dry soil was followed the dull whump of packages of damper soil that rained down—the cast from the tunnel, thrown up by the rapid exit of the worm, which had been flung high and far on a trajectory that brought some of it down to the point where they lay prone on the ground. The cast was heavier, and the larger deposits were more dangerous. At such speed, they were likely to cause a more serious injury if they hit home.

"Hot pipe," Dean exclaimed, rolling onto his back, "watch out for that!" A large lump of damp soil hit the ground where he had lain but a moment before, the damp cast spreading as it splattered into the dry topsoil, making an impression where his head would have been and raising enough dust to suggest that it would at least have concussed him.

By this time, the others had also turned, and were trying to judge where the larger deposits of cast would fall as they moved around on the ground, wriggling from side to side. There was no time to actually get up and run, only to try to avoid the possibly damaging lumps of cast while still prone.

But it was because they were in such a position that, when the initial rain had ceased to fall, they were able to comprehend in its full and awesome glory the sight that confronted them.

The disturbed mutie worm had come straight up from the hole and was now erect, perpendicular to the sand and awesome in its length. At a glance, Dean judged it to be about fifty feet long, the tail end disappearing into the hole. It waved and undulated in a rippling motion, the continual movement of its segmented body the manner in which it was able to keep aloft. The end segment that acted as a head—although, as with all worms, this was arbitrary—moved around as if trying to detect the recce party. Of course, this was patently absurd, as it had no sensory organs with which to see or hear them as they lay on the desert surface. But it did have a mouth, just like the specimen that Jak, Dean and Doc had seen at the redoubt, and the strange rows of fleshy teeth rippled and undulated in its open mouth like a miniature version of the whole body. It had no vocal cords, but the movement caused resonances that ran through its whole body, amplified and then directed outward by the open mouth.

It was an eerie and disturbing sound, a high, keening wail that had a bass note running beneath that was only semiaudible, so that it could have been imagination that added it. The sound had waves of rippling notes and glissandi in it that echoed the worm's moving body. It was almost hypnotic, freezing them where they lay.

The creature was gigantic, its sheer size somehow magnified by the luminous nature of its body as it stood in the encroaching darkness. If it should, by chance or design, cause to fall across them and come down onto the desert floor, then it would crush them beneath the mucus-covered flesh of its body.

The thought of this caused Doc to snap out of his reverie. It was curious that it should be Theophilus Tanner, but on consideration, perhaps not so strange. Doc was used to drifting in and out of states where the real and the imaginary interacted and overlapped, leaving him in a space where it was difficult to judge the real. So when a real state that seemed hallucinatory occurred, then why should it not be Doc who would instinctively grasp the nature of the real?

None of which mattered to him then, although he would perhaps ponder it later. Now all that he could do was to take action to try to save his life, and the lives of his companions.

Doc moved with a swiftness remarkable in someone who appeared so old. He reached across to Mik, who was carrying a supply bag, and took it from him. Mik had been placed in charge of carrying spare ammo, grens and plas-ex. Doc opened the bag and picked out a gren. For good measure, he took a lump of plas-ex and wrapped it around the gren, hoping its sticky properties would make it hold to the smooth gren surface for long enough.

Scrambling to his feet, Doc launched himself toward the monster mutie. Somehow, the creature detected the movement and turned toward them, seeming to focus on the moving Doc. Its head section tilted, the teeth moving with a fearful viciousness within the otherwise bland and expressionless mouth, and the keening note changed again with the shape of the creature against the darkened skyline.

Crying out with the effort, Doc pulled the pin on the gren, drew back his arm and threw the explosive toward the open mouth. The head section lifted slightly as it detected the motion of the gren through the air, moving with the arc of the small object as the mouth opened and welcomed it.

The gren, still with the plas-ex wrapped around it, entered the mouth of the giant mutie worm, the sudden appearance of a foreign object changing once again the note emanating from its body.

"Down—duck and cover!" Doc yelled, dragging the phrase from somewhere within his unconscious, from something he had once heard.

All the members of the recce party threw themselves onto the desert floor, covering their heads from the rain that would inevitably follow, and to stop the noise making their eardrums ring too much.

The gren exploded inside the body of the giant mutie worm, the plas-ex wrapped around it boosting the power of the explosion so that it was at least doubled in intensity.

If they had been facing it, they would have marveled at the fact that one second the worm seemed to be rearing up in all its awesome glory, and the next it had simply disappeared, to be replaced by a rain of white, luminous flesh and mucus that seemed to radiate from one central point. The explosion spread down the worm, the shrapnel in the gren ripping the segments in such a way that it would make it impossible for them to survive as anything other than the smallest creatures. Even if they did possess a mutated version of the older worm genetics that would enable a chopped-up worm to regenerate into smaller, separate entities, then these would be so small as to not cause the recce party any problems. As the explosion spread, so the particles of exploded mutie worm rained out, too small to cause harm but uncomfortable as the flesh and mucus landed on their legs, backs and arms.

As the gren exploded, the noise was at first contained within the body, a dull roar that grew within a fraction of a second into a deafening clap as the wet, sickly sound of flesh slapping on flesh with extreme force blended into the sounds of destruction. The last high, keening notes of the undulating voice were also blended in with this before being subsumed by the sounds of the gren and the plas-ex.

It was over as quickly as it began, the last echoes of the explosion dying away on the night air, the last, far-flung particles of worm flesh falling to earth. Lonnie raised his head.

"Shit. That I could easily have done without, my friends," he said with a remarkable understatement.

Jak, always practical when it came to such matters, ignored this and asked, "How far from ville? Any chance hear that?"

Tilly considered this. "It's an empty old space between here and there, but I reckon it won't reach that far. Even if it does, you get trading parties traveling across this desert. They might expect a wag in a few hours at the most, but they won't expect us in about a day."

Jak nodded. "Good." He sniffed the now cold night air. "Should move on some, then set camp. Too cold travel now."

Lonnie agreed. "A half hour's walk should get us well out of range of that bastard hole—just in case there are any other of those mutie bastards ready to poke their ugly heads out. Let's move out."

The members of the party assembled, checked that they had everything they needed and nothing was left behind in the confusion—Doc handing the ammo bag back to Mik—and they began to march back onto their prescribed route to Charity.

A few miles passed before they felt safe enough to pitch camp in the partial shelter of a dried scrub oasis. Jak set a fire for warmth and they erected their tents, Lonnie allotting a watch rota.

Now calm after their encounter, they settled down to rest until morning, hoping that the remainder of the journey could be quick and incident free.

THE SUNRISE next morning was sudden, the night dissolving into day in a matter of minutes as the engorged orb of the red sun rose in the rad-blasted sky. Jak was on watch, and woke the others as the light infused the atmosphere.

"Eat, then go, yeah?" he said. "Make good ground before sun hot."

Lonnie agreed with the albino, and after they had breakfasted on their rations and taken as much water as they could to keep them going until their next break, they packed the tents and were ready to leave.

"Let's hope we don't have any more problems today," Danny remarked in a weary tone.

"Don't be such a baby," Tilly admonished. "We just keep our eyes open and deal with what comes...no more, no less, yeah?"

"'Spose..." Danny agreed reluctantly.

Lonnie took his bearings with the minisextant, and they began the long march to Charity. At present, although they were exposed, there was enough space around them for any distant wags to be spotted long before they would be spotted on foot. So it was safe for them to march in the open, although they all kept a watch for activity on the horizon, and for any shelter that might be close enough to provide them with shade from the burning sun when they rested.

The march was tedious, like the day before, and although they endeavored to keep alert, it was all too easy to fall into the stupor of following the beat of their footsteps and walking and thinking to that rhythm and that rhythm alone.

The only one of the party who avoided this was Jak. The albino teen's hunting senses told him to keep alert. Something was warning him that there was danger ahead, but he couldn't tell as of yet what that may be. So, as he walked, he kept all his senses on triple red, his eyes scanning the horizon and to all sides, no matter how much the harsh, bright light may hurt his pigmentless irises; he listened above and beyond the tramp of their feet and the sound of their breathing, filtering that out so that all other sounds came within his provenance and were analyzed for any possible signs of danger. More than that, he allowed his whole body to become attuned to the environment and the elements. Years of hunting in the bayou and after were brought into play by his subconscious mind.

He didn't know what it was, but something was bothering him. And while all this was operating on an unconscious level, his conscious mind was focusing on the events of the previous day, trying to remember anything that may give him a clue as to why he was feeling this way.

At one point, keeping their distance to an extent that he wasn't sure whether they were wild dogs or cats of some kind, there had been a pack that seemed to trail them for a while. Then they had simply disappeared. But Jak knew that creatures that took the time and trouble to track didn't just disappear. They faded into the shadows and bided their time. All creatures, including man, were the same.

So where was the pack now? Holed up somewhere, waiting?

Jak figured that this was a distinct possibility. He couldn't hear or see them, but he knew that they were there. And even if the rest of the recce party didn't know it yet, at least he'd be prepared for them.

The recce party had been marching for a little over three hours without a break when Lonnie held up a hand and stopped them. The line had straggled out a little over the past few miles, with fifty yards between Lonnie and Dean.

"'Kay, I figure we need a rest and water break," Lonnie husked through a cracked and parched throat, which attested to the truth of his statement. "See that crop over there? I reckon that'll give some shade. C'mon," he finished, keeping his words to a painful minimum. He turned and began to walk to the northeast of their chosen path, deviating slightly to reach the small outcrop and scrub about half a mile away, which would give them a minimal shelter while they rested.

The rest of the group followed, except Jak. The albino waited until the last of the group—Danny, inevitably—had passed him and stood facing the rocks.

The albino slowed his breathing, filtering out the sounds of his own nervous system and concentrating everything he had on the rocks ahead. He could hear little other than the sounds of his own companions as they walked and respired, but there was something underlying that he could barely make out. A scrabbling noise, as of small mammals moving with care. He could see nothing, but then again, his eyesight was poor at the best of times, let alone in such bright light. No, the important thing was smell.

Jak had a superb olfactory sense, and as he sniffed the air, he became certain that there was something lurking in the shelter of the rocks. Something musky and animal, something more than one or two in number. A pack, in fact, to judge from the confusion of odors that underlay the scent of the recce party.

Could it be that the pack he had noticed the day before somehow had the intelligence to work out their route and then ambush them? It seemed far-fetched, but any animal with enough sense to survive in this hostile environment would have learned behavior patterns that would ensure food, shelter and water. If other parties, on foot or in wags, had gone this way, then the animals—whatever they were—would have learned this.

So they were waiting for the recce party in the shadows and shelter of the rock—and the unsuspecting party was heading straight for them.

Jak was a few paces behind by now, and his lagging back had been noticed. Both Danny and Dean had turned to question his sudden halt. Danny had no way of knowing, but Dean knew the albino hunter well enough to realize that something was seriously wrong. He saw the way Jak was standing and the poise of the albino as he took in what was happening by the rocks.

Even as Dean watched, Jak sprang into action. From a standing start, he began to sprint toward the front of the party. He knew he couldn't yell, as the noise and the tone of his voice would alert the waiting creatures that something was wrong, and yet he couldn't let Lonnie walk into a trap.

The sound of Jak's feet pounding on the hard desert surface, raising clouds of dust in the late-morning air, alerted the recce party leader that something was amiss. He turned, as did the others, on hearing Jak approach.

"What—" he began.

It was then that Dean made a serious error of judgment. Not realizing in the heat of the moment why Jak had not alerted Lonnie by yelling at him, the young Cawdor raised the alarm.

"Watch out! Something's wrong!" he cried.

As soon as the first syllable escaped Dean's lips, Jak changed his tactics. Knowing that the creatures would now be alerted, the albino hunter drew the .357 Magnum Colt Python blaster from out of the depths of his jacket.

"Waiting behind rock," he yelled in a clipped, terse tone, hoping that he hadn't wasted precious fractions of a second by having to explain his actions. Wasted because, even as his mouth opened to utter the first sound, the creatures had begun to swarm from behind and over the rocks, alerted by Dean's cries.

Lonnie began to turn back to the rocks, his hands gripping the H&K he carried slung over his shoulder as he shrugged it into position with a practiced ease. What he saw made him freeze for a vital half moment. And in that time, the creatures were upon him.

For what he saw was a swarming posse of wild cats, more than he could ever recall seeing in one place. They had obviously evolved a kind of group or pack mentality that enabled them to communicate and work together in some fashion, for it was only by such a manner could they have contrived to have held their peace so well while waiting for the party to approach the rock. Come to that, knowing that they would approach the rock—or were at least likely to—was in itself a sign of an evolved group intelligence.

Although this flashed through Lonnie's mind, it wasn't the thing that impressed itself upon him the most. As he got the H&K into his hands, he was almost frozen to the spot by the sight that he beheld. What had been an empty expanse of rock a scant few moments before was now a heaving mass of multicolored fur, the surface of the rock seeming to ripple as the undulating mass of flesh and fur scuttled down and around the rock face, heading for the group.

They were wild cats, mostly dark-gray-and-black tabbies, with long fur that was matted and in some places bald, the pale gray skin showing through. A few of the cats showed white patches or touches of ginger in their coloring, which, en masse, just made the whole carpet of fur seem more amorphous and sinister. And the noise was immense. They yowled in fury and hate as they moved, a hunger seeming to permeate the very tone of their massed voice, the previously quiet desert air now rent asunder by the sounds of a hungry pack in full cry.

For, make no mistake, these were creatures in a feeding frenzy. From the look of those few that it was possible to pick out from the pack, either because of some different marking or because they rose from the pack to look around, the pack hadn't fed well for some time, and now they saw their opportunity.

For a moment, the entire recce party, apart from Jak, was frozen in awestruck horror by the sight. It was fortunate for their collective well-being that the albino hunter had his wits fully about him and was focused, as always, on survival.

Taking a combat firing stance to one side of where Lonnie was standing, the H&K frozen in his hands, Jak raised the Colt Python and fired into the pack. He aimed for the center of the front ranks as they poured off the rock and onto the desert floor. He squeezed the trigger until the blaster exploded deafeningly, the slight echo of it resounding against the rocks, but being deadened by the wall of fur that now covered the outcrop.

The powerful handblaster cut a swathe through the front ranks of the cats, ripping through thin flesh, splintering bone, and turning organs into a bloody mush. A couple of the cats took a full impact in their heads, skulls exploding in a shower that adhered to the matted coats of the animals around them.

It stopped the cats for a fraction of a second, as confusion spread through the pack, the smell of death hitting them strongly. Their collective purpose was for a moment lost as they scattered, a small gap on the rocks forming around the chilled animals.

That fraction of a second was enough. The sound of Jak's Python was enough to shake the recce party from the stunned inaction that the sight of the cat pack had caused.

"Nukeshit bastard—chill them now!" Lonnie yelled, beginning to fire with his H&K into the cat posse.

Mik and Tilly also opened up with their blasters—Tilly was carrying an Uzi, and Mik had a H&K like Lonnie. Danny also carried an Uzi, but showed his ineptitude in yet another inopportune moment by jamming the Uzi as he began to fire. Cursing, he fiddled awkwardly with the blaster while Dean stepped back to cover him, concentrating on precision shooting with the Browning Hi-Power that would keep the pack well back from them, even though his blaster alone couldn't put much of a hole in their numbers.

Doc, on the other hand, was more than able to do some serious damage. The older man stepped forward, his eyes glittering with anger as though the attack of the cats was in some way a personal affront. It would have been baffling to the others if they had noticed—if their attention had not been focused on the pack in front of them—but to Doc it truly was a personal matter.

In his head, Doc was no longer standing in the middle of the New Mexico desert after skydark, but was in the backyard of his home in Vermont, some two hundred years before. Young Jolyon was standing to one side of him, crying in pain and fear, his arm scratched hideously by a feral cat that had wandered from the nearby woods—the same creature that had been responsible for the death of Rachel and Jolyon's pet cat Matilda a few days before—and had responded to the young boy's desire to pet him with a vicious rake of the claw. That wild cat had been killed with a single shot from the Remington that Doc kept in the house for emergencies.

That cat; young Jolyon, whom he would never see again and who had probably died well over a century before and may never even have seen adulthood for all he knew; the danger posed by this motley crew...all of these things went through Doc's mind as he stepped forward and fired the shot chamber of the LeMat into the posse of wildcats.

The shot from the percussion blaster spread through the pack, ripping into them and generating high-pitched and terrible yowls of pain as more of the animals were wounded or chilled. Yet the fact that they were confused, and now were either in a feeding frenzy or a panic over the danger, made them disperse from pack movements, and made them harder to fire upon, their actions harder to predict or second-guess.

Some of the cats had turned upon themselves, either beginning to sate their hunger on the chilled animals, or sensing injury, fear and near death in others who had been hit, turning on them as easy targets. Others had taken fright at the sudden explosions of the blasters and the molten death that had passed among them. Driven wild with hate, hunger and fear, they were moving erratically, running between the legs of the recce party but not attacking, while others were trying a concerted approach to their actions, their claws and teeth attempting to scratch and bite through the tough material of the clothing worn by all the party members.

"Shit, they're feisty little fuckers!" Mik exclaimed, shaking one cat loose from his leg and then following through to kick another in the head as it tried to leap at him, the force of his combat boot dislocating the animal's jaw so that it sagged uselessly as the creature hit the ground.

"Yeah—watch jaws, though," Jak yelled back.

Dean, hearing this, took a closer look at the creature that approached him before taking a shot that cleaved the head of the creature. As it came toward him, while he took aim, he noted that the jaws of the cat were slightly enlarged in order to accommodate larger than usual fangs. And these fangs dripped with a viscous fluid that suggested they were designed for combat in some manner.

It was something Doc needed to hear and take heed of, but the older man was no longer in the New Mexico desert.

"Harm my child, you pernicious and ugly beast?" he yelled in a hysterical tone. "Nothing can come between me and my family ever again, not even a mangy scrap of fur like you, do you hear me?"

He tried to fire again at the cat that was making directly for him, but the LeMat had discharged both the ball and shot chambers, and the hammer clicked on a dead charge. Holstering the pistol with one hand, Doc decided on a hands-on approach to the problem of the charging cat. As it leaped at him, he thrust out his free hand and with a display of timing that would have been spectacular and damn near impossible if he had intended it, he caught the beast by the throat in midleap. The animal hissed and yowled at him, drool and viscous fluid dripping from its jaws, the noise slightly distorted by the way in which his grip was beginning to choke the beast. Its body writhed and twisted with a preternatural strength as it sought to free itself, a strength matched by Doc's own maddened grip. Its front paws lashed, the back legs coming up as it squirmed, kicking at him with sharpened claws. But all it hit was the thick cloth of his jacket, his exposed wrist and hand frustratingly out of reach for the creature.

His grip tightened, then squeezed. The cat's neck broke, life dying in its suddenly dull eyes. And yet, even in its death throes, it took one last chance. Aided by the manner in which its neck was distorted by snapping, its dying move was to sink its fangs into his wrist. It was a feeble bite, not painful as it broke the skin, but enough to deposit some of the viscous fluid into Doc's bloodstream.

Doc's arm burned, then numbed, and he screamed in pain as he dropped the chilled cat, suddenly pulled back into the world of the Deathlands by the burning sensations sweeping through his body, followed by the numbness of sudden paralysis.

Jak saw the dying cat bite Doc and saw the stricken man fall to the ground. He immediately knew what had happened and knew that he had to get to Doc and get him clear before the remains of the cat pack fell upon the prone man.

By now, the Uzi and H&K fire was beginning to tell on the cat pack, and those that weren't injured or chilled were beginning to thin out and scatter, their courage and pack instinct now shot to pieces by the continuous blaster-fire that had decimated their numbers. But there were still enough to attack Doc where he lay, with enough venom in their fangs to chill him before they ripped him apart.

"Cover me—get Doc out," the albino hunter yelled, moving toward Doc before he had finished barking out his instructions. As he moved, he holstered the Colt Python and palmed two of the leaf-bladed throwing knives, which he would use to fight off the surviving cats at close range. Stooping low as he ran in, Jak flicked his wrists so that the knives became whirring blurs that caught the flesh and fur of the cats that had clustered around Doc, closing in for the kill.

But then again, so was Jak closing in for the kill—and he was a far more experienced and ruthless hunter and killer than anything the posse of cats would have previously faced in the desert. As he stooped in and ran, the whirring blades made short work of the cats around Doc. Jak kept an eye on the cats, keen to make sure that none of them got another bite in at the prone man, always angling his blade to drive them clear as much as chill them. Behind him, the rest of the recce party kept the immediate area clear by firing at any of the posse that were still in the area. Those of the cats that Jak cut that weren't chilled by his razor-sharp blades ran, their terror and pain deflecting their attention away from the food that Doc represented.

The blasterfire echoed away in the desert air to silence as the last of the living cats disappeared, melting into the desert as though they had never existed. The only signs that there had been a cat attack were the vast number of mutilated cat corpses and the prone Doc.

Jak dropped to his knees beside him, pulling at the old man's arm and exposing the bite wound. It was swollen and red, with a buildup of venom in the lump that surrounded the two fang marks. Although the venom had been swift acting, the fact that there was such a large lump surrounding it suggested that there was more still contained within. It was imperative for Jak to remove it. Slipping one of the knives back into its hiding place, Jak kept hold of Doc's arm and transferred the remaining knife to his free hand, immediately slitting the red lump, which spilled out a pressurized mixture of blood and venom. Doc tried to scream in pain, but his vocal cords were paralyzed enough for him to produce little more than an agonized squeal.

Jak bent his head and applied his lips to the open wound, sucking out the poison that remained in Doc's wrist, then spitting it out onto the dust—once dry, but now moistened by the blood of the chilled cats.

Dean was by Jak's side immediately with a canteen of water. The albino swilled the remainder of the blood and venom from his mouth and spit it out onto the earth.

"What do you think?" Dean asked.

Jak shrugged. "Doc live, but mebbe have to carry while. Take time poison sweat out—give him water."

Dean bent and forced some water into Doc, even though the old man's paralyzed throat found it hard to accept the liquid.

"Fuck, I thought this was going to be a rest stop," Mik said with a sardonic manner that verged on tired hysteria.

"Rest up for a while, then we should get going," Lonnie said softly, running his hands over his closely cropped head. "We can't lose time now, especially if we need to carry Doc."

While they took a rest break, keeping away from the scene of the carnage, Dean and Jak constructed a makeshift stretcher from parts of the lightweight tents. Tilly and Danny agreed to take the first leg carrying Doc. The only good news during the rest period was that Doc already seemed to be regaining some use of his muscles, as his legs were already beginning to twitch involuntarily.

Finally, they were ready to begin again. Tilly and Danny lifted the stretcher, and Lonnie took the lead.

The sun overhead was past the halfway mark of the day, and they still had a lot of ground to cover. The plan was to be on the edge of Charity by nightfall, using the cover of darkness to bypass the irregular patrols of Baron Al, and to camp overnight before staring their recce mission properly when the dawn broke, by which time they could only hope that Doc would be back to full mobility.

Chapter Nine

Dawn broke with a rapidity that caught them all by surprise. Jak was on watch, and roused the rest of the recce party, including Doc.

"I feel a little stiff in the muscles, but otherwise ready to take on anything," he reassured them, although the deathly pallor of his skin told another story.

"Well, you do know that we can't carry passengers when we're in there," Lonnie told him, but with a sidelong glance at Jak and Dean just to let them know that he was sure they would be loyal to Doc, but his people couldn't afford to be if they found themselves up against it.

"Okay," he continued after they had agreed. "We need to scout the whole ville, see if there's any big sign of sec activity, find the base where the convoy will set off from, and assess the amount of wags and armory being used."

"You know where we're headed?" Dean asked.

Lonnie nodded curtly. "Know this place all too well. And I know a way in."

Charity was built around the remains of an old New Mexico town, the name of which had long since been forgotten. But it had been a one-horse town, and possibly a one-wag town, in the days when such things counted. Not being big, it had been isolated and off the beaten track for any enemy attacks during the nukecaust. As such, it had only been the nuclear winter that swept the Deathlands that had damaged the old buildings, and this was in places minimal, as the town had been built to withstand the harsh heat and desert winds, with low adobe buildings, and very little over two stories. When the ancestors of the current baron and the interbred families that made up the ville's elite had first come to the old town, they had taken over the most repairable and least damaged buildings, which were those that were residential, and thus smaller than the more damaged shops and small businesses that were either directly on the main street, or clustered on the edge.

These larger and more damaged places had been taken over and used by the trickle of outsiders who had come to the ville over the preceding years: to such an extent, in fact, that smaller buildings made of waste rubble and corrugated iron had been built into shacks that ran off the main drag and into the areas around the old business area.

As well as housing the overspill of newer residents to Charity, these places also played host to a different kind of business. Before skydark, the main drag of the town had been home to the grocery store, the tourist-trap gift shops, the clothes and furniture stores of a normal ville. Now, the trading for food and clothing was carried on in other quarters, and there were no tourists, only outsiders. The business that was carried on in these areas was the sale of jolt and derivative chemicals and hallucinogenic plant extracts—this was, after all, New Mexico, where such plants grew in abundance and were stronger than ever after rad mutation. There were also saloons where you could drink cheap liquor until you dropped, and gaudys where you could sate your carnal needs if you had the ability after spending so long in the saloon.

There was no law anymore, so these businesses couldn't be outside any law. These were violent times, so the idea of a no-go area for Charity residents was ridiculous—on the contrary, they loved the main drag and the old business district. But there was a distinct purpose to making the main drag and the business district the areas where there were bars and gaudys and drug dens. By containing all these activities strictly to within these areas, Baron Al Jourgensen and the barons who had preceded him had been able to control the amount of jack that flowed in and out of Charity with a firmer hand than in many villes. People knew where to buy, and where to sell, and even at seven in the morning, it was always party time down on the drag, and party time in Baron Al's private vault.

But all the jack in the world wouldn't buy seed crops, wouldn't buy food, if there was none to be had—hence the deal with Summerfield and the sale of the ville's women and hence the trade caravan that the Hellbenders were out to raid.

Gaining access to the ville had been absurdly easy. It was isolated and off the main roads and trails that ran through these parts. Only those who truly wished to visit the ville, either for trade or for pleasure, would come this way. So the sec guards who patrolled the perimeter were inclined to be slack at times, especially as the land was flat for miles around, and any wags would be easy to see from a distance.

Not so a party of seven who traveled light and had selected a sheltering place to hide out. Once they had packed their tents away and eaten from some of the self-heats they had carried as supplies, they assembled around Lonnie, who told them that from his knowledge of the sec routine, there would be a gap in less than an hour where they could just walk in.

It seemed a long time to wait as the sun began to blaze hot. The sec guards patroled the ville perimeter on old motorcycles, fuel being one of the few things Baron Al had a supply of, and one of the things that he had tried to use for trade.

"There they go," Lonnie whispered triumphantly as two sec guards on old choppers, with belts of ammo across their chests and old Thompson blasters resting in the crook of their arms, crossed virtually right in front of the spot where the recce party was concealed. The two guards stopped to talk briefly, the hum of their conversation buried beneath the guttural growl of their bikes. Then they throttled the choppers and moved off in opposite directions.

"And that's it?" Dean asked incredulously as the noise of the bikes receded into the distance.

"Yep, that's it," Lonnie confirmed. "See, most people

only come to this ville to trade with Baron Al or to visit the drag. And they're pretty few and far between."

"But isn't Al worried about you or Correll or anyone?"

Lonnie gave a twisted grin. "He thinks we all bought the farm when we left. In his world, no one survives without Baron Al...which is kinda useful for us, when you think about it. C'mon, let's go."

He came out from cover and led them across the few hundred yards of desert soil that ended abruptly with the beginning of the ville, in the shape of a few old adobe buildings that were quiet.

"Residential. No one's up yet," he commented as they walked past and begin to hit the old tarmac and pavement of the preDark town.

This area of Charity was all quiet, and as they walked along the paved sidewalk, Dean wondered if they would be noticeable as being the only people out on the streets at this hour.

"'S'okay," commented Lonnie, "we'll head for the drag. That's never quiet."

It took them only a few minutes' walk to negotiate the back streets of the ville and reach the town center, Lonnie knowing exactly where he was headed. Dean realized that they knew nothing of Lonnie's personal history, and he wondered what the man's grudge was against Baron Al. Whatever it was, now that they were here he seemed as fired up against the ville as Correll had been when they first encountered him a few days earlier.

"C'mon, let's blend in," Lonnie suggested, steering them toward a saloon.

"What about sec wags for convoy?" Jak questioned.

Lonnie shrugged. "I know where they'll be, all right, but we need to leave that till later in the day, when there's some action on them. The yard'll be empty by now. We've got till nightfall—yeah, if we get separated, we rendezvous where we camped last night, okay? Now," he added with a malevolent glee as he pushed open the doors of the saloon, "it's time to shake some action."

As soon as the doors were opened, the noise increased to a deafening volume. A long, makeshift bar constructed from old shop counters and covered with chicken wire was being propped up by a number of men and women with prominently displayed blasters. They were all downing home-brewed spirit at a rapid rate, and the smell of the grain used for the brew permeated the room with a decaying stink. The boom box behind the bar, guarded by the bartender, a fat man with a graying beard as long as his belly was large, was playing an old song with soaring guitars that seemed to be about a man leaving home, feeling he wouldn't be remembered, but that he would rather be a free bird than tied down. A sign proclaimed that each drinker was limited, due to shortage of brew and shortage of grain to make it, to three drinks only. A quick head count of those sunk into corners, either unconscious or near to it, suggested that the brew was strong enough that very few drinkers would not reach their limit.

Lonnie strode across to the bar, and the fat man looked

at him with a curious stare, as though he half recognized him.

"What can I do for you?" he asked, a note of suspicion creeping into his voice.

"Drinks for all of us, Jem," Lonnie replied with a grin.

The bartender's eyes narrowed at the use of his name. There was also something about the voice that reminded him...

"Say, I'll give you the drinks if you've got the jack," he said slowly, "but mebbe I shouldn't. There's something a mite too familiar about you, boy. Something that rings a danger bell in my head."

"My friend, the only thing that rings bells in your head is that brain rot you've been serving for too long. Always said that you shouldn't drink your own brew."

The bartender said nothing for a moment, then a slow smile spread across his face. "Wouldn't have recognized you, Lon. Never did see you without a beard or all that hair. But voices don't change, do they?"

"They don't," Lonnie agreed. He put some jack on the bar. "Now, how about you do the business and give us what I'm paying for?"

"Sure," the bartender replied, taking the jack with one hand while he laid out a row of glasses with the other. Raising a bottle filled with the murky spirit, he poured along the row of glasses with practiced ease, slopping very little between glasses. "What brings you back here? You know that Baron Al would be pleased to see you back."

"Yeah, and he'd be pleased to know how little of your profit actually goes into his coffers, and about the way you let the gaudy sluts use the bar without giving him his share of the jack," Lonnie added, indicating a corner of the room with his head.

Both Dean and Danny, curious, followed his movement and saw a woman in one corner, taking two customers at once. Her head was buried in the lap of a semiconscious man who seemed not to know what was taking place, while her short dress was hiked up above her waist and another man moved rhythmically behind her, his movements pushing her head into the other's lap farther and farther.

"See, Baron Al likes to keep his businesses under strict control down here, so he can get his share of the jack. Jem here isn't supposed to run gaudys, and she sure as shit won't be giving the jack she fleeced from those dudes to Baron Al, will she?"

"I don't take jack from her," Jem said.

"No, but you take favors," Lonnie pointed out. "In Al's book, that's more jack she don't declare."

"I knew I'd rue the day you came back—if you ever did," Jem muttered, passing the glasses to the recce party. "So what do you want from me?"

"Not much," Lonnie said, sipping the strong spirit from the glass and wincing at the sour taste. "But enough. Do the sec still drink here in force?"

"'Course they do," Jem replied. "Why d'you think I can still have gaudy sluts on the house and get away with it?"

Lonnie nodded. "Figured as much. So what do you hear when they get to the third glass?"

"About what?"

"About the big convoy and the trade-off with Summerfield."

"What d'you want to know for?"

Without warning, Lonnie reached across and grabbed the fat man by his beard, pulling him over the counter.

"Because, fucker, I do. Ask me no questions and I won't slit your porky little throat."

The rest of the recce party was astounded by this sudden turn of events. They had all, in their own ways, assumed that Lonnie would want them to blend in with the other ville inhabitants until such time as they had gleaned the necessary information and got the hell out. They had assumed that to enter the bar was part of that process. It would seem that Lonnie had a personal score that he wanted to settle while he was back in Charity, an assumption that was confirmed by his next few words.

"I should've chilled you when I had the chance before, Jem," Lonnie growled. "Mebbe I'll finish the job this time."

Jak noted that, despite the fact that brawls were commonplace in bars and people usually didn't interfere in case they got themselves chilled, the atmosphere had changed in the bar through the course of Lonnie's discussion with Jem. Their exchanges could barely be heard by the rest of the recce party, let alone by anyone else in the bar, over the noise of the boom box. However, it was startlingly obvious to even the most intoxicated and junked-out inhabitant of the bar that there was something going on here that was beyond the normal bar brawl.

An undertone of clicks sounded around the bar as blasters were drawn and safety catches clicked off. Jak nudged Dean.

"Be ready—get out quick," he whispered.

"What about the others?" Dean replied.

"We have got a rendezvous," stated Doc, who had been listening, "and we know a time. I suspect we may very well have to leave the rest to chance."

Meanwhile, Mik and Tilly were trying to stop Lonnie from going any further.

"C'mon, man," Mik whispered hoarsely, pulling at the recce leader's arm, "leave this. We can't risk a firefight before we've even started, can we?"

"You don't know what this fucker did," Lonnie replied without taking his eyes off Jem.

"You're right, I don't," Mik said softly. "And guess what? I don't fucking care. I just want us to get this mission accomplished and get back to Papa Joe, okay?"

"Uh, I think it may be too late," Tilly murmured as one of the drinkers, holding a remade snub-nosed .38, wandered closer to them.

"There a problem here, Jem?" he asked in a lazy drawl.

"Could say that," the fat barman replied in a voice choked by Lonnie's grip.

The disheveled drunk held the Smith & Wesson up to Lonnie's head. Considering how drunk he was, and the fact that he looked to be a physical wreck, his arm was highly muscled under the strip lighting of the bar, and his hand was rock steady.

"Let him go," he said slowly and gently.

"Make me, shithead," Lonnie replied, the veins bulging at his temples.

Danny leaned over to Dean, keeping an eye on the rest of the bar. Even the gaudy slut had stopped, and was looking up from her position, the semiconscious man's limp member in her hand while the customer behind her had withdrawn and was doing up his pants and trying to fumble his blaster from its holster.

"It's gonna go up," Danny said, "and I think we should get the fuck out before we all get chilled."

"What about Lonnie?" Dean replied.

"Leave him," Jak interjected. "All have job, right?"

Tilly, turning, nodded. "Scatter, and try to assemble later," she agreed.

Jak nodded. "Take Doc with me."

"Obliged," Doc said, his LeMat firmly grasped in his fist.

"You come with me," Danny said to Dean. "While they check the convoy, I think there's something else you should see."

Dean was about to ask what that might be, but was forestalled by what happened at the bar.

Mik had a Walther PPK handblaster in his fist, and it was pointed at the head of the disheveled drunk who still had his Smith & Wesson at Lonnie's head.

"You chill him, and you're on the last train west, too, fucker," Mik said steadily.

"New Mexican standoff, eh?" the drunk said. Then, louder, "What y'all say to that?"

The words had barely escaped his mouth before the first blaster went off. The gaudy slut had a small derringer of her own, which she kept tucked into her dress between her breasts. The recce party wouldn't know this, but the disheveled drunk was one of her best customers, and she wasn't about to lose that source of income. Fortunately, she was a lousy shot, and the small-caliber slugs took out the strip lighting above the bar.

It was the signal for chaos to descend.

Blasters were raised and shots fired off with absolutely no sense of direction. In the heat and dark of the bar, there were shouts and screams of pain from those of the customers who were hit by stray or badly aimed slugs. The only ones not to fire were the members of the recce party. Jak and Doc had already hit the floor and were threading their way toward the exit as the firefight began. Behind them, Dean and Danny had also hit the ground, but as the young Cawdor made to follow Jak and Doc, Danny grabbed him by the arm.

"This way," he whispered with urgency. "We'll take the back way."

Dean turned and followed Danny, figuring that they could catch up with Jak and Doc back at the rendezvous. As for Mik, Tilly and Lonnie—anything could be happening to them, for all that he could see or hear in the dark, dense atmosphere of the bar, which now stank of cordite, blood and fear.

In fact, the disheveled drunk who had been aiming his blaster at Lonnie's head had been distracted by the slut's loose shooting to such an extent that he had turned his head away for a fraction of a second, his arm slackening just enough to alert Mik to an opening. The rat-faced recce man had raised the blaster he had aimed at the drunk's head and brought it down again butt-first, the force of his wrist and fist driving the heavy stock into the drunk's skull, parting his greasy hair with a force that cleaved an open wound in the flesh and left him with blood coursing down his forehead. The drunk crumpled under the blow and fell away. At the same moment, Lonnie slammed Jem's head onto the bar with a force that drove it down through the chicken wire and the glass; the bartender's face suddenly opened up into a thousand tiny and painful wounds by the wire and the shards of glass that were driven into his eyes, blinding him with blood and pain.

Mik turned and loosed Lonnie's grip, while Tilly grabbed the recce leader by his other arm and yelled, "Let's get the fuck out of here!"

Pulling him away, assisted by Mik, Tilly directed him toward the exit that Doc and Jak had used.

"Let's move it, and keep him down!" she yelled at Mik, who nodded rather than waste breath.

Which just left Danny leading Dean through the confused and drunken crowd toward the rear exit from the bar.

They reached the door leading out to a back alleyway

that was littered with garbage, and housed a few rats that scuttled for cover as they emerged into the daylight. Out front, where the other members of the recce party had been making their escape, a crowd of curious drinkers, sec men reluctant to walk into a firefight before it had run its course and those who just wanted to join a fight, had gathered. Danny and Dean, however, had a clear getaway.

They were out into the alleyway, and both young men scrambled to their feet, slowing as they gained a few yards from the bar's back door.

"Don't draw attention to yourself," Dean muttered in a low undertone to Danny. "We don't want anyone coming around the back to wonder why we're in a hurry and blast first before asking any questions."

"Fuck it, I think I may have gathered that. I know I'm not that great at this, but I'm not a complete idiot," Danny replied with testy edge to his voice. "Anyway, who got us out the easy way?"

"Okay," Dean replied with a placating gesture. "There is one thing that bothers me, though. How the hell did you know about the back door, and where it was?"

They reached the end of the alleyway and turned into the main drag. Danny was leading them back into the crowd that had gathered around the bar. They skirted the far edge of the crowd so as not to get noticed by those gathered around, or recognized by those now emerging from the bar who could point them out to the sec men. Dean tried to keep an eye out for the rest of the recce party, but it was too confused and rowdy around the bar to see anything definite.

"This way," Danny said, taking Dean down the first turn that led away from the main drag. "Now just stick with me and trust me."

"It's not that I don't," Dean countered. "It's more a case of not knowing what the hell is going down here. After all, you said—"

"Said nothing," Danny interrupted. "Listen, everyone who ever lived in Charity knows all about the drag, and remember my dad did sec over the whole ville. Anyway, I've seen the plans of this ville, back in Baron Al's little private sanctum. And that, my friend, is where we're going now."

"But what about the others?" Dean questioned. "We're supposed to be on recce for the trade convoy, not chasing after—"

Danny stopped walking and turned heatedly on Dean. "Listen," he snapped, "there's five of them going after that information. I figure that the real way forward is to get more info on the old tech. And I figure that's what your people want, as well. So we leave the scouting to them, and we try to get our hands on something a little more interesting, right?"

"But there'll be time for that when we've raided the convoy," Dean reasoned. "Right now the best thing is to—"

"The best thing is to cover as many bases as possible," Danny interrupted once more. "Just trust me on this." He held up his hands. "If I'm wrong, chill me already. But we could do everyone a few favors. I know where the storehouse is, and I know how to get in there. So do we go, or do we not?"

Dean nodded firmly. "Let's do it," he said simply.

Danny grinned and turned to go, leading Dean away from the main drag and into the main body of the ville.

In a matter of just a block, the drag seemed to be forgotten, the commotion around the bar fading into the background as the rest of the ville went about its everyday business. By this time, most people were up and about, and the trading posts and businesses were open. People moved slowly in the heat, the pastel colors and whitewash of the adobe buildings, stained by age, reflecting the heat back into the streets while the few unpainted brick buildings absorbed the heat, their surfaces already like kiln ovens that radiated heat back onto the street and into the path of passersby, including Dean and Danny.

The younger Cawdor noted that the businesses concerned with services such as clothing and shoe repair, ironmongery and blaster maintenance, were doing well. There were more than a few people availing themselves of these services. On the other hand, the businesses and trading posts concerned with food were devoid of both stock and customers. Water was being sold, and slate boards that had recently wiped and rechalked prices on their surfaces, told of the drought that had started to bite into the ville.

Dean was conscious that they were dressed differently from the everyday ville dwellers of Charity. Their dark,

thick clothing was not only uncomfortable and swelter-
ingly hot in the increased temperatures of the ville streets,
but also stood in sharp contrast to the lighter clothing—
both in material and color—of the other people that passed
them on the streets. At one point, Danny suddenly changed
direction and led them down a side street. From his body
language, Dean understood that Danny had seen someone
or something that he wished to avoid, and so kept his head
low and followed suit. A few yards down the street, Danny
pulled Dean into a quiet doorway and watched as a man
walked down the end of the street.

"Knew my dad...and me," he said by way of explanation before leading Dean out into the street again.

"Where are we going?" Dean asked as they turned back
to their original direction.

"You'll see," Danny replied enigmatically.

The streets became quieter the farther out they went,
until they were nearly out on the edge of town, entering the
old industrial area. Like the main drag, this part of the ville
was now given over to bars and gaudys like those on the
main drag. There was now more activity on the streets, and
a number of gaudy sluts and drunks littered the streets. The
sluts tried to proposition Dean and Danny as they passed.

"Hey, sugar, want a piece of ass?"

"Action sweetie, real cheap, yeah?"

It was difficult to know how to reply without attracting attention to themselves. The usual response in this part
of the ville would be to pay jack and use the service. Any

attempt to avoid buying a woman would seem out of place, yet neither young man wanted to waste time by even appearing to make a transaction. Their brief dismissals were met with insults and curses, and attracted attention from some of the drunks.

"Shit, how much farther?"

"Not far," Danny replied in an undertone. "Baron Al loves to keep his stock of old tech hidden in plain sight. I reckon he doesn't know anyone else is aware of it outside of him or his sec."

"Let's hope so," Dean muttered.

In a few moments they arrived outside an old factory building that looked to be as decrepit as any of the bars and gaudys that surrounded it. However, it didn't escape Dean's notice that the building was less used than any of the others, with gaudy sluts hanging around outside but not entering, as they did the other buildings, and drunks sprawled unconscious outside it rather than coming in and out with brew and spirit.

"That's it?" Dean asked.

Danny nodded. "And, my friend, I know the way in that bypasses the sec guard," he said with a grin.

Dean took note of the guard who was positioned by the main entrance, posing as a drunk but noticeable to Dean's combat-trained eye by the manner in which he held his blaster, deceptively close to a firing position. Danny took them away from the building and past the bar next to it, weaving his way in and out of the drunks who were loitering outside. The two young men slipped around the side of the bar and walked along the rear of the bar until they reached the alley that ran between the two buildings. Dean could see another supposed drunk lurking at the rear of the old tech warehouse, also cradling his blaster in a manner that would make it easy for him to come into a firing position.

"How do we do this?" he whispered.

Danny looked at his wrist chron. "We wait. Unless they've changed the routine drastically in the time I've been away, the guy at the back should saunter around to the front in a few minutes, just to check with the guy at the front."

"Hot pipe," Dean exclaimed, "how can they be that slack!"

Danny smiled slowly. "It's like that here. No one much ever comes to Charity, right? So there's only ever problems with out-of-hand drunks, and they either get chilled or beaten, and are too fucked to really be a threat."

Dean shook his head. "Shit, what a way to run a ville."

"Be thankful this bit is this easy," Danny replied. "'Cause the raid on the convoy sure as shit won't. I'd say Baron Al is so paranoid about outsiders that he'll have sec hyped up on jolt and armed one for ten."

Dean shrugged. "So let's do the easy bit."

The two young men waited for a couple of minutes until the "drunk" at the back of the old industrial building got to his feet with an ease that belied his apparent state, and began to wander around the front of the building via the far side from where Dean and Danny waited.

"They'll talk awhile, but not long, I'd guess, just in case Baron Al comes calling," Danny whispered. "Let's go."

Dean followed Danny as the young man moved out of the shelter of the building beside their target and slipped across the gap constituted by the alleyway until they were at the back of the building that housed the old tech.

Looking up at the outside of the building, Dean could see that the old two-story industrial block had only one apparent exit at the rear: a door on the upper story that could be accessed by an old metal fire escape. All the windows had been covered with sheets of corrugated iron or metal salvaged from other parts of the industrial area, and these had been welded into place over the previously open areas. Even the door at the top of the fire escape had been covered and welded, on closer inspection. On the lower story, the windows had been filled in with brick and concrete block from rubble, and the huge double doors that would, in the days before skydark, have been where wags picked up whatever the building produced were now welded shut, with large metal girders across the join between the doors.

The two young men were at the rear of the building, listening for any sign of the sec guard approaching, and Dean couldn't for the life of him work out how Danny could get into the building.

Danny grinned, looking at Dean, and said, "Trust me on this, dude."

He went down on his knees at the juncture where the bottom of the wall disappeared into the earth.

"Should still be here," he muttered to himself as he burrowed in the dust. "Got it!" he added triumphantly as he pulled a concealed ring from beneath the topsoil. Turning to Dean he said, "Got to do this carefully, in case we leave too little on top when we go in."

"What the hell is it?" the younger Cawdor asked, helping Danny to carefully lift what appeared to be a narrow trapdoor.

"Access shaft," Danny replied. "This gets us down into the basement of the building, where the generators are. I think it must have been for maintenance at one point, but it was mostly forgotten. See, my dad was thorough and made a good recce of the whole place when Baron Al put him in charge, but I don't think he ever reported everything he found. This was always kept covered, and it looks like it hasn't been disturbed since."

"Be triple hard to cover when we go down, though," Dean pointed out as Danny slipped into the narrow causeway. "The ring's gonna stick out when the sec comes back."

"Have to trust that," Danny said simply. "There isn't any other way to get in, and with a bit of luck they won't notice it. Hell, they don't know it's there, it's at ground level and they have no idea what it's for. We just try and keep as much soil on top as possible."

With which, he started to slide between the partially opened trapdoor and the ground, trying to keep the trapdoor as level as possible and so keep the covering layer of soil intact.

Dean watched Danny disappear into the hole and, shrugging, followed him.

The shaft was dark and airless, the atmosphere incredibly hot and it stank of decay. It was obvious that it was rarely used. In fact, Dean figured, it probably hadn't been in use since Danny had left the ville. There was a metal rung ladder that was bolted to the concrete side of the shaft, and Dean felt his way down it gingerly, hearing Danny's boots on the metal a few feet beneath him. Then he heard his companion's feet touch dull-sounding concrete or brick, and he knew that they had almost reached the bottom.

"Duck when you get to the bottom," Danny whispered, "the shaft is only about four feet."

"I hope you know the way from here," Dean replied. "I don't want to end up heading back out into the center of the ville."

"It's only one way we can go, don't worry," Danny replied with amusement in his voice.

It was pitch black at the bottom of the shaft, and the heat subsided into the coolness of a subterranean tunnel, the stifling confinement of the entry shaft now past. Dean bent forward and followed Danny's footsteps, unable to see him as his eyes still hadn't adjusted to the darkness. The boy had been right about there only being one direction they could head. The bottom of the shaft had been a tunnel in one direction, and a wall at the other, although Dean could feel, as he lightly ran his hands along the sides of the shaft to try and detect its width, that there were pipes and cables running along it that ran straight into the wall by the shaft.

"What the fuck was this for?" he asked.

"Dunno for sure," Danny replied. "I figure that it must have been to do with the power supplies for the building before skydark, and mebbe the generator Baron Al's got going when he moved in later. I do know that this runs under some of the other buildings, too. We need to take the first shaft up, which should be about here," he added with a distracted tone, as though looking for something where he couldn't see. "Shit, found it!" he exclaimed triumphantly, adding, "just in front of you, about five yards. You need to pull yourself up."

Following the sound of Danny's voice, Dean reached up into empty space and groped for the bottom rung of the metal ladder that, once again, was bolted to the side of the shaft. Pulling himself up, he winced as strong light penetrated the shaft, then flooded it, as Danny opened the trapdoor at the top of the shaft.

"This is it?" he asked as he followed Danny up into a bare side room that was only ten feet by ten.

"Ah, that's the joy of it." Danny laughed. "The shaft is put out of the way of general use so it can't be a hazard. Which means it gets hidden away from the prying eyes of any sec—especially those who can't be bothered to check too well."

Dean replaced the trapdoor in the floor carefully and looked around the empty room. Dust motes were visible in the air, and like the entire building, it was lighted by ceiling panels, a few of which were either dead or blinking erratically. In one wall there was a simple metal door.

"This should bring us out into the ground-floor corridor—most of the tech and all the paperwork is on the upper level," Danny stated, opening the door slowly and scanning the empty corridor. Both he and Dean listened intently, but could detect no signs of activity. Danny indicated that they should move, and readied his Uzi in case he needed it. Dean had his Browning Hi-Power to hand, checked and reloaded. Given Danny's inability with a blaster, as he proved during the fight with the mutie cat pack, it was precaution Dean felt to be more than necessary.

The building seemed deserted. There was no sign of activity, and the only sounds were the low hum of a generator and distant electrical activity, none of which indicated a need to be on triple red. Nonetheless, neither of the young men was willing to take a chance.

The lower story of the building was little more than an open factory floor, with scattered benches and debris giving no clue as to what had been manufactured there in the days before the nukecaust. Dean felt uneasy with the floor being so open. It would be all too easy for any sec to enter and see them immediately. The sooner they were past this obstacle, the better.

Danny led them to a staircase that spiraled up the far wall, leading to a door set in the wall. Dean followed him, eyes scanning the walls and the door set into the front of the building for any signs of activity.

"Come on, let's move it," he murmured to Danny.

"We're there," the youngster replied as he opened the door. Dean swung through after him, taking one last recce before closing the door gently. They were on a mezzanine, with a washroom and more stairs leading to the upper level. The hum of the generator and equipment was louder now, but there was still no sign of any life, for which Dean was grateful.

"How the hell does Baron Al get the fuel to run the generator all the time?" he asked of Danny.

"I don't really know. The weird thing is that fuel's the one thing Charity's never been short of for trade. I think he has some good trading allies for that, because he cultivated them. But that's why he's in the shit over the lack of food. He's been too busy chasing this dream to look out for the people he rules over. Which is kinda dumb in the long run, 'cause there's more of them than there are of him and his sec."

"Yeah, sure," Dean answered, not bothering to add that he had seen fear rule over many a ville, and numbers and manpower weren't necessarily the most important things.

They took the last few steps from the mezzanine to the upper story, and Danny opened the wooden door at the top, pausing only to check the room before turning to Dean with a huge grin on his face.

"Welcome to wonderland," he said, ushering Dean into the room.

"Hot pipe!" Dean whistled, all other words failing him at the sight with which he was greeted.

The room ran the length of the building, and like the floor below was open plan. Rich velvet drapes and hangings ran around the walls, blocking the windows and giving the room an altogether richer, warmer feel. The floor space was occupied by vast banks of comps, vids and other electronic pieces the use of which was, at this moment, a mystery to Dean. In front of the drapes in one corner stood a row of battered old metal filing cabinets, with an ornate wooden writing desk to one side of them.

"This," Danny said, encompassing the old tech with a gesture, "is the hardware. But that—" he pointed with his Uzi to the filing cabinets "—is where the real treasure lay, I'd say. I didn't pay it much attention back in the day, 'cause I was only young. But now...that's a different matter. I'd say that those drawers probably contain all the secrets to make this stuff viable again. And that, my friend, is where we should be looking."

He strode across the room, pointedly ignoring the winking lights and gentle hum of the comp consoles, and the flickering images that played again and again on vid and terminal screens. Dean followed him, although he couldn't help but be distracted by the old tech equipment, the likes of which had always held a fascination for him. Some of it he recognized from redoubts, or from the Brody school, where there had been a certain amount of old tech that some of the teachers had tried to teach to the students, most of whom had more pressing concerns. But, like his father, Dean had always had an interest. Ryan had always been fascinated by the snippets of preDark culture that he could find, almost as though he could somehow unravel the secrets of the past and use them to make the present better for himself. Without anything ever being said between them, Dean had always shared this interest, with a more practical bent toward the old tech.

"Dean, come and take a look at this," Danny said softly. Dean stopped poring over the console of a terminal, trying to get into the programming, and hurried over to the writing desk, where Danny had a pile of books and papers that he had taken from the filing cabinets, and which may or may not relate to the electronics in the room.

Dean looked over Danny's shoulder at the myriad of paper, covered with figures, sentences that looked almost incomprehensible in their complexity, and colorful drawings of the comps along with diagrams of their schematics.

"It's all here," Danny said, not without a note of awe in his voice, "but the trouble is working out which bit belongs to which. I wasn't old enough then to really get a grip on any of the theory, but it strikes me now that although the boxes and circuits are working, it's the stuff that makes it all work—software, wasn't it?—that's the problem. Sometimes, you can't immediately tell what each comp has running it, and how to connect them to each other."

Dean nodded. "I know what you mean. The problem is that not all the software recognizes each other, so you have to find ways of doing it. I was taught something about that...networking, Mr. Brody called it. He had a few old comp books."

"Did it work?" Danny looked at him with eyes glittering intently. The young man had forgotten about the world of Charity and the Deathlands outside the room, forgotten about their companions in the recce party, forgotten about any dangers that may be facing them. All that mattered to him now was that he may be close to cracking the secrets of the comps, and making them slaves rather than adversaries.

"Yeah, not that we had much in the way of equipment," Dean replied, catching the mood. "Listen, if we can find a couple of cables, I could show you quickly, and we could mebbe find out a little more about what Baron Al's got here."

"Okay. What sort of cables do we need?" Danny asked, but Dean was already rooting around the hardware, emerging with a couple of connecting cables.

"These," he said. Then, indicating two of the comps, he added, "We'll take those two. You connect that one." He pointed to the one nearest Danny.

"Sure," the youngster replied enthusiastically, taking the cable. "How do you actually connect these things?"

"You look for the right socket on the back," Dean replied. "You put the male lead into the female port."

"What?"

Dean smiled. "You never heard that? The triple stupes who invented these things had male and female ends to them. The male is the one with prongs, and the female—"

"Is the one with the hole," Danny finished, shaking his

head. "Shit, with jokes like that, no wonder they tried to blow up the fucking world."

With the two comps connected, the young men hunched over them, each keeping an eye on his terminal while Dean tapped in commands to try to identify the software on each, and get them to communicate.

"This may not work," he said to Danny. "We really need more time for this. We should wait until we get back to the redoubt," he continued, beginning to feel the pressure of being stuck in enemy territory.

"Best to find out as much as possible now, and take as much of the paperwork," Danny said firmly.

"Why?"

"Because..." Danny began, then stopped. He looked at Dean in a completely different manner from any way he'd looked at him before, as though he were assessing how much he could tell him. Finally, he decided. "Because I don't trust Papa Joe, that's why. See, he's spent so long with nothing to do except dwell on revenge that I figure he'll go over the top when he gets his hands on Baron Al. If it don't chill him, or everyone else, in the attempt, then he'll torch the ville, and all this'll be lost. And this is the future. But he's spent so long brooding over revenge that I reckon he may just be a little loco by now."

Dean nodded briefly. "I figure most of us feel the same. Trouble is, we've got to go through with it because he outnumbers us...if you're with us on this."

Danny smiled. "Figure it's the other way around."

But the smile was driven from his face when a voice

from behind them caused them both to whirl round in shock.

"I figure it doesn't matter which way around you want it, 'cause neither of you may get out of here alive—especially if you get smart," the voice added as Dean went for his Hi-Power.

He let his hand drop as their adversary, now stepping from behind one of the drapes, showed herself. Danny cursed. That was always his hiding place, and he should have figured on checking that one.

Chapter Ten

Apart from the fact that she was holding an old Thompson submachine gun—immaculately polished but still with a dulled air of danger about the gray gunmetal—and had a set, hard expression, Dean would never have imagined her to be a threat. But threat she most certainly was. He carefully withdrew his hand from his holstered Hi-Power.

"It's okay, don't panic. I'm just taking my hand away, okay?"

"I can see that, stupe, I'm not blind," she spit pithily, without changing her expression.

"Shit, I can't believe that I was that much of a stupe not to check it out," Danny said, ignoring the other two and banging his hand down on the bench that held the comp. At the sudden slap, the girl turned the barrel of her Thompson away from Dean, and the young Cawdor reached immediately for the Browning. Catching this from the corner of her eye, she swung the machine blaster back toward Dean, but not before he had the Browning clear of the holster and leveled in her direction.

"Stalemate?" he questioned, echoing something his father had said a few days before.

"Mebbe...mebbe not. What's to stop me blasting you now?"

"You don't want the sec coming in here. If we're not supposed to be here, then neither are you, right?" he asked, directing the last toward Danny.

"Nice try, dude, but it won't work," Danny replied, shaking his head slowly. "Not if that's who I think it is."

"And who's that?" Dean shot back, his confidence rattled.

Danny looked the girl up and down. She was about fifteen, dressed in a cropped T-shirt with sequins that clung to the swell of her breasts and left exposed a tanned and taut abdomen. Her jeans were old denim, bleached and ripped by use, but sewn through with golden threads. On her feet she wore exquisite velvet pumps that had enabled her to move quietly, but also suggested that she hadn't come from a great distance, or that she was used to roughing it across rough ground.

"She's a few years older now, and a shitload more beautiful—"

"That ain't gonna pull no weight," she interrupted.

Danny held up his hands. "Who says I was trying to? Mebbe I mean it. But you are, aren't you?"

Her face split into a lopsided grin but the blaster remained steady. "Yeah, and I remember you, too. Hell, you were the reason I learned to get in here. You were how I learned to get in here! Never thought I'd see you again, Danny."

Dean sighed, and looked to the ceiling. "You know, I'm sure this is all fine and dandy for you two, but seeing as we're standing here at blasterpoint and we may get interrupted any second, it'd be kind of nice if someone told me what the hell was going on?"

Danny cut to the chase. "Her name's Ayesha, and she's Baron Al's youngest sprog. Only daughter, too. Hence the fine clothes and the ability to carry such a fancy blaster. But not why she's here."

Her brow furrowed. "In what way?"

"Well, I remember what Baron Al was like, right? Now, I may have been away awhile, but I'd be willing to bet my life that the old bastard hasn't changed that much. And the two things he was sure of were that he didn't like girls hanging around anything important, and that this place was out of bounds to everyone in the whole damn ville unless he was with them."

Ayesha pursed her lips. "Fuck it," she said softly. "I guess you've got me there." But her grip on the machine blaster didn't waver.

"Okay," Dean said carefully, starting to get a little weary of the situation. "Let's see if I've got this straight. We're not supposed to be here, and you're not supposed to be here, and we're all in the shit if we get found. Am I right?"

Ayesha nodded agreement.

"Right," Dean continued, "so I reckon it'd be better for all of us if you put that blaster down and we started from there. It's not going to do any of us any good if we get snuck up on by the sec because we're so busy eyeballing each other. Am I right again?"

Reluctantly, the girl lowered the Thompson. "Guess so," she said simply.

There was an almost palpable lowering of tension in the room.

Dean returned his attention to the cables, linking them and tapping a few commands into the keyboard of the comp he was manning as he said, "So I guess you know why we're here. You were listening, right?" he added to her quizzical expression as he looked up. "So you know about Correll, the Hellbenders and everything?"

"Kinda," she answered. "I didn't know that they existed. I figured—like everyone else here, I guess—that once all you guys disappeared into the desert, then that was it. Time to buy the farm."

"Should have been," Danny agreed, "but I guess we got lucky." Despite his best efforts, he couldn't keep the slightest tinge of cynicism from invading the latter statement.

Ayesha seized on it. "I heard what you were saying about Correll being obsessed...mebbe he is, but mebbe that's a good thing."

"Why?"

She shrugged. "I've got reasons."

Dean moved over to the other comp and tapped in a few commands on that keyboard. "Check it out," he said, trying to bring the conversation back onto some kind of track. "They're networking, Danny."

"Shit!" The teenager's attention was immediately taken by the old tech. He looked at the monitor. "Sweet fuckin' murder, you've actually done it. How the hell did you do that?" he added, glancing at Dean.

"If you were paying more attention to this than to her,

then you'd know," Dean said in an acid tone. "Now look, I can show you how to do this when we get back to the redoubt, as long as we have these," he continued, detaching the cables and putting them in his backpack along with a sheaf of papers from those Danny had taken from the filing cabinet. "That isn't a problem. Getting out of here and back to the rendezvous in one piece is—especially now that we have this little problem." He indicated Ayesha.

"She's not a problem," Danny said softly. "Shit, I can remember when I used to sneak about in here and I'd see her sometimes with Baron Al, if she was tagging along with him. And then I'd see her in his palace, when I was with my dad. She's only a kid, Dean."

"With a big blaster," the young Cawdor pointed out.

"Mebbe, but—"

"But nothing, you stupe," Ayesha butted in. "Listen, you think I never saw you when you were hiding here? I always wondered how you got in, what you wanted. I used to follow you. Why the fuck do you think I come here now? Because I got interested in trying to use this shit, that's why."

"But you never gave me away," Danny said, incredulously.

"Of course not, you fuckwit. I was fascinated by you, and then by this. I wanted to learn, I wanted to come out and tell you I was watching. And now you're here with this story about these guys called Hellbenders—"

"No story—it's truth," Danny said quickly.

"Whatever, it's come at just the right time."

At first, neither Dean nor Danny caught her meaning. Then it dawned on the young Cawdor, who said slowly, "You mean your own father would sell you?"

She nodded. "Hell yeah. I'm a big prize to those cold-heart bastards. Daughter of a baron and not yet been screwed? Prize meat and big jack...the full shit. That's why I haven't chilled you or called sec. I could always make some excuse about seeing someone come in here and following them in, if it came to it. No, I've got other ideas. What do you say we make a bargain?"

"What kind?" Dean asked.

"You're gonna be mounting a raid on the convoy, right? Well, when you do, you make sure that me and the girls get away—the wag we're being carried in gets left alone and we get the chance to make a run."

"You've heard what Danny said about Correll," Dean replied, shaking his head. "I can't make guarantees about someone like that."

"That's okay." She shrugged. "You do what you can. It's a better chance than we'd have anyway."

"Okay, so that's what you get. What about us?" Danny questioned.

"You get to get away from here right now." She smiled. "I can guarantee you safe passage to wherever the hell you want to go. And when the raid takes place, you don't have to worry about the wag with the girls as I'll take care of the sec."

Dean eyed the Thompson and tried to figure the chances on the sec guard being back on duty at the place where they had made their entry. He looked at Danny. "I figure we could go for that, right?"

Danny assented. "Not that we get a lot of choice," he added, giving Ayesha a look that suggested he was quite happy with that option.

She grinned. "That's settled, then. So if you've finished frigging around with all those cables, I figure we'd better get our asses out of here triple sharp."

"Any reason?" Dean queried as he shouldered his backpack.

"Way things are at the moment, my beloved father has been taking solace in this building, away from the troubles outside. He's really gone into himself, and turns up here at all hours of the day and night. It's okay for me, 'cause I can use all the hiding places, but three of us trying to hide in here may get a touch noticeable."

"Fair point," Dean agreed. "So how do we get out of here?"

"Not the same way you got in, if you're still using that stupe method you used to," Ayesha remarked to Danny.

"Sounds like it served you well enough," he countered, unable to keep the irritation out of his voice.

"That was until I found this," she returned with a grin. "Follow me."

Leaving them almost in her wake, Ayesha turned, shouldering the Thompson as she did, and made her way toward the door they had used on the way in. She paused at the mezzanine, listening for any sec that may be outside, on the main factory floor. There was no sound.

Unwilling to speak in the quiet, in case it reverberated and in some way alerted anyone outside, Dean gave her a questioning expression. Ayesha returned it with a smile, and beckoned them on with a crooked index finger.

Opening the door, she went onto the fire escape, which led to the mezzanine from the floor of the old building, but instead of continuing down the staircase, she swung herself over it and hung underneath. Once there, holding herself by one hand, she opened a window that should have been barred and covered like the others.

And so it would appear from the outside, but the nails that had held the thin metal covering sheet in place had long since oxidized into rust, and it had been simple for Ayesha to prise the sheet loose. Dean wondered why and how she had discovered this, but decided that now wasn't the time to ask such questions.

The sheet swung, pivoted on one nail, revealing an open frame to the outside that was high enough above eye level not to be noticeable unless you looked up, and faced onto the alleyway at the side of the building, where there was little chance of anyone passing by, and where the sec men, softened by years of inactivity, never thought to look.

Ayesha swung herself through, balancing on the frame as she reached out to pull at a silken thread that hung close to the wall. This was attached to an old fire-escape ladder of the retractable sort, which should in theory have been rusted up and noisy to extend.

The manner in which she turned and winked at them

before pulling the thread suggested that she had returned several times under the cover of darkness to grease the metal. The ladder extended swiftly and silently to the ground. Ayesha swung herself out onto the ladder, and beckoned the two young men to follow with a gesture. Dean was first, negotiating the obstacle with ease and coming out onto the ladder. Danny was a little more hesitant, but gritted his teeth and followed. When both of them were on the ladder, Ayesha leaned across and pulled the metal sheet into place. She covered the alleyway as Dean and Danny dropped down to the ground, and then followed them, sending the ladder back up to its destination with a tug of the cord. When the ladder had settled, the cord hung limply against the wall, and if anyone had noticed it, they would have assumed nothing more than that it was just a piece of old twine hanging from part of a decaying and disused building.

Ayesha led the way to the front of the old building, checking that the sec man on duty was paying little attention to the side, and then beckoned the two youths to follow her as she slipped onto the thoroughfare which, although by no means crowded, was busy enough for them to get lost in quite easily.

"That wasn't at all bad," Danny sniffed dismissively.

"Bad nothing, you stupe bastard," Ayesha snapped back. "I'd like to see you do better. That method you had of getting in—you went by the old tunnel, right?—is so frigging dangerous. Second time I tried it I nearly got caught, and I vowed that I'd find a better way then."

"So how the hell did you find that the window barrier was loose in that position?" Dean asked, unable to contain his curiosity any longer.

She shrugged. "It let in light where it wasn't tight anymore. Saw it one day when I was trying to get in—trying to avoid the sec by going your way," she added with a grin directed at Danny. "Just had to take a look at the outside, see where the window came out. It was perfect."

"You're pretty damn smart," Dean remarked.

"For a girl?" she snapped back, with anger flashing in her eyes.

Dean pulled a pained expression. "Hot pipe, Baron Al must have given you some shit for being a girl. That wasn't what I meant at all. Fact is, you're pretty damn smart for anyone, I'd figure."

"That's okay, then," she said, calming slightly.

By now, they had moved away from the old industrial area and back into the main residential and barter sector of the ville. As they passed by, there were a few glances shot their way by people who had recognized Ayesha as the baron's daughter. But such was the fear they had of Al Jourgensen that they dare not approach her.

"Is it me, or is this getting a little uncomfortable?" Dean commented.

Danny was busy looking at Ayesha, who was returning his admiration. "No, I don't reckon so," he answered.

"That's because you haven't been paying attention to the people around us," Dean snapped. "Listen, Ayesha, you're going to land us right in shit with the sec, because we need to blend in with the background until we get back to the rendezvous point, and you're really making us stand out."

"Tough," she answered with a pout. "Look, I just want to get some reassurance from the others in your party that the deal's on."

"I've said so, haven't I?" Danny said.

"No offense, but you're not exactly in charge, are you?" Ayesha pointed out bluntly. "And neither are you," she added to Dean.

"Fair enough," the younger Cawdor commented. "I can understand that—but you're gonna get us into trouble before we reach the rendezvous at this rate."

"Okay, tell me where the rendezvous point is," she said testily, and when Dean had informed her, she continued, "I can get us there without anyone seeing, so stop moaning, stupe."

Dean shrugged. Looking at the way Danny was staring at Ayesha, and her determination to relay her terms to the rest of the recce party, there was little he could do. He agreed with ill grace, and let her lead the way.

Ayesha took them away from the main drag of the ville, circumventing the crowded center, and around quieter areas that were not occupied during the day, as the inhabitants of Charity went about their daily business in the centers of commerce and trade. They were able to make rapid and unseen progress, and were soon at the edge of the ville.

"We've just got to wait for the sec patrol to pass, and then we can make the distance," she whispered as they waited by a low adobe wall, sheltered from the track around the outer edges of the ville that was used by the motorbike sec patrol. There was no sign of their companions by the outcrop that they had used as shelter, but then, they wouldn't expect it any other way.

The minutes seemed to crawl by until the sec patrol roared into view, coming from opposite directions. Despite this, they all knew that there wouldn't have been enough time to make the distance without being spotted; and so they waited impatiently for the bikers to cross, cursing every word they paused to mutter to each other in their boredom, unaware that their perimeters had been breached.

Finally, after what seemed like an eternity, the bikers set off in opposing directions, to continue their sec circuit of the ville.

"Let's go," Dean barked, breaking into a jog trot as they began to cover the distance to the outcrop cover that was being used by the recce party. As Ayesha and Danny tried to keep pace, Dean wondered if the others had fared well in their part of the mission—indeed, even if they had made it back alive.

A question that was answered as they reached the seemingly deserted rendezvous. From out of nowhere— at least, nowhere they could see—Doc's voice sounded low and amused.

"Well, well, my young gentlemen, what do we have here? I had no idea that we had to bring back souvenirs."

Chapter Eleven

"What the hell have you done now, Danny?" Lonnie growled as he moved from out of cover and into an area where Dean could see him.

"I've done nothing," Danny replied defensively.

"Then what do you call that?" Lonnie countered angrily. He came down from a point of cover, his blaster waving angrily. Behind them, and to one side, Doc, Jak, Mik and Tilly also slipped out of cover until they formed a circle around the returning trio.

Considering the hostility she faced, and the fact that she was now surrounded by the recce party, Ayesha kept herself cool. The Thompson remained on her shoulder, and although she felt anger at the reaction, she didn't let it show.

"I've got a name...and I've got a reason for being here," she replied calmly. Dean noticed that her cool manner made Danny cast further admiring glances at her.

"It's gonna have to be good," Mik murmured, making sure that Ayesha was more than aware of the fact that his blaster was leveled at her by gesturing with it as he spoke.

Doc interjected, "I feel sure that Dean would not have

allowed a stranger to endanger this mission. If he is assured that she is safe, and that there is a reason strong enough for her to be here, then the very least that we can do is hear her out."

Lonnie shot Doc a look of venom. If the old man was trying to undermine his authority... Jak caught this, and fixed the patrol leader with his fiery, piercing red eyes.

"Doc right—let's hear," he said simply, but in a tone that would brook little argument.

Lonnie looked away, unable to hold the albino hunter's gaze. He knew that during the preceding few hours, the combined skills of the albino and the old man had been useful, and that he owed them that much.

"Well, spill it," he barked at Ayesha.

So the baron's daughter told them everything that she had already told Dean and Danny. When she explained how she had caught them, Dean saw that Doc was gazing at him speculatively. He knew that the old man would be amused that Dean had allowed himself to get caught in such a manner, but also anxious for the young Cawdor to explain how much of the old tech he had been able to unlock. It had been unspoken among the companions since the start of their mission, but the CD-ROM that the friends possessed was an item that held their curiosity. Could Dean have discovered how to unlock its secrets? Doc would be anxious to question the young Cawdor when they had some privacy, or when they were back at the redoubt with the rest of their party.

Meanwhile, Ayesha had reached the end of her tale, and

had told the rest of the recce party about the deal she had struck with Dean and Danny. Instead of it being greeted with the consent she had expected, she was astonished to find Lonnie whirl around to the bespectacled teenager.

"You nuke shit cretin," Lonnie screamed, white with rage. "What the fuck gives you the right to make deals without telling the rest of us? Who runs this fucking recce party? What, you want to let us do the business while you sneak off and then come back with some kind of stupe scheme that could give everything away?"

"It's not like that," Danny began, but was cut short by the enraged man.

"Shut the fuck up! Where the fuck were you when we needed you? We thought you'd got chilled in that bar and went on to make the recce, and all the while you were in danger of fucking things up for us and for Papa Joe by getting yourselves caught by Baron Al's sec—"

"The sec couldn't catch a stump-legged mutie running backward in a sandstorm," Ayesha spit in disgust. "They're shit, and they know it. Lazy mothers, all of them. Day I can't get past them is the day I deserve to buy the farm," she added.

Lonnie, stopped in midtirade by this outburst, stared at Ayesha speechlessly for a moment, then burst into peals of laughter.

"Shit," he said finally, "you sure don't sound like there's much love lost between you and your ville."

"A ville and a baron who'd sell his own daughter down the river?" she replied bitterly. "What d'you reckon?"

"Mebbe she's got a point there," Mik said. "Anyway, it's too late to worry about it now. We've got three choices—chill the bitch, take her with us or figure she's telling the truth."

Dean watched Danny out of the corner of his eye. The bespectacled youth stiffened at the mention of chilling Ayesha, and Dean figured that this could be a problem. If it came to a choice between the group and the girl, Dean had no doubts where Danny's loyalties would lie, and the last thing Dean wanted was to see him chilled at this stage.

"She's telling the truth," Dean said with a flat, even tone.

"How d'you know?" Mik questioned, his small, beady eyes narrowing to points in his sharp face.

"I don't," Dean answered. "But then again, I don't know that she's lying, either. She could have turned us over to the sec, and she didn't have to bring us back here."

"It's a fair point," Tilly said. "I reckon we should go with this one—it'll make things a little easier when we attack, having one less wag to knock out. Kinda evens the odds a bit."

"Which is no bad thing," Doc interjected. "So I suggest, if I may be so bold as to address our group leader, that we wrap this up and hit the trail. Time is tight, as I believe the saying goes...went."

Lonnie frowned. "You are one crazy old bastard, but there was some sense in there somewhere." He directed his attention to the girl. "Seems everyone wants to believe you, kid. And I guess I should go along with that. Triple fuckin' stupe of Danny to bring you here, but that's done. You go and get yourself and your girls ready, if you can trust them—"

"Only the ones I tell," Ayesha interrupted. "Most of them would be shit, but there's a few of us, and that's all it needs. The others will just be glad to be saved."

"Okay. We need to hit the road, so you get back and get ready."

Ayesha nodded, then turned to Danny. "Guess this is it," she said simply. The teenager nodded dumbly, too choked on conflicting emotions to really speak. "Mebbe I'll see you in a while, if we both get out of this without being chilled. And mebbe you can teach me something about the old tech, okay?"

She left before Danny had a chance to answer, heading back to the edge to the covering rocks, the Thompson still slung across a narrow shoulder. She didn't look back. Surveying the empty area across the desert between the outcrop and the edge of the ville, she stared up at the sun to judge where the sec patrol would be on their bikes. Nodding to herself as she worked out that she had the time to traverse the distance safely before they came around again, she began to walk out into the searing desert heat of the middle of the day. Slow at first, and then building to a trot to cover the distance as quickly as possible, she still didn't look back, preferring to concentrate her attention on the expanse of ground ahead, focused on her task, a small cloud of dust raised by the velvet pumps as she sped across the dry, sandy soil.

Danny watched her go, and then started when he felt a hand on his shoulder. Dean was standing next to him.

"Don't think about it," the younger Cawdor advised. "If you see her again, then it's supposed to be that way. Concentrate on keeping yourself from being chilled. That's all that any of us can do, right?"

Danny answered with a nod, and Dean continued, "Okay, so when we get back to the redoubt we'll try and unravel a few secrets before we have to get into a firefight. Sound good to you?"

"Yeah, guess so," Danny replied. But for the first time in a long time during his young life, he realized that there was something pulling at his attention that was more than just a hunk of old machinery.

The two young men returned to the main body of the party, where Lonnie was issuing his commands. "I was figuring on taking some rest here until the cover of night, but now we can't be certain that this is safe. I don't know whether or not to trust her, or whether or not she'll be spotted coming away from here, so I figure we need to head out triple fast."

"In this heat?" Mik questioned, adding with a whine, "and how the fuck are we going to get any cover in the middle of the day?"

"We aren't," Lonnie answered. "We just move at a regular pace, and keep ourselves triple alert. If she's found, or says anything, then the mission's blown anyway. The attack on the convoy won't be a secret. So it's even more important than ever to get back to Papa Joe and report what we've found."

"Guess so," Mik agreed reluctantly.

"Then let's do it," Lonnie said with an air of finality.

The sun bore down with an unrelenting gaze, the heat seeming to settle around their feet and work up their ankles in tendrils of heat that grabbed at them and sucked them down, draining them of their energy, each step sapping their strength.

Tilly stared up at the sky, squinting and covering her eyes as she looked toward the sun, trying to determine its position and so work out how much longer they had until the cooling balm of the night. She turned and shook her head at Mik, who was giving her a quizzical stare. The burning red orb was still almost centered in the sky, and although it was past the midway point of the day, there were still many, soul-destroying hours of heat to go before the night could descend.

Lonnie led, with Tilly and Mik at point, Danny sticking to the middle with the three companions. As they walked, using as few words as possible so that they could conserve energy and not run their throats ragged in the dry heat, Danny and Dean filled in Doc and Jak on the details of their part of the mission.

Dean confessed that he was surprised to find the others waiting at the rendezvous when he and Danny had returned. They had only spent a few hours in the ville, and the rendezvous time was set for the next morning.

"Didn't even know if you were alive," he said shortly to preserve precious breath, "but even so, didn't expect to see you waiting."

"Things triple fast when pressure," Jak said, shaking his head, the tendrils of his stringy white hair dripping sweat in the overwhelming heat.

"I must confess, I hadn't expected us to achieve our objective as quickly," Doc mused.

"When we left the bar, it was touch and go whether the sec would get us...and if not them, then certainly those drunks and jolt fiends who were gathered on the sidewalk outside. Fortunately, there was enough smoke and covering fire from within to confuse them, so when we tumbled out in the midst of a few other customers who were placing discretion over valor, then there was enough of a general melee for us to achieve safety. I fear the poor bartender may, however, have bought the farm.

"In the safety of a side alley—possibly the very one you had used scant seconds before, though that is mere supposition on my part—we were able to regroup, and Mik and Tilly were able to calm Lonnie. It would seem, although I can claim no authority for this, that the bartender was one of those responsible for him falling foul of the baron, and thus being exiled. I fear he wanted to settle that old score before we began our mission.

"However, that notwithstanding, once we were out of immediate danger, he managed to regain calm and outline a plan of recce that we could follow. It would appear that he allotted a whole day to the enterprise in case we should find ourselves having to wait for a window in which to carry out the mission. Myself and Jak, of course, expressed our concern about your good self and young

Danny, but Lonnie rightly pointed out that you may be chilled or alive, but that you knew the rendezvous point, and the rest was up to you. There was little to do but concur with such an opinion.

"We headed off to the area where the convoy was being prepared. It was in an area of the ville that was not so heavily populated, and it would seem to me that it was an old sports arena that was being used to house the wags. Even from some distance, you could hear the noise of engines being tuned and maintained by grease-laden mechanics, and the smell of wag fuel became almost overpowering within a block of the arena itself.

"I was struck by the paucity of the sec guard that was being mounted. We were obviously strangers to the area, and yet we encountered only the barest minimum of sec patrols, and as the area was largely deserted it was a simple task to find cover, either in a building or a side alley. I would hazard a guess that the good baron is either slack through lack of threat, or is pouring all his resources into the convoy and its preparation, and hoping that no one will threaten him in the meanwhile. Whatever his view, it was simple for us to approach the arena.

"Gaining access to the area where the wags were being prepared was, however, another matter. The arena is not large, but it does have a central stand that is still intact, and a building that housed the box office once upon a time. I should imagine it was a baseball stadium rather than football, and one's mind does go back to the golden days when the boys would step out to the diamond, bat in hand, ready to face the pitcher, hiding the secrets of his tricky grip behind his glove...a war of wits between two men, the fielders poised—"

"Doc, stop and tell story," Jak murmured in a low voice, interrupting the old man's flow.

For a moment, Doc looked blankly at Jak, as though the albino hunter had interrupted a dream from which he didn't wish to emerge. Then his eyes, misted over by his own imaginings, cleared, and he grimaced.

"Of course, of course... We had no way of knowing if there were any sec posted at the windows of the block, keeping a lookout. It did not seem likely, given the lack of force we had so far encountered, but nonetheless, it was a necessary measure.

"Jak volunteered to take the role of decoy, and set out to draw any fire as he headed for the side of the arena at an angle, using what little cover there was. I fear that, even given our friend's skills, it would have been difficult for him to escape injury if there had been anyone on guard. But, quite amazingly, he attained his objective without drawing a single blaster shot. It would seem that any sec was concentrated on the interior of the arena.

"We hurried to the front of the arena, where Jak joined us, and it was simple task to gain entry without being seen.

"Inside the arena, on the space that would once have been occupied by the grassy field of play, there was a sea of churned up and rutted mud and dust, the mud no doubt caused by spillages of water and wag fuel used by the mechanics.

"And this is where it becomes a matter of some concern to us. There are twelve wags in the Charity convoy, one of which looks large enough to convey the body of women that are to be the prize for Summerfield. There is another, armored wag that will carry the jack. Of the others, four are for the transfer and safe return to Charity of the crops and supplies that Baron Al is purchasing. The others are sec wags, and they are a formidable sight.

"Six wags, all of them armored and reinforced with the addition of metal shielding and wire mesh across the windows to make it hard for any grens to be thrown into them. They are mounted internally with a variety of machine blasters, and two appear to have rocket launchers also fitted. They were covered with a swarm of filthy, sweat-begrimed mechanics, who are working flat out to prepare them.

"There was a heavy sec presence within the arena, but such is the work rate being demanded of the mechanics that they were being pressed into action to help mount blasters and carry cans of fuel and boxes of ammo to and from the central stores, which seems to be located under the main stand. It did cross my mind that to knock out this stand would be to cripple their operation, but I was vetoed by Lonnie on this notion. I fear a head-to-head conflict would be a necessity for the Hellbenders to achieve satisfaction, no matter how else the result could be achieved.

"We were able to secrete ourselves around the arena and make notes and observations, and also to hide in plain sight among the sec and mechanics. It is such chaos as they struggle to meet the deadline imposed on them that the firefight to come may be aided by their inability to ensure the full working order of every wag and blaster.

"Having achieved our objective, retreat was a simple matter, as was regaining the rendezvous. The rest you know."

Doc finished his story, and Dean contemplated it in silence as they continued across the hot desert, keeping watch on an empty horizon and praying for dusk to fall.

It would be interesting to see what Ryan made of this, as compared to Papa Joe.

Chapter Twelve

It took less than two days to make the return journey, the recce party hastened by its initial trip into the desert during daylight hours. When night fell, they were glad to rest up, dehydrated and overheated by the rigors of the day's march. After building a fire, they ate and then slept while a watch rotated, rising with the dawn the next morning to complete the trip back to the hidden redoubt.

The last few hours, those spent scaling the winding road that stuttered in and out of existence around the side of the mountain, were in many ways the worst, as they found themselves making a journey upward in the blazing sun, the incline and the heat conspiring to draw any strength that was left from their calf and thigh muscles, each step weighing heavy and dragging what little energy they had from their bodies.

Apart from the sheer hard slog of it, the journey had been uneventful. There had been no more giant worms to disturb their passage, no packs of wild cats luring them into a feeding frenzy trap and certainly no other humans or muties such as stickies who were traversing the vast wastes of dust-blown desert, either on foot or by wag.

They had been completely alone, and this sense of desolation hadn't added to the ease of the journey, making them feel as though they were the only people left alive. By the time they had reached the small plateau of rock shelf that stood before the camouflaged entry to the redoubt, they felt as though this may actually be true. Doc, already partly delirious from the heat and the dehydration, was sure that this was so, and that those who accompanied him were mere shades—ghosts of those he had set off with, but who had perished along the way. Within the recesses of his mind, Doc was aware that he was starting to lose the thin thread of sanity, the silken cord to which he desperately clung, and prayed fervently that they would soon attain the air-conditioned cool, the water and food sources of the redoubt, and that he would be able to rest and recover, grasping once more that silken thread.

"Sec cameras should have got us on the last turn," Lonnie remarked to Dean, Jak and Doc as they walked—more shuffled after the last grueling ascent—toward the large sec doors set in the rock face. "There should be a party waiting for us."

His assumption was proved correct. As they came within a few yards of the doors, they began to open, scrolling upward to reveal a party of Hellbenders, accompanied by Ryan and Mildred, and headed by Correll himself.

"Weren't expecting you back so soon," he said briefly. "Must've been a hell of a journey." Gesturing to the rear of him, he indicated that two of the party go forward to assist Doc, whose will to carry on had collapsed now that the doors were open. The old man was buckling at the knees, and Travis and Rudi rushed forward to support him, closely followed by Mildred.

"Jeez, you old coot, you can't keep doing this at your age," she whispered to him as she checked his vital signs quickly before indicating to Travis with a nod that they transfer him to the med lab.

Doc was able to spare her a distant smile. "Not bad for someone breaching a third century, though, my dear doctor...."

"No, mebbe," she replied, ignoring the puzzled looks of Travis and Rudi. As she said nothing by way of explanation, they put it down to the ravings of sunstroke, and disappeared down the tunnel, transporting the ailing Doc.

Correll watched them go, then turned back to the rest of the recce party. "You've done well," he said briefly. "To be truthful, I didn't figure on the old man coming back with you. Shows guts. But all that counts for shit if you didn't get results."

"Oh, we got results all right," Lonnie said, replying as leader of the recce mission. "Full details of the wags Baron Al's sending out, some old tech stuff that the boys picked up—we got separated, and they ended up taking an alternative route—and what's more, we've got ourselves an ally in the convoy."

Correll tried to stay impassive, but Ryan noticed that he stiffened at this last sentence, as though a raging torrent of conflicting emotions were running through his mind and body, and he was fighting to keep them under control. A vein on the side of his neck throbbed, causing an eyebrow to twitch, and the one-eyed man guessed that Correll's blood pressure had just shot out there past the bloated, rad-red sun.

But despite this, the Hellbenders' leader fought to keep an even tone in his voice as he said, "Okay. We debrief in forty-five. You take a shower, eat and drink, then meet me in the office." With which brief utterance he turned and walked back down the tunnel, leaving the rest of them standing in the hot desert sun.

"Aw shit, doesn't sound like he's happy about that," Mik complained, the whining tone returning to his voice after so long.

"How can you tell?" Ryan queried.

Tilly shrugged. "If he wasn't pissed, he would have had us debrief without the option of showering and eating first. Guess he needs to cool off and get himself together before tackling this. It's unexpected, and Papa Joe doesn't like unexpected."

"Not even when it's good," Danny finished in a flat tone.

Ryan pondered that as the recce party wearily passed him on its way back down into the redoubt. If Correll was resistant to any changes in his plans, that could cause problems later, when they had to go into combat. As Jak passed, at the end of the line and still looking fit comparatively, his red eyes met Ryan's monocular gaze.

"You think what I do?" he said quietly, knowing that his own observations on the exchange that had just taken place would be the same as those of the one-eyed man.

Ryan gave a brief nod. "We'll talk about it later, in privacy."

Jak returned the nod and proceeded down the tunnel without looking back.

Ryan was left standing alone on the plateau in front of the sec doors, the rest of the recce party and the welcoming group having retreated. He stared out at the vast expanse of desert in front, stretching to where Charity lay, beyond the horizon.

It was going to be an interesting debriefing.

IT TOOK the recce party just under an hour to shower, change into clean and cool clothing, and eat and drink enough to bring back up their water and salt levels, both of which had been depleted by the long trek. Doc had showered with them, and then eaten in the med lab, where Mildred had monitored him and put him on a saline drip she had found in the well-stocked lab. That restored Doc's body, and enabled his brain chemistry to regain its delicate balance.

At the end of an hour, the recce party had reassembled in the office that Correll used as his base of operations. The walls were decorated with maps and diagrams, and new ones had been added over the course of the preceding two days as he ran through new plans for staging the attack. As he sat there, behind the large desk that had, at one time, housed the military commander of the redoubt back in the days of the Totality Concept, he toyed with a pencil that had been sitting on a piece of paper on the otherwise bare desktop.

Lonnie, Mik, Tilly, Danny, Dean and Jak were joined by a refreshed Doc, with Mildred along to keep an eye on him. Also in the room were Ryan, Krysty and J.B., as well as a select few of the Hellbenders who were obviously Correll's high command: Rudi, Travis, Jenny and the injured Cy, who—although still in no fit state for combat—had been a longtime and highly trusted associate of the Hellbenders' leader. His shoulder was heavily bound, but the fact that he was up and about was a testimony both to the skills of Mildred and her assistant, Travis, and the fact that the redoubt's med lab had still been well stocked, and the remaining supplies well maintained by the highly disciplined group.

Correll fixed Lonnie with a cold eye. "So tell me about the convoy," he said simply.

"I will, but first you've got to know what happened when we arrived, as it leads on to why we've got the extras," Lonnie began.

And so he began to explain the events of the previous day, beginning with their entry into Charity. He left nothing out of the account, bearing the withering and angry stare of his leader when he explained about Jem, and the reasons why the group became separated. But this was soon forgotten as he got into the details of what they had seen in the old sports arena, and reeled off the full specifications of the amount of wags that would be used in the convoy, and the extent of the armory that they would carry. Correll's pencil moved rapidly across the paper, making notes. Not many people were able to read and write, for education was the last thing that most needed in order to survive, and so came well down the list of priorities. The fact that Correll seemed to be able to write so rapidly and fluently suggested that he had, at one time, received an education exceptional by Deathlands standards, and once more Ryan wondered about the full story behind the driven man.

When Lonnie had finished his description of the potential convoy, he handed the account over to Danny, who explained why he had led Dean to Baron Al's secret stash of old tech—leaving out his explanation to Dean about not trusting Correll to keep his cool in the heat of confrontation—and so to the appearance of Ayesha.

As he explained the agreement he had reached with the girl, and how she had accompanied them back to the rendezvous point, he began to falter, sensing the growing anger in the Hellbenders' leader, and noticing how Correll's tightly compressed lips were a deathly white, all color bled from them.

He began to stammer so badly that Lonnie, sensing trouble ahead and wishing to avert it if only for his own sake, as recce patrol leader, took over and detailed the agreement he had reached with the girl, and stressing his view that she could be trusted because she was desperate to get away.

When he had finished, Correll gave the briefest of nods, and when he spoke his voice was strangulated by the desire to keep it even.

"So we know the strength of the Charity force, now,"

he began. "We can assume that Summerfield will match that, as they sure as shit have spies in each other's camps. What they don't know about is us, and what we've got. Jenny? J.B.?"

The Native American and the Armorer exchanged glances. J.B. had spent some time during the day examining the collection of wags housed in the old garages of the redoubt. Some of them were vehicles that had been used by escapees as they drove across the desert and found the redoubt, or had been found by Hellbender scouting patrols, and others were the wags that had been in the redoubt since before skydark. Some of these were just transport wags, which the community had been refitting using weapons from the armory; others were purpose-built attack and defense wags, heavily armored and armed. J.B. expressed his opinion that these would be more than a match for the cobbled-together wags of Charity, if—and he stressed the word—the tactics were right. Despite their superior firepower and the element of surprise, they would be outnumbered by the combined convoys of both villes, and so keeping their flanks protected was a must.

Correll nodded his agreement. "I've taken all of that into account," he said simply. "The final battle plans will be drawn tonight. The convoys will rendezvous in less than forty-eight hours. I want everyone in the base to get a good night's sleep, 'cause we're sure as hell gonna have to be wide awake and full at 'em tomorrow. Group briefing will be at sunup tomorrow."

With which, he dismissed the group gathered in his office and returned to his papers, scribbling furiously and muttering incoherently to himself as they left him.

While the Hellbender group went off to their own rooms and immediate companions, Ryan gathered his people together.

"Back to our space, and I think we may just need our own briefing first," he said softly.

It was something with which the others could all concur, and when they reached the office space that doubled as their living quarters, Jak took guard by the door, keeping one ear on Ryan while he made first watch.

"So I've heard Lonnie's and Danny's view of things— what do you think?" he asked of Doc and Dean.

By turns, they expressed opinions that differed little from those already heard, Dean adding the all-important coda of the opinion Danny expressed concerning Correll's ability to keep calm and focused in the heat of battle.

"Yeah, I'd kind of figured that one out myself," the one-eyed man said wryly. "I'm not too sure of anyone else other than Danny has that opinion, though...and that could make things difficult in the middle of a firefight."

"The only thing we can do is keep triple alert for when it starts to happen and have plans of our own," the Armorer added.

Ryan agreed. "That's why I wanted this. What do we think of the setup here? J.B.?"

The Armorer considered this for some time. "The

weapons have been well kept, and the wags are maintained well. There's a good supply of ammo and grens— better than I've seen for a long time. The hardware won't be a problem. There's enough to go around and then some. It's a question of whether they can use it."

"They can," Krysty interjected. "They've got good blaster sense and know exactly when not to fire. But the thing that worries me is that they're arrogant—not in an obvious way, but because they've been isolated for so long that it seems like Correll's hyped them up to a point where they really believe they're unbeatable."

Mildred agreed. "They can shoot well, but they can't take the idea of someone being better than them. So if they come up against forces that are better in a firefight, some of them might go to pieces." Although she didn't add any names, Mildred thought of the blond Catherine, who had tried to make her look stupid in front of Rudi.

"Same goes for unarmed combat," Krysty mused. "You saw it yourself," she said to Ryan, before going on to detail her experiences with Juan.

"It would seem to me," Doc commented with a degree of humor, "that we are dealing with a community that is a trifle unstable—and if anyone is qualified to see that, then it must be me. I fear they have been in isolation and infected with the good Mr. Correll's brooding on perceived wrongs."

"And that's what makes them dangerous," Ryan finished. "They're like a damaged gren that could go off in your face as soon as the enemy's."

He turned to Dean. "You reckon we can trust Danny to be with us if we have contingency plans?"

"Yeah. All Danny really wants to do is spend his time messing around with old tech and trying to get to the bottom of it...and mebbe spend the time doing that with Ayesha helping him."

"And can she be trusted?"

Dean shrugged. "Who can say? It's kind of hard to get an idea about her just from a couple of hours, but I'm sure she wants to get out of that convoy alive and not be a slave to Summerfield. And I'm also pretty sure that she'd pretty much like to spend all her time messing with old tech as well—especially if Danny's around."

Ryan grinned. "I guess that's a yes—but has she got the capability?"

"Provided the other women in the wag don't turn against her, then yeah—she's hard."

"They aren't going to stop her," Mildred added. "Turn away from a chance to get free and not be a slave? That's got to be worth risking a chilling."

Ryan sucked on his hollow tooth thoughtfully. "Okay. Problem is that we can't make any plans of our own until we know what Correll has mapped out—and by then, we probably won't get a chance to get together and work out an alternative."

"We should try and keep together as much as possible," J.B. said. "Keep close contact."

"May not be that easy," Krysty mused. "Correll's not

a stupe—he wants our abilities, but he won't trust us enough so soon as to let us keep together."

"Then we're just gonna have to try and mess with those plans in the heat of the moment," Ryan mused. "Play it as it comes."

Jak, who had been silent up to that point while he kept watch and listened at the same time, turned his face to the others in the room. His scarred face was set and serious, but there was a light in his eyes that may have been amusement, or may just have been the anticipation of a hunt.

"Always play as comes," he said flatly. "That why not yet bought farm."

Chapter Thirteen

"Ryan—Ryan Cawdor," the voice whispered, harsh in the almost total silence of the room, broken only by the breathing of the others.

The one-eyed man awakened in an instant, his arms coming up and grabbing at the source of the voice, still half in a dream of his brother Harvey and Front Royal. His strong fingers grasped at soft flesh, feeling the arteries and windpipe of someone's throat.

Small hands shot up to grip his wrists, the countergrip incredibly strong for the size of the short, stubby fingers. There were no nails as the grip tightened, as if whoever owned the hands was a compulsive nailbiter.

"Fucking stupe—let the fuck go," hissed the whisperer, the voice now strangled by his grip.

Ryan, still not fully awake, could feel the blood cutting off in his wrists as the grip of the other tightened, desperation lending strength. His vision adjusted to the gloom of the room, only a faint patina of light penetrating from the redoubt corridor as the door to their quarters wasn't fully clothed. In the faint light, he could see a blond head before him, with green eyes dark in the shadows but still piercing enough to be defined.

Suddenly realizing where he was and recognizing his alleged assailant, he released his grip.

Catherine staggered back a step or two, coughing as quietly as possible and trying to force air back into her closed throat.

"Nuke shit, what were you trying to do?" she husked hoarsely when she was able to speak once more.

"I was in the middle of a nightmare," he replied quietly. "Triple-stupe thing to do, sneak up on a man like that—"

"Yeah, well, it's not something I'd do from choice," she returned bitterly. "I usually like 'em to know when I'm coming."

"Then what are you doing here?" Ryan asked, rising from his bunk.

"Papa Joe sent me to fetch you. He figures there's something you should see, but he said not to disturb the others. Which is why I was trying to be delicate and gentle about it. And all you do is try and fuckin' chill me."

Ryan grinned, made crooked by the scar down his face—the scar of which he had been dreaming so vividly.

"You don't get much in the way of delicate and subtle on the outside," he said.

"If that's the best I'm going to get from you by way of an apology, then I s'pose it'll have to do," she answered, still rubbing her throat. "But it's a bit—well, crap, really. Anyway, stop pissing around. There's things to do."

She turned and left the room, slipping out through the door by opening it to the barest minimum and letting in the least possible light. Ryan figured this was to enable the others to stay sleeping, and did likewise as he exited the room, blinking as he came into the stronger light of the corridor.

Catherine was already some way down the corridor ahead of him. She turned and hissed, "Come on, fuckwit, we haven't got all night."

Ryan allowed himself an inward smile at the bad temper of the small blonde, and also allowed that such spirit would probably make her good in a firefight as he quickened his pace to catch up to her.

She led him through the deserted corridors and down a level to where one of the berths contained old sec camera equipment. Ryan followed her into the room, to find two of the Hellbenders sitting in front of the screens, with Correll standing behind them. He turned to acknowledge Ryan as he heard them enter.

"You were slow," he admonished Catherine.

"Sorry about that," she replied, rubbing her still sore throat, "but some people think that trying to wake them in the middle of the night means you want to fuckin' chill 'em. And mebbe you should."

Correll allowed himself a rare flash of humor. "Mebbe Rudi'll figure that one out one day," he said to her. "Subtlety isn't your strong point, is it? Still, he's here now."

"So can I go and get some sleep, and dream about my neck being covered in hot tar all night instead of getting ready for a firefight, then?" she said with a heavy sarcasm that was directed at the one-eyed man.

Correll assented, and Catherine left them with a glare

at Ryan that could have struck him down as stone if preDark mythology had been accurate.

"I apologize," Correll said as she retreated. "I should have sent someone better, but she was the first to hand as she'd just come off watch. That put her in a bad temper anyway, as she does like to sleep. A good and true fighter, though."

"I don't doubt that," Ryan said, recalling the iron grip of her small hands as they tried to tear his fingers from her throat. "So why did you bring me here?"

"Look," Correll said simply, standing back so that Ryan could see the monitors.

Most of them were for the interior of the redoubt, as he recalled from the occasion when the companions had viewed this room earlier in their sojourn. At this moment, they showed a skeletal watch preparing some last-minute details for the attack to be mounted on the morrow, and little else. The vast majority of the Hellbenders were, as had been Ryan himself, getting some much needed and all-important rest.

But four of the monitors on the bank were for the outside. They covered north, south, east and west, rotating through almost 180 degrees on their respective mountings, and taking in almost all the territory that surrounded the rock outcrop where the redoubt was based. There could be little, if any, of the surrounding desert that wasn't covered—no blind spots where potential attackers could hide.

It was, however, no human or animal agency that had taken the attention of Correll. The night was lit up by the raging clouds of a chem storm, the chemical reactions inside the rad-blasted clouds creating flashes of light that made the outside seem almost as bright as day. Rains lashed down horizontally onto the rock, eventually scoring across the sandy and dry soil, churning it up with the winds and the force of the water into a quicksand of mud and deep puddles that would make the journey treacherous as they set out the following day. As the sun came up and burned into the earth, then the soil would dry out and make the going easier, but it would also harden the tracks they had left behind them—tracks that wouldn't have existed on the dry earth, and tracks that could give away their position and movement, and thus betray the ambush.

That was always assuming, of course, that the chem storm would abate by morning. It was also highly possible that it could continue for hours, even days, and so completely wipe out the planned rendezvous for the two convoys.

All this raced through the one-eyed man's mind as he watched the monitors.

"How long has this been going on?" he asked.

"About two hours," Correll replied.

"How long do they usually last?" Ryan queried.

Correll shrugged. "Hard to say, friend. We don't really get much in the way of chem storms out here. This is only the third I can remember in as many years."

"Fireblast," Ryan cursed softly to himself. "You've got to admire the timing of it."

Correll nodded, his lips set grimly. "There's no way they'll rendezvous if this continues," he said in an artificially even tone, trying to keep his temper. "It'd be suicide to try and move through that."

They remained silent for a moment, watching the images on the screen. The storm was awesome in its fury, with the rolling clouds crashing together, sparking off flashes of lightning colored by the residues of chemicals carried within the acid rain that beat strange patterns into the soil, fashioned by the conflicting drifts of wind that beat into each other, causing eddies and whorls of dust and mud to whirl around the sparse vegetation, which was being ripped from its fragile rooting. Any animals or reptiles that wished to risk the storm were soon chilled, the majority opting to take whatever cover they could find. The unearthly, orange-gray sulfurous light that spread and suffused across the land cast an unearthly pallor on the landscape, making it seem even more alien and unfriendly than it had ever seemed before.

"If it abates before the sunrise, then we've got a chance of things going ahead," Ryan mused. "I can't see the rendezvous not taking place unless it's as absolutely impassable as this."

Correll shook his head slowly. "Jourgensen and Hutter both have a mutual need. They've taken long enough to get this far with each other. They're not likely to blow it out their asses unless necessary. For a start, they need to communicate with each other to arrange a mutual point and time, and that won't be easy...especially as they won't know whether or not the other has sent their convoy out."

Ryan mused on this for a moment. Things were starting to get complicated. Should they risk a move?

"How about us?" he asked, turning to face Correll, tearing his eye away from the terrifying spectacle that was taking place outside the redoubt.

"What—should we stay or go?" Correll posed.

"No, I mean what about your spies? Is there any way that they could let us know about changes of plan?"

"No reason why not if it's a rearrangement," Correll said tightly. "Thing is, they can't let us know in this bastard chem storm. This is when I wish we already had the secrets of the old tech."

"I don't know," Ryan said quietly, stroking his chin as he scanned his memory. "I can't think of anything I've ever come across that could penetrate successfully through the rad interference you get with such a storm. You've got spies in both villes?"

Correll nodded. "One in each. And up to now they've been able to keep us informed with some old radio equipment that we worked out how to use—well, Danny did. That boy's useful to us, despite the fact that I reckon he'd buckle in a firefight. But these old handhelds are only so effective. The signal gets too broken up too easily, even with the usual rad shit that's in the atmosphere, let alone with some bastard storm like this."

Ryan nodded. "If it abates before morning, they'll get in touch as soon as they can to let us know if it's still on, won't they?"

Correll smiled mirthlessly. "They know they have to—let us down at this point, and they might as well kiss their asses goodbye about ever linking up again. Same reason our man in Charity didn't help the recce party. No way could he afford to blow his cover, not at this point. If they got into trouble and got themselves chilled, well; that was their problem, right?"

Ryan nodded almost imperceptibly. "Had to be," he replied; but he did wonder if Correll's hardline discipline didn't run the risk of engendering rebellion. As long as it held for the next day, then they would be okay. On reflection, it did seem that, despite his tendency to harsh judgment, he had little to fear from his people, all as driven in their own manner as their leader.

All the while he and Correll had been exchanging views, the other two inhabitants of the room had been sitting in silence, monitoring the storm. Now one of them spoke.

"Look at that!" he whispered in awe.

Outside, the storm was showing no signs of abating. If anything, it had decided to whip itself into even more of a frenzy than ever before. Two banks of clouds, tinged in alternate shades of orange and blue, were buffeting each other from opposing directions, the cross winds that drove them making them clash with a force and speed that caused the dense mass of liquid contained within them to visibly shake, the chem-ridden clouds shuddering at impact, raining all the more heavily and driving their packets of chem-ridden water into the earth. The immovable objects and forces of the clashing clouds caused great sparks of static electricity to shoot across the sky, bolts of orange, red and blue lightning clashing and lighting up the sky until the images from the monitor screens in the dark-

ened room were bright enough to show every line of hate
and revenge etched across the face of Correll as Ryan cast
an eye over the Hellbenders' leader. The man's eyes blazed
almost as bright and fierce as the storm.

"Shit," Correll whispered. "If this doesn't calm down,
there won't be any Charity or any Summerfield to fight
against. I figure we must be safe enough down here—unless a bolt of that lightning hits the rock full on and splits
it—but it must be hell on earth to be in those villes right
now." But despite the words, Ryan could detect not a single note of sympathy in Correll's voice.

"Let's hope they hold out—come to that, if there's casualties, let's hope that your spies in each ville aren't
among them," Ryan added. "No way we'd know if it was
being chilled or fucked-up equipment that stopped them
getting in touch."

Correll didn't reply. He snorted, almost a sigh as he
breathed out heavily. There was an almost imperceptible
shaking of his head as his eyes, unblinking, stayed fixed
on the screen.

"Nothing we can do," Ryan said eventually, his attention divided between the screen and the Hellbenders'
leader. "I figure we should try to get some rest and prepare in the morning as though we were setting out. If the
storm's still raging, or if we hear the rendezvous is off from
either side, then at least we're practiced for the real thing."

His words were practical, but he tried to frame them in
a manner that Correll would also find soothing. Not for
the first time, Ryan was aware that the gaunt man beside

him was walking a knife-edge of sanity, driven almost beyond human endurance by his desire for revenge. If Correll went over the edge, then they would all be doomed, for there was no way that the companions could detach themselves from the Hellbenders at this stage.

For a few moments, it seemed as though Correll hadn't heard Ryan. Then he turned to face the one-eyed man, his eyes at first cold and blank, then firing with recognition as he dragged himself back from his own personal hell.

"Yeah," he said finally with the briefest of nods. "Guess you're right."

Ryan turned and left the room, but as he paused on the threshold and looked back, he saw that Correll wasn't about to follow. The gaunt man had turned back to the monitors, his eyes still unblinking.

RYAN FOUND IT difficult to get any more rest during the remaining few hours of night. The memory of Correll's gaunt, unblinking stare haunted him. The Hellbenders' leader was reining in all his anger and rage, all the hatred that drove him on. The problem was, if he kept doing this, then there would come a point when it would explode. And the likelihood was that it would explode when they mounted the attack on the twin convoys.

Danny had been right to point this out to Dean, as the younger Cawdor had told them. It was something of which the rest of the companions had also been aware. But Ryan felt, as the leader of the group, that there was little he could do to avoid confrontation over this matter. Their only chance of getting out was to go to the mat-trans and jump, but if they did that they would have to fight their way past Correll's people, in all likelihood, and this would just exacerbate the man's rage and bring it out earlier than they had otherwise thought.

Ryan hoped that the chem storm would abate, so that the convoy rendezvous could go ahead, and so that the attack could likewise proceed. At least they could cover their own backs out in the field, with a wag of their own, no matter what may happen to Correll and the Hellbenders.

But having to fight their way out of a three-cornered fight wasn't the best way to end this encounter. And still the CD-ROM they had in their possession needed to be decoded. From what Dean had described, the stash of old tech that Baron Al Jourgensen was holding could actually contain the key to unlocking the CD, and perhaps tell them all they wanted to know.

Ryan had a bad feeling in his gut. So many things to juggle, so many variables to go wrong. And at the head of it all, a man who was becoming, more and more, completely unstable and unpredictable.

So it was that, when Travis poked his head around the door of their berth a few hours later and briefly informed them that the hour had come to rise and prepare, Ryan had managed little rest and was in the middle of a shallow, dream-filled sleep where Correll had turned into a stickie whose sucking fingers were ripping at his heart, trying to tear it from his body.

When the rest of the companions had risen, and Ryan

was on his feet, his eye looking sunken and red, Mildred took one look at him and nodded.

"You too, eh? Can't say I was able to get much rest thinking about Papa Joe's team talk coming up. I'd be much happier if we could play this our own way."

Mildred was aware that Ryan had discussed with Correll the manner in which the attack could be mounted, and the tactics that could be used. She was also aware that, although ostensibly taking notice of the one-eyed man, Correll was liable to dismiss them all for his own, tunnel-vision aims.

Even more so when Ryan told them of the chem storm.

J.B. shook his head, pushing his spectacles onto the bridge of his nose. "It would have to stop right now for us to get out there—and there'll still be enough rad interference in the atmosphere to make radio communication impossible right now. If it's over, we'll have to assume they're going ahead."

Ryan agreed. "That's how I see it, but how's Correll going to read it?"

"I think we'll go," Krysty said. Her hair was waving slightly, as though caressed by a breeze despite the fact that the redoubt's air-conditioning didn't disturb the air in such a fashion. The movement could only mean that her mutie sense was telling her that there was a dangerous situation ahead. "I can't see Correll stopping now. Not after waiting so long. This is the culmination of all his dreams. He's not going to throw this away unless it's totally impassable out there."

It was a view with which the rest of the companions could only concur. So when Travis reappeared to summon them to eat, they left their berth in silence, anticipating what could lie ahead.

The entire community was gathered in the large room that served both for the feeding of their minds and bellies. The latter was the case at the moment, as the forces of the Hellbenders ate heartily, readying themselves for the confrontation that lay ahead. Certainly, they were acting as though the chem storm had abated.

Correll was in his usual position, flanked by Jenny, the redoubt armorer, and Lonnie, who seemed to have established himself as second in command. On seeing the companions enter, he beckoned to Ryan and J.B. to join him. As the leader of his group, Ryan was an obvious choice, and J.B. was picked because of his ability with weapons. Indeed, while the others had been engaged either in training or in the recce mission, J.B. had forged a good working relationship with the Native American woman who now acknowledged him with a smile. Despite her initial misgivings and hostility, she was now sure that J.B. was invaluable. He had helped her to maintain and repair some of the weapons that had been damaged during training, and had also given her invaluable advice about the best times to use concussion and shrapnel grens in enclosed environments. She had learned from him, and as a result her respect for the man had grown.

Ryan and J.B. collected their food and joined the table, while the rest of the companions found spaces around the room. Dean, Jak and Doc joined Danny who, as usual, was seating himself a little apart from the rest of the group.

"Heard about the chem storm?" he said in an undertone as they joined him. When they acknowledged this, he continued, "I figure that Papa Joe would send us out whatever the conditions, way he feels about things. But the good news is that it's stopped out there. At least we won't have to fight our way through a shitload of acid rain."

"Not good conditions, though," Jak noted.

A sentiment that was being echoed on the table where Mildred and Krysty were now breaking their fast. At the request of Rudi, they had joined the table where he sat with Catherine and Cy, among others. Mildred regretted it almost as soon as she had sat down, as he put his arm around her to "settle her in." She didn't know which was worse, the feel of his unwelcome hand, knowing that she couldn't deck the mother with a roundhouse punch in front of all his fellow Hellbenders, or the glare she received from Catherine, as the last thing they needed to do at this stage was to make enemies—not before going into a firefight.

"You ready for some action?" he asked her, with a wicked grin on his face.

"You'd better be," Catherine added in a venomous undertone.

"I'm ready to go out there and fight, if that's what you're trying to say," Mildred replied with a faked ingenuousness, shrugging him off.

"We're all ready, aren't we?" Krysty added, trying to change the subject.

"I'd like to say I am, but I dunno," Cy said with a tinge of regret in his voice, gesturing to his still bandaged shoulder. "I can fire a blaster, but not a real heavy-duty one. You did a good job on this, Doctor, but there hasn't really been enough time for it to heal, y'know?"

"Just take it easy, and pick your shots," Mildred said to him, glad to sidle away from Rudi and change the subject and focus of her attention. "Worse thing you could do is get carried away and end up opening up that wound—then you'll be no good to anyone except the other side."

While she handed out these words of advice, at another table Correll was filling Ryan in on events following the one-eyed man's return to his rest.

"The chem storm carried on for another three hours, and believe me, my friend, it got to the point where I believed that we would have to postpone the mission. But when it cleared, it cleared with a speed that was breathtaking. It was as though the winds that drove the clouds together had suddenly reversed poles, like magnets. Where they had been driving themselves together, now they could think of nothing but driving themselves apart, and the faster the better. Within minutes, the sky was clear and dark, only the stars lighting the sky."

"That's good," J.B. mused, "but what about the villes— would they still go?"

"More importantly," Ryan added, "have you had any signals from them?"

Correll shook his head. "Not much chance of that, friend Ryan. The rad interference is still far too strong.

Nothing going across that air except ear-blasting static. There's no way I'm gonna hear from either of my spies this side of next week, if the strength of the interference is anything to go by."

"So how can you be sure the convoys will be going ahead?" Ryan queried.

Correll shrugged. "Can't be a hundred percent sure, I guess, but I do know one thing—Jourgensen and Hutter both need to meet badly. Badly enough for them to risk taking their convoys across ground that has been hit by a chem storm. If the ground hasn't dried out, then it'll be muddy and hard going, and mebbe both of them'll be late at the rendezvous point. But you can sure as hell bet that they'll be going. And if they go, then we go."

"I reckon that it'll take them longer, but if you work out the distance and the likelihood of us having the same problems over the territory, it'll kind of even out so that we don't have to worry too much about changing our time of departure in order to reach them at the same time as they arrive," Jenny added.

"That seems a fair assumption," J.B. commented. "But how will it change our tactics? What are the conditions like out there?"

"Just as you'd expect," Correll replied simply. "The desert is like a swamp right now. The earth has been turned into mud and quicksand, so we'll have to be careful as we negotiate the old tracks, but it's drying out rapidly. I figure that we'll leave some tracks, but mebbe by the time we get to where the rendezvous is taking place we'll have been out there long enough for the desert to have dried out and not leave any telltale tracks."

J.B. nodded. It was more or less as he had thought it would be should the rains cease, and he knew that Ryan felt the same. Their main concern was never going to be the conditions if they were anywhere near good enough to start out.

After they had eaten, Correll had the room cleared of all the tables, and the Hellbenders arranged their chairs so that they were seated facing the one direction—the part of the hall where Correll had set up his maps and charts. He waited for the group to settle before beginning.

"Okay, people," he said, staring at a point somewhere over their heads. "Now I know you all know about the chem storm, and the effect that it's had on the terrain out there, but I have to tell you that I feel that it doesn't affect the basic plan. We can still get there in plenty of time to mount our ambush, and then to claim our rightful reward.

"And that reward is ours. We have all been unjustly exiled from Charity—a few of us from Summerfield—and we have been driven from our homes, family and friends by the idiocy and maliciousness of the barons, particularly that coldheart son of a gaudy piece of scum called Jourgensen. When the time comes, I don't care how or who metes out his chilling, but I sure as shit hope it's me.

"We leave here in approximately ninety minutes, which should give us all that we need to finish loading and checking the wags. Thanks to Jenny and our good friend J.B., we know that the tools will not be found wanting, so it is to ourselves that we have to look. Have we got what it takes, people?"

He turned and faced the map he had pinned up on the wall, tracing the route with his finger as he spoke.

"This is the route we'll be taking. It's more or less direct, but as we get nearer the rendezvous we'll be avoiding the more obvious tracks so that we don't leave any sign of our arrival. This is something that has become more of an imperative since the chem storm, as the land around here may still be churned up and wet enough for us to leave wag trails. The other thing we have to watch for is any signs of quicksand. We don't have the time or manpower to devote to getting anyone out of trouble like that. There's gonna be a hell of a lot more of them than there is of us, so we have to conserve our energy and hit them hard and efficiently. When we arrive at the rendezvous point, this is what we do."

He pulled the map off the wall and replaced it center stage with a hand-drawn chart that showed his tactical maneuver for the attack.

"We form a pincer movement at the rear of these two outcrops, and as both convoys converge on the valley where they plan to meet, we close it down from each end, attacking them from the rear and hitting them hard. Then, before they have a chance to regroup, we come around the sides of the convoys, each group splitting to two, and hit them from each side, so they have no idea where to turn. And while they're turning, we hit them so bastard hard that there's nothing of the scum left. We know that both Hutter and Jourgensen are attending the rendezvous because of the importance of the trade, so that means they'll all be carrying their best sec. We hit them and wipe them out, then the ville of Charity is wide open.

"It's a simple plan because simple is best. Make it too complex, and everyone has to remember what the fuck they're doing in the heat of battle. Make it too complex, and it's hard to adjust if something happens that we don't expect. But I'll tell you one thing—it's simple enough for us to chill the fuckers and finally gain vengeance."

As he finished, a roar swept the room, along with cries of hate against the barons and their villes. This seemed to spur Correll on, as he yelled above the noise, "We've been screwed for too long, we've waited too long. Lives have been destroyed, people we love have been chilled, lives we wanted to live have been denied us. Now we can take all that back and show them that they had no right to take it away from us. We're hell-bent on vengeance and we will have it."

The room was deafening as the cheers and whoops rose to a crescendo.

Ryan and J.B. exchanged glances and looked around the room. The only people whose eyes weren't lit by the fires of fanaticism were those of their fellow travelers...and also Danny, who looked distinctly uneasy with the whole affair. It was Danny whose crestfallen and bemused expression summed up their feelings as Correll spoke again.

"I hate the fact that the fucking chem storm threatened to ruin the whole plan. I hate it that the fuckers we've got in those villes can't tell us shit because of rad interference stopping transmission. I hate the fact that we're going into this blind compared to what it should be, but I'll tell you all something—we have right on our side, and that's what's going to see us through and help us defeat those bastards and avenge all those we've lost. Now let's get this show on the road," he yelled, whipping the enthusiasm and fire of his people into a frenetic state as they began to filter out of the room and down to the wag bays, where they would pick up the last of their traveling supplies and gun the wags into action.

The companions were among the last to leave the room. Mildred made her way over to Ryan and whispered urgently to him.

"I don't have to tell you, do I?" she began. "I've seen that so often in the old days. Papa Joe is about as unstable as you can get, like a volcano about to blow. Trouble is, we're going to be right in the path of it this time."

"Yeah, I know that," Ryan returned in an undertone, "but what can we do? We've got to roll with it for now."

"Listen, if he carries on like this, I wouldn't like to bet on our chances of reaching the interception point in one piece with him in the lead, let alone winning a firefight."

J.B., who had heard their exchange, interjected. "It's no use worrying about that, Millie. Ryan's right, we can't back out now. We've got to run with the pack and then play it by ear. Thing we've got is that we can stay cooler than them. They're all as fired up as Correll is. We've got to trust to our reactions being better."

Mildred fixed the Armorer with a sardonic stare, her eyebrow raised. "John, don't you realize that the last thing I'm worried about is our ability? We're not the ones giving orders, and he's got superior numbers. What I'm worried about is the few of us having to fight on three fronts instead of two. That could be stretching things a little too thin."

"We'll have to see," Ryan replied. "We don't have any other option."

With which decision, the one-eyed man led them after the retreating Hellbenders, toward the wag bay.

Chapter Fourteen

In the wag bay, the heat, smell and noise were intense. The Hellbenders were checking the wags, loading up the last supplies of ammo and grens, and settling themselves into the variety of vehicles in order to begin the trek to the ambush point.

As the companions entered, Jenny approached them.

"Papa Joe wants you and Krysty to go with him," she said to Ryan. "J.B., he wants you to go in the second wag with Mildred. I'll be in that one, too. Dean, you and Jak and Doc are to go in the third wag out. Each of the first three will form a lead point for the different parties when we reach the destination. He values your experience in different environments, and wants to spread you out to be as effective as possible."

"Of course he does," Mildred murmured, although there were other thoughts that occurred to her. Ryan had wanted them to keep together as much as possible, and although it was as well that they weren't spread across the entire convoy, splitting them into three would make it harder for the group to maintain unity if they had to find a way of pulling out. It also suggested to her that perhaps Correll had a notion that they might be watching their own backs in this manner, and wanted to keep them separated to some degree.

The one-eyed man felt much the same about this, but knew that dissent in such a situation, surrounded by the Hellbenders, hyped up to fight and believing totally in their leader, wouldn't work. If anything, the way the Hellbenders were feeling it may just get them chilled before they even left the redoubt. Although they had been accepted by the group, he was as aware as the rest of the companions that they were treading a thin line in a group that was riddled with mass hysteria and insanity.

"Sure," he said simply, nodding briefly and turning to his people, a signal to Jenny that her task here was done. As the woman walked away to resume her last-minute chores, Ryan spoke softly.

"Looks like the three wags we take are all equipped with radio..." He indicated the wag with Correll already seated at the wheel, staring stiffly ahead and almost in a trance, and the two wags immediately behind it. They were of the stock from the redoubt, and were military sec wags, fitted with machine blasters and antitank weaponry. "That's good, 'cause at least we'll have a direct link if shit happens. We need to keep triple hard out there, especially when we reach the destination and move into position. I figure it'll blow, if it's going to, when they get first sight of the convoys converging. Until then, we keep it down and wait. This is a situation to react rather than act, okay?"

There was a murmur of agreement from the rest of the

companions, and they parted, moving off to their allotted wags.

Ryan and Krysty climbed into the wag that was already
occupied by Correll. He was at the wheel, staring straight
ahead out of the front windshield, and didn't acknowledge
their presence. On his lap was cradled a metal box, sealed
and welded all around. It was about three by three, and had
no identifying marks. With no seeming point of entry,
Ryan wondered what it was for. Did it contain some kind
of weapon that Correll had not told them about? Some kind
of mysterious old tech invention that he had found in the
redoubt? If this was so, then perhaps Doc would recognize
it, as he had seen so much during his time as a captive of
the whitecoats of the Totality Concept. But on reflection,
Ryan thought it unlikely that it was weapon. The box was
too crudely constructed, too amateurishly welded to be
something that was legacy of the military-industrial complex that had left the world in such a condition. No, this
was something that Correll himself was responsible for,
and from the manner in which he was gripping the box, it
had some intensely personal meaning for him.

The one-eyed man turned to Krysty, but she had already
seen the box on Correll's lap. The same things had run
through her mind as through Ryan's, and she knew what
he was thinking. It wasn't a good idea to ask—her hair
wrapped itself tight to her when she thought of this, and
without him having to even frame the question, she shook
her head almost imperceptibly.

Ryan and Krysty took their places in the wag. There

were two other Hellbenders there besides Correll: Travis and Cy, who was manning the blasters and antiwag hardware that sat at the back of the wag. The comps glowed green and yellow in the dark of the vehicle, casting a sinister light on his features as he smiled a greeting. Krysty wasn't sure that she wasn't imagining it, but it seemed as though the entire party was set on a suicide mission, and didn't really need Papa Joe to go over the top. They could manage this quite easily by themselves.

As the one-eyed man slipped into the seat beside Correll, it seemed to snap the gaunt man out of his reverie, and he turned to face Ryan.

"Ready?" he asked, his voice no more than a hoarse husk.

"If the rest of the party are ready to go," he stated.

"They will be," Correll said simply and, without even bothering to check if this was the case, gunned the engine of the wag. It had been ticking over while they boarded, and now the powerful engine roared deafeningly in the enclosed space of the wag bay. The noise grew in intensity as it was joined by the roaring of the other wags in the war party.

Correll put the vehicle into gear, and it began to move toward the exit ramp that would take them up the necessary levels of the redoubt and out onto the rock plateau.

As the leading wag approached the sec doors, Correll leaned out, punched the exit code onto a small console and jerked the lever that would open the door. As the door lifted, he took the wag through and out into the chem-raddled morning.

Ryan winced as the change in light hit his eye. The low-level lighting of the redoubt was replaced by the scorching sun, which hit them with no mercy as they exited the redoubt, the red, rad-bloated orb distorted even more through the haze of chem fumes that rose from the rapidly drying earth. The air stank of sulfur and a sickly sweet undertone that couldn't be identified as the quality of the air changed. Instead of the cool, cleaned air that was passed through again and again via the air-conditioning and purification system, they were hit by the heat, dust and chem-soaked air that came after a storm.

The wag turned sharply on the rock plateau, gravel and loose shale moving under the large, heavy-tread tires and shooting over the edge of the rock table, down to the base of the outcrop. It was a sharp turn to maneuver the large wags on the relatively small space and take them down onto the road that wound around the far side of the outcrop.

In the second wag, J.B. gritted his teeth as he swung the steering wheel, the wheels locking as the wag spun on the loose surface. He righted it, hoping that the rear tires would hold on the shale, and followed Correll's lead. Already clouds of loose earth and dust were being thrown up by the motion of the wags, and it crossed the Armorer's mind that the wags that came at the very rear of the procession were in danger of being blinded by the opaque clouds that were being raised.

Correll had already hit the road that wound down the far side of the rocks. It looked a steep and narrow path, and he took it at a speed that—to Ryan—verged on the suicidal. The wheels locked on the angles of the road, the rear of the wag sliding across toward the edge of the precipice, back end of the wag waving wildly into space.

"The one problem with being so secure is that it makes it a bastard to get down again," Correll said with a humorless grin that spread across his thin, drawn face.

"As long as we get down the right way, and not the quickest," Ryan returned.

Correll laughed harshly but said nothing.

The convoy of wags from the redoubt spread out down the mountain track, other drivers following J.B.'s lead in hanging back from the wag in front, allowing the dust some time to settle before they hit the lowering clouds. It also stopped the spray of loose shale and stone from battering the windshield of each preceding wag. Although the shields were of a material that could not be broken by the missiles, they could nonetheless obscure the driver's view with their constant hammering.

In the leading wag, Ryan and Krysty both breathed a sigh of relief when Correll took the wag onto the flat of the desert floor, coming out of the final turn and gunning the engine as he hit a straight trail, intending to eat up as much ground as possible with the minimum of delay. Correll himself, and Cy and Travis, seemed not to have noticed the perils of the descent. Each was in his own little world, focusing on the firefight to come.

J.B., sweat glistening on his forehead, spectacles slipping down his nose, took the final turn with a feeling of relief. After that descent, at that speed, any kind of firefight would be by way of light relief. Able at last to take one hand from the wheel, he pushed his glasses back up his nose and gunned his engine, changing gears and increasing speed to try to make up the rapidly widening distance between himself and Correll. He breathed out heavily through his mouth, sparing a moment for a swift glance at Mildred.

The woman pulled her plaits tight behind her, rolling her eyes at the Armorer in a gesture that spoke of relief.

Jenny watched them both, then said, "That ain't scared you already, has it?"

J.B. grimaced. "Given the choice between a shoot-out with a bunch of coldheart mercies on one side and ravenous stickies on the other, and taking that road again, I'd choose the firefight. Know better what I'm doing then."

The Native American nodded. "You'll soon get a chance to prove that, I'm thinking."

A similar conversation took place in the third wag, driven by Lonnie. Catherine and Danny made up the numbers, along with Dean and Jak.

"Hot pipe, anything's got to be better than that!" Dean exclaimed.

"You're not going pussy on me, are you?" Lonnie asked without humor. His close-cropped head was rigidly set on the road ahead, and his eyes stared with a dark intensity at the wag in front. He put his foot down, gaining ground on J.B. as the Armorer increased his own speed to catch up with the leading wag.

"Not a matter of that," Dean replied sharply. "Shit like that is stupe—get us chilled before we even get a chance to fight."

"We don't pull out of anything," Catherine snapped. "If you go, then you go big."

"Bit stupe to go before you get to the enemy, though," Danny said quietly.

"Whose side you on, son?" Lonnie barked without looking away from the road.

"It's not a question of sides," Danny replied, keeping his voice level. "It's a question of meeting the objective. Isn't that what Papa Joe has always said?"

"Just mind you remember all that Papa Joe says," Lonnie returned. "Make up your mind where you stand, boy."

Dean and Jak exchanged glances. Would they have to start watching their backs against the Hellbenders, as well as the convoys from Summerfield and Charity?

Convoys that they could only hope had actually left their respective villes.

ELIAS TULK WAS A FAR from happy man. As a sec man for Baron Tad Hutter, he had been selected to ride shotgun on the leading wag to leave Summerfield, laden with food supplies and seed crops, headed for the rendezvous point. He wasn't anticipating much trouble from the sec forces accompanying the convoy from Charity. They'd be too busy trying to stop any of the women they were trading from stepping out of line. What's more, the device Hutter had his men rig on each wag would more than dissuade them. For, on each of the wags carrying a crop or supplies, a very obvious primitive flamethrower had been erected, pointing down toward the merchandise loaded on the wag.

One wrong move, and everything they wanted and needed so desperately would be torched.

So the problems wouldn't come from that quarter. There were more likely to be problems with the rest of the Summerfield sec wanting to stop and screw all the women they were trading before the convoy reached base again. That wouldn't go down well with Hutter, as the women were to be saved for breeding stock, and they weren't to be touched or damaged in any way. The women in the ville had proved barren for some time, and new blood was necessary if the ville was to survive. However, all the reasons in the world wouldn't stop some of the sec men going on the rampage if the rumors proved true, and the daughter of Baron Al Jourgensen was part of the trade. Not yet sixteen, still a virgin and supposed to be a looker. Unless strict discipline was maintained, she would be fucked ragged and left for dead by the entire sec force before they reached Summerfield.

But that wasn't the problem that occupied Elias Tulk. He actually didn't care whether the girl—whose name he knew to be Ayesha—was raped and possibly chilled. Hutter wouldn't be able to stop it on his own, even though he sat beside Tulk right now, with an Uzi across his lap and a Sharps slung across his back.

Elias Tulk was not a happy man because of the chem storm. The interference was so bad that he had been unable to contact Papa Joe and let him know that the convoy had left as planned, undeterred by the aftermath of the storm. The radio that Correll had given him when he had first been recruited by the Hellbenders was now lying in his bunk back in Summerfield. It was too risky to carry it with him, and it had proved useless earlier that morning, when he had made one last attempt at contact.

Tulk had been recruited by a recce mission, willing to change sides and act undercover because Hutter had taken Tulk's wife for his own, simply because he took a fancy to her. But the woman had been unwilling, and for disloyalty to the baron, Hutter had made Tulk shoot her in the head. The memory of her eyes, staring imploringly into his own as he squeezed the trigger on the 9 mm Luger and blew her brains from the side of her head, still haunted him. He hated himself for not refusing the baron, and hated the baron for turning him into the kind of spineless automaton that would follow from fear. He didn't care whether he bought the farm on this day, only that Hutter's little empire should collapse.

Which was why he was fretting about not being able to contact the Hellbenders. He hoped that they would take the same chance as Hutter, and set off anyway.

The concern had to have shown on his face as he piloted the wag across the desert, for Hutter spoke.

"Elias, you look like something's troubling you, boy. Why don't you tell your old daddy what it is, now."

"Nothing much, Baron," Tulk replied, resenting the patrician attitude of Hutter, who thought of himself as the father of his people, and acted accordingly. That's if you believed in the sort of father who raped and chilled his daughters at will, and delighted in setting man against man to divide and conquer any opposition against him in the ville. Tulk knew how much Hutter was anticipating the arrival of Ayesha, and had almost walked in on the baron masturbating while he repeated her name like a mantra.

Hutter looked patrician. A large man, standing over six feet with long gray hair and matching beard, and nursing a huge gut from overindulgence, he sat uneasily on the narrow wag seat, in direct contrast to Tulk, who was a few inches shorter and lean, with a sharply defined musculature that stood out well under his olive skin. His dark, saturnine brow remained fixed on the road ahead, not wishing to give anything away until the time he could gain his own personal vengeance.

Hutter wouldn't accept Tulk's answer. "Say, you ain't actually afeared about what we're gonna do, are you?" he asked with a sly sarcasm infusing his voice.

"Why would I be, Baron?" Tulk answered with as little expression in his voice as he could manage.

Hutter shrugged. "I dunno. Mebbe it's just that you don't have the balls for this sort of thing. Mebbe I should think about demoting you—but then again, if you ain't worth where you are now, then why would you be worth anything in the sec force?"

Tulk sighed inwardly, but kept a stone face. This was one of Hutter's irritating habits, part of his divide-and-rule philosophy with his sec force. If he set one against another, and kept petty rivalries and jealousies afloat, as well as threatening the position of his sec hierarchy, keeping them at one another's throats, it was easier for him to keep control over them all, as none would ever form alliances to end his reign.

Except, of course, if they chose to align themselves

with an outside force. Emboldened by this knowledge, Tulk did something that he had previously always been mindful of—he spoke back.

"Mebbe I'm not worth anything, Baron, but just mebbe no one else is, either, because we've never had the chance to be a proper sec force."

Hutter was silent for a moment. Confusion crowded his brow. The one thing that had never occurred to him was that one of his sec crew may actually talk back to him. Confusion gave way to anger, and his hands tightened around the Uzi he cradled in his lap. From the corner of his eye, Tulk saw that, and allowed the ghost of a triumphant smile to flicker across his face.

"I wouldn't think about that, Baron," he said mildly. "You chill me now, and who's going to drive the wag? You certainly can't, and besides, by the time you clean the wag out and throw my body out, plus get it back on the track after my chilling body has thrown it off course, you'll be late. And then you'd lose face. And we can't have that, can we?"

"No, we can't," Hutter replied in a low, flat tone that was so quiet it was almost lost under the roar of the wag engine. His eyes bored into Tulk, and there was nothing in them except the cold flint of hatred and finality. Elias Tulk wouldn't be going back to Summerfield.

Tulk ignored the baron, and tried to keep the smile from his face, although inside he felt more elation and freedom than he had for, well, for probably all his life, but certainly for the past few years. He, too, knew that he wouldn't be going back to Summerfield—at least, not with Baron Tad Hutter. But the men had entirely different reasons for thinking this.

Tulk drove on, with Hutter beside him, sunk into a brooding and heavy silence. Toward the rear of the wag sat two other sec men, who had listened in bewilderment to the exchange that had just taken place. Neither would ever risk what they called their lives by talking to Hutter in such a manner, knowing that there were always other sec men willing to avenge petty rivalries by doing the baron's bidding and assisting them to buy the farm. So the fact that Tulk had just committed suicide—as good as—in front of them made them both feel uneasy about the mission ahead.

They weren't the only ones to be feeling ill at ease.

AYESHA SHIFTED uncomfortably on her seat. It wasn't the wooden bench, hard and unwelcoming as the wag bumped over the rutted road surface, that made her squirm uneasily. Rather, it was the closed flick knife that she had concealed about her person before the women had been gathered and put into the wag, where they now sat huddled and crammed together, ten on each side of the armored wag, with three sec men on hand—one to drive, one to ride shotgun and one to man the machine blasters that were mounted through slots in the side of the armored wag.

It was stiflingly hot, as the wag offered no protection from the beating sun, the heat gathering and collecting on the bare metal of the roof and sides, turning the interior into an oven. The women sat in mostly sullen silence, with only the odd complaint, slapped down hard by the sec men, sometimes with a word, sometimes with the back of the hand. It was also dark in the enclosed wag, and in the poor light Ayesha could study the downturned and trammeled faces of the women, and the anxiety on the face of the sec man who sat with them in the rear of the vehicle. Because of the gloom she could do this without being observed too closely.

Baron Al had trusted none of the women, or their men. Many of them had husbands and lovers who had been unwilling to let the women go. They had been "persuaded" by force or threats to let their women go, but as the women themselves were also unwilling—incredibly so, in the eyes of Baron Al—it was more than possible that, starving as they were, the men and women involved would hatch some kind of plan for escape, or at least an attempt at it. So he ordered that each of the women be strip-searched before she got on board the wag.

In the middle of the old sports arena where the wags had been prepared, the women were gathered and then stripped naked, their ragged clothes examined for any weapons they may conceal. The sec men conducted the cavity searches, Baron Al joining in this part of the search, which he saw as a bit of extra fun for him and his men.

Except when it came to Ayesha. She was stripped like the others, but because she was Baron Al's daughter, and the prize of the merchandise because of her virginity, none of the sec men assembled were willing to conduct the cavity searches, particularly in front of Baron Al himself. One wrong word, one wrong move—the slightest touch of blood proving that she had been despoiled, and thus taking the prize cachet away, and the sec men knew that Baron Al was likely to come down hard on them. So when it was her turn to be searched bodily, Baron Al stepped forward himself.

Knowing that Hutter would test her immediately by screwing her as the exchange took place, Jourgensen was aware that no blood coming from the sexual encounter would convince Hutter that she was no virgin, and the deal would be off. So Baron Al trod carefully.

"You better not be trying to shit me, girl," he whispered as he approached her.

"Why would I do that?" she answered, barely able to keep the contempt from her voice.

"You know," he said simply. "I'm just gonna have to trust that you've got nothing up your pussy—or that you never have," he added. "But I can still see."

And before the girl had a chance to move, he bent her over and thrust his fingers up her anal passage, probing as his sec men had with the other women to see if there were any weapons concealed.

Although she was empty in that orifice, Ayesha clenched the muscles in her pelvic floor and prayed that he wouldn't be able to feel the knife she had concealed in herself before leaving his palace. It was a slim, mother-of-pearl-handled knife with a rapier thin blade that she had honed until it drew blood from her fingertips with the slightest of pressure. It would be a formidable weapon in an enclosed space, where the sec men would be unwilling to use their blasters. The only thing she had to worry about was whether it would open involuntarily before she could remove it. With an air of resignation, it dawned on her that even if it did open, the internal hemorrhaging would probably cause her to buy the farm, so she wouldn't have much to worry about in that event.

Baron Al had withdrawn his fingers. "I dunno whether or not to be disappointed in you," he said softly. "You ain't causing trouble, but I'd expect it from any daughter of mine."

"Glad I let you down, then," she said with a sneer, not betraying her triumph at deceiving him. She'd keep that pleasure to herself.

And now she was aboard the wag as it rolled across the rutted, churned-up desert, shifting ever more uncomfortably on the bench seat, and hoping that the motion of the wag wouldn't cause the knife to open. She had to get it out soon, but quite how was another matter.

"What the fuck are you doing?" the sec man on the machine blaster snapped with irritation, watching her move.

"I need to piss," she snapped back.

"Shit, you pick your fucking moments, don't you?" the sec man replied with exasperation. "We're not going to stop the wag and let you out behind a rock, no matter who you are," he continued with more than a hint of sarcasm in his voice. "You'll have to do it as best you can in the corner." He pointed to a slops bucket in the corner of the wag, near the bolted rear doors. He felt safe offering her this, as the wag was in the middle of the convoy, and even if she felt inclined to try to risk her luck diving out of the rear door, there would be a wag on their tail that would pick her up—if it didn't chill her first by running her over.

Ayesha stood unsteadily, her legs numb from the journey, and her balance unsure as the wag swung across the rutted desert. As she steadied herself, she took the opportunity to look around at the other women in the wag. Most of them looked as though they were already beaten and defeated before any fight had even begun. One she recognized, and this woman was typical of them all. A tall, broad woman with a large bust and wide hips, her sharp-nosed face and prominent teeth were framed by a shock of blond hair that fell in a mane over her shoulders and down her back. Despite the lack of food that had plagued Charity, she had still kept a lot of meat on her bones, and the same basic shape that she had always had. And yet, if you looked closely, you could see the folds of loose skin beginning around her neck and shoulders, and the sag of her bosom where the flesh was falling off, leaving baggy, empty skin behind. She was looking down—had been for most of the journey—and only looked up on hearing Ayesha move.

The girl recognized this woman as Anita, who had worked at the palace as a cook and had also whored for Baron Al when he had felt the urge in the still of the night. She had thought that lending her favors to the baron may save her from being sacrificed, but she had already born two children to different fathers, proving that her fertility was down to herself rather than any one man, and the baron had picked her as one of the first to board the wag. She was only in her middle thirties, with plenty of time to bear more children for the desperate men of Summerfield.

Ayesha despised the woman, as she had been sly and bitchy to the girl when the baron had been absent, yet sweet and nice to her when he was around. Yet it gave her little pleasure to see the woman so defeated. As she gazed up, her eyes meeting Ayesha's, the girl could see that Anita had been crying the whole time since they had left the ville, her eyes little more than bloodshot orbs rimmed with sore, puffy flesh. Her cheeks were streaked with grime that had run under the onslaught of the tears, and her whole bearing was of one who had already accepted her fate...whatever that may be.

The resignation and defeat of this woman she loathed made Ayesha even more determined to meet her side of the bargain with the Hellbenders—with Danny—or to be chilled in the attempt. Anything would be better than to end up like this pathetic specimen.

Casting a swift yet penetrating survey over the rest of the women in the wag, she could see that the vast majority of them fell into the same category as Anita. There were only a couple of exceptions, one of them being a tall and lithe girl who was of mixed white and black parentage. She had a firm figure, lightly muscled and highly toned, with large brown eyes that met Ayesha's with an unflinching gaze. As their eyes met, it was as though some kind of understanding was reached between them without the need for words. Both recognized the will to survive, and seemed to agree without even acknowledging it that they would back each other up if the need arose. The girl had long plaits that were tied back into a ponytail at the back of her head, accentuating her perfect cheekbones. She had a pride and hauteur in her bearing that told Ayesha that she wouldn't be found wanting. The ponytail moved slightly behind the girl's head as she nodded almost imperceptibly.

Ayesha moved to the back of the wag and turned to face the sec man, who was watching her intently.

"So what d'you think I'm going to do, try and overpower you with a jet of piss?" she said, sneering at him. "Or is that how you get your kicks? Watching young girls?"

The sec man tightened in his seat, his body rigid with rage at her taunts. "You better watch your mouth, bitch," he growled, "or I'll forget who you are."

"And why you can't touch me?" she finished.

The sec man was about to say something when the sec riding shotgun turned and addressed him. "For fuck's sake, let her do it in peace," he said wearily. "Anything to stop that damn whining. She'll get what she deserves soon enough."

"Mebbe you're right. I'll hold that thought for a while," the sec man replied with a cold smile that spread humorlessly across his lips. "Why not? Let the bitch piss in peace."

With which he turned away, facing the front of the wag, although his grip tightened instinctively on the Uzi.

Instinct—that would be her enemy. She had to hope that the sec man didn't have an inkling of what she was about to do, or else the whole thing was blown before she had even begun.

Ayesha unbuttoned her jeans and let them fall from her hips. She had forsworn underwear for ease at this moment, and thanked whatever had made her choose this as she reached into herself and fumbled for the end of the knife stock. Looking up desperately, she could see that some of the women were watching her with puzzlement, while others were still looking away and were downcast. The beautiful dark girl was looking directly at her, but as she was in the eyeline of the sec man, she kept her face stony so that he wouldn't be alerted. Mostly, it seemed that the women, if they cared at all, were puzzled in a lackadaisical way as to why she seemed to be playing with herself rather than pissing. She was aware that the sec man would become suspicious if he didn't hear her, so when she had extracted the knife she tried to force something out to sound in the bucket, but nothing other than a brief trickle could be forced from her unwilling bladder.

The knife sat in her palm as she rapidly hitched up her jeans and secured them. She took two strides forward, palming the knife so that the blade shot out away from her body as she triggered the mechanism with a soft clicking sound.

It was little, but enough to attract the attention of the sec man, who recognized the sound of old, and swung around in his seat to face her, bringing up the Uzi.

Ayesha knew she would have to move fast, and ironically it was Anita's stupidity that saved her.

"Ayesha, what are you doing with that?" she asked in a voice that was pathetic and stupid, hiccuped still with her sobbing.

The words were enough to distract the attention of the sec man—distract him enough for his head to turn toward the sound of Anita's voice and give Ayesha the vital fraction of a second to slice across his exposed throat with the knife. Her arm was well muscled, and she put enough power and momentum behind the stroke to slice across the exposed flesh cleanly and deeply. His windpipe and carotid artery were opened, and the blood pumped from him in gouts as he opened his mouth to speak, only a choking husk emerging through the damaged flesh as the light faded in his eyes.

The dark girl was swift, her reactions sure. As he choked, she shot out of her seat and grabbed the Uzi, wrestling it from his grasp and turning to cover the sec man riding shotgun, who had turned at the sound of activity in the rear of the wag. She clicked off the safety and held the blaster firmly and in a manner that suggested she knew exactly how to handle it.

"Don't even think about it unless you want to be spread over the windshield," she said quietly but firmly, adding over her shoulder, "I think we're in charge now—right, babe?"

Chapter Fifteen

The journey was proving long and arduous. It was approaching the middle of the day, and the sun bore down on the Hellbenders' convoy with a relentless force. Inside the wags, the heat built up to a humid, stifling pitch. For those who were using the old preDark military wags that had been left in the redoubt, it was slightly more bearable, the insulation inside the wags cutting down some of the heat that was stored in the metal. But although these wags also had air-conditioning, the drivers had been instructed by Correll not to use it, as it would eat up more fuel, and the gaunt man wanted to make sure they had enough to get them to the rendezvous point and also to carry out any maneuvers they may need to make without the wags running dry and spoiling the military action.

But it wasn't just the heat. The track they were taking was across desert terrain that had been muddied by the lashing chem rains and churned up into a quagmire. This was now drying, the ridges of wind-driven mud now becoming hard obstructions beneath the wheels of the wags, making steering hard and bumping the vehicles and their contents uncomfortably across the desert floor. They also had to keep an eye out for those patches that had turned into quicksand and were proving less willing to dry out. Spotting anything was hard, as the powdery soil was becoming dust, driven up in clouds from the hard ridges by the constant disturbance of the wag wheels, the resultant dust clouds making visibility poor at times.

It was easiest for the front wag, piloted by Correll. For J.B., Lonnie and those wag drivers that followed them, things were proving to be at times disorienting.

"If we all make it to the right place at the right time, and in one piece, that'll be the biggest achievement of all," Mildred commented sardonically as J.B. had to swerve hard to avoid a deep rut that came out of a dust cloud at the last moment.

"That's when the difficult bit starts," Jenny countered, fixing Mildred with a piercing stare. "We have to be disciplined and motivated."

"Sweetie, you sound like a machine," Mildred returned, a wry smile crossing her face. "You can be as disciplined and motivated as you like, but you need to get to the enemy first. And this is a real bastard."

"You're not kidding, Millie," J.B. muttered. "This is bad enough for me, but for those behind?" He let the question hang in the air.

Jenny shifted in her seat and looked to the back of the wag. It was closed in, with no windows but a sec monitor that gave them a rear view via a camera in the frame of the vehicle. The monitors still worked, and one of Correll's men watched it.

"What's happening back there?" the Native American asked.

The Hellbender shrugged. "Fuck knows. He's right, Jenny. There's nothing but dust back there. I wouldn't mind betting they can't see a thing."

THE SENTIMENT WAS ECHOED by Lonnie, the driver of the next wag back, but with a little more exasperation.

"Fuck it, why don't they watch where they go?" he yelled—more to himself than anyone else—as he hit the wheel of the wag hard with the palm of his hand. "Shit, how are we supposed to know where we are when there's nothing but dust all around?"

"Just follow, for fuck's sake," Catherine said wearily, leaning against the side of the wag, then wincing as a jolt over a rut caused her to crack her head against the metal side.

"How can I?" Lonnie snapped. "I can't see what I'm supposed to be following."

Dean pondered for a few seconds, then leaned forward to Doc.

"You wish a few moments of discursive diversion?" Doc asked with a raised eyebrow.

"I want to talk about something," Dean replied.

"Then pray tell me what it is."

"I've been thinking, Doc, and I'm wondering if I should mention this."

Doc beamed at the young Cawdor. "Certainly, I would be only too pleased to advise you—provided, of course, you tell me what it is that you wish advice upon."

"Yeah, funny, Doc, really funny. But it could be important."

Doc's attitude changed, immediately becoming more serious. "Then go ahead, young Dean," he said softly.

"Well, if Lonnie's having this trouble, and all the wags behind are getting it worse, then what's it going to be like when we mount the ambush? There won't just be our wags, there'll be convoys from Summerfield and Charity, as well."

"That's a lot of dust, and a lot of confusion," Doc agreed.

"Exactly."

"I think this needs mentioning," Doc said gravely.

"You hear that, Lonnie?" Catherine said. Although feigning disinterest, she had been listening in to their conversation.

"Yeah, I caught the general idea," Lonnie acknowledged between gritted teeth, steering wildly to try to negotiate a reasonably clear path along the track. "Think the two-ways will work yet?"

"They may over a short distance," Dean said, moving to the front of the wag. "I'll keep it brief, 'cause you never know who may be listening."

"I don't reckon that they've got radio equipment," Lonnie answered.

"Mebbe if find spy," Jak chipped in. He had been apparently sleeping, but as was his way he had kept his senses alert and had awakened at the sound of Dean's voice.

Lonnie blew out his cheeks. "Fuck, I hope not."

Dean picked up the handset of the radio and put a call through to the leading wag, knowing that the exchange would be heard by all the wags, as Correll had made sure that they were all tuned to the same wavelength before leaving the redoubt. The use of old tech like this was rare, but Correll, with Danny's help, had been able to make sense of what he had found at the old military installation, and right now, Dean was glad of this.

When Correll responded angrily, asking why the hell Dean was using the radio, which was only for emergency use, Dean quickly explained his concern. There was a pause before Correll answered.

"If we stick to the basic plan, then we'll be in close enough to see what's going on in the clouds. If we move swiftly, then we'll pin them down in such a way that they won't be able to move out of formation without running straight into us...in which case we just blast the fuckers anyway. Besides, the rendezvous point is hemmed in on all sides by outcrops. The chem storm won't have been able to blow up so hard in there, so the ground shouldn't be so churned up."

With which finality, Correll put down the handset and returned his attention fully to the vast expanse of desert that lay ahead. In the far distance, almost over the horizon and approximately another half hour's drive away, Ryan and Krysty could see a small cluster of rocks.

"That's it," Correll said so softly that it could almost have been to himself. He kept one hand on the wheel of the wag while, with the other, he cradled the box on his lap. "Soon," he added in a gentle tone.

Ryan wasn't sure, but it seemed as though Correll was addressing the box.

ELIAS TULK HAD DRIVEN in silence across the plains, avoiding the ruts wherever possible and skirting the patches of quicksand. Baron Tad Hutter sat next to him in silence. Tulk was setting a fast pace as the leading driver, and the sec men who sat in the rear of the leading wag were keeping a close watch on the wags that followed.

"Shit, man, slow down," once of them implored. "Those dudes back there are really having problems keeping the pace up."

"Not my problem," Tulk said shortly. "Not my fault if the bastards can't drive."

"But Baron," the other sec man added, addressing the silent Hutter, "we don't want to lose them."

Hutter was silent for a moment, then said, "If they can't keep up, then they've got no place on my sec."

The two sec men in the rear of the wag exchanged puzzled glances. It didn't make sense. If they lost the rest of the party, it would put the baron at risk if they arrived at the rendezvous point alone and found the opposing force there in full.

Neither, however, felt brave enough to question Hutter on this. Instead, they lapsed into an uneasy and uncomfortable silence.

Hutter, however, was much keener to talk now that his long silence had been broken. He spoke in a low undertone that could be heard over the sound of the wag engine by Tulk, but not by the sec men at the rear of the vehicle.

"So what d'you think you can prove, boy?"

"Who says I want to prove anything?" Tulk replied, keeping his eyes on the road and not pausing to glance at the baron.

"I'd say you want to prove something pretty badly," Hutter mused. "You've never spoke to me like this before—no fucker with any sense has," he added.

"Mebbe I've lost any sense I ever had," Tulk replied. "Mebbe I've got some for the first time. And mebbe you should make your mind up about that, eh?" he added.

Hutter narrowed his eyes and didn't speak for a time. He studied the whip-thin sec man beside him, his eyes concentrating on the road ahead with an intensity that was out of place.

"Can't think of anything to say now?" Tulk added after a while, without looking around.

"No," Hutter replied truthfully. "If I thought it was possible, I'd say you had some plan to get rid of me, but I can't work out how the fuck you'd manage that on your own. And you sure as shit wouldn't get any of the others to join you. I've made sure of that, making them all shit scared of each other more than me."

There was a note of puzzlement in the baron's voice that made Tulk want to smile. However, he managed to keep any sign of his inward amusement from showing on his face.

As he drove, Tulk's mind wound back to the moment when the recce party had taken him back to the redoubt.

It had been some months after he had begun spying, and it had taken until this point before he had been truly accepted, and any suspicions that the Hellbenders still held had been allayed. By night he had left the ville, and had met with the recce party at a point several miles from the edge of the ville. His cover story to explain his absence was that he had been conducting a survey of the outlying areas to plot any points from where the ville could be attacked. To this end, the recce party, which already knew the area, gave him a detailed map of the area surrounding the ville that would only omit their own personal camping spots when on recce. Armed with this, and the wag he had used to leave the ville, Tulk was able to cover his own back and make the time to follow them on the day-long journey to the redoubt, where he had first met Correll.

The memory of the gaunt man's unsmiling visage as he explained his personal—and therefore group—mission still haunted Tulk. He had no doubt that Correll was insane, and yet he could understand that. He had no idea of Correll's own personal history, but he knew from his own experience that to have to internalize the intense emotions that a baron abusing privilege could bring was to skirt close to insanity. Some stayed the right line—as he believed he had—because they had to keep living with the enemy. Others, like Correll, didn't, and so were allowed free reign to their feelings, and perhaps the descent into madness.

After a briefing, Tulk had returned with the personal knowledge that Correll was as insane as Hutter, just in a different way. But this was, in a sense, irrelevant. Correll's madness allowed Tulk to unleash his own, and gain his revenge.

And that was priceless.

The knowledge that it was nearly time filled him to bursting, but—mindful of the still puzzled baron beside him—he allowed himself only the expression of putting his foot down on the gas, and coaxing more speed from the wag's protesting engine.

"AYESHA, THIS ISN'T going to make things any better for us. We'll just get beaten before they screw us, and it'll hurt," whined the big blonde from her seat in the back of the wag.

"Shut up, bitch," snapped the girl with the Uzi. She didn't turn to glare at Anita, but the big blonde could feel the hostility coming off her, and immediately shut up, even trying to stifle her sobs.

"Thanks for that," Ayesha murmured as she spared a glance for the sniveling blonde. "Any more of that shit, and I probably would have slit her throat, as well."

"Anytime, babe," her ally replied. "But I hope you've got some sort of plan, 'cause I've just seized the moment, and I don't know what the hell to do next."

"First thing is to get their blasters," Ayesha said decisively, moving down the middle of the wag. She addressed the sec men in the front directly. "I want you to hand your blasters over the back, holding them by the business end with your fingertips only. I don't want you getting any ideas, or else my friend here may just blow your mother-fucking head off. Okay, boys?"

The sec men complied without a word, the one who had twisted in his seat dropping his H&K over the back, while the driver unholstered his Walther PPK handblaster and dropped it over the back, straining to keep the vehicle on track as he leaned behind him.

Ayesha moved in front of her ally and pulled the blasters back, crouching low but keeping her head up and her sights firmly on the sec man who was still facing her. The knife, still dripping, she kept in her left hand, the blade angled up ready to strike if attacked.

Gathering the blasters, she pulled back and stuck the Walther in the waistband of her jeans. The H&K she held on to, looking around at the women on the benches. Most of them still looked like Anita—downtrodden and resigned to their fate, fearing it would now be worse because of her actions. But a couple of the women had brightened con-siderably, and although they had nowhere near the courage of the girl holding the Uzi rock steady, they could be use-ful.

"You," she said, indicating a slim woman with sharp features and short, cropped hair who had begun to take an interest in events. "What's your name?"

"Adrienne," the woman replied in a tone that was nervous, but had an underlying bite of insolence that could be useful.

"Consider yourself recruited to our little women's lib-eration army," Ayesha said, tossing the H&K to her. "Know how to use that?"

"It's a blaster like them all. Just give me a second or two to work out its little peculiarities," Adrienne replied in an offhand manner.

The sec man facing them spit down onto the floor of the wag. "Don't think you bitches are gonna get away with this."

Without a word, the girl with the Uzi took half a pace forward and swung the barrel of the blaster up in an arc, catching him in the mouth and nose, which gushed crimson. Before he had a chance to react or even register the agony he felt, she had stepped back out of range and resumed her position, with the blaster trained on the pair of sec men in the front of the wag.

"Don't you think at all, asshole. That way you may not get chilled yet," she muttered with savage venom.

"Nice work," Ayesha murmured approvingly. "Listen, just who are you, girl?"

"Name's Claudette. I used to work in the kitchens for the sec, and I know what fuckpigs they are," she said shortly, adding, "and you still ain't said if you've got a plan."

"I've got a plan, Claudette, don't you worry about that," Ayesha said. "By the way, I'm—"

"Hell, you think I don't know who you are?" Claudette snapped. "You're the prize package. I've heard this scum talking about what they'd do to you before Tad Hutter had the chance, and then about what he'd do to you. Gotta say, girl, that was a smooth move you pulled. But you'd better have a good plan, 'cause I can't see how we'll get out of this alive. And if I was you, knowing what I know, I'd chill myself now and save the humiliation and pain if we don't get out and Hutter gets his hands on you."

"No worries about that," Ayesha replied simply. "We just need to stay on course to the rendezvous and wait."

Claudette didn't look around, preferring to keep her eyes firmly fixed on the sec men, but Ayesha could feel—almost see—her look of disbelief.

"Girl, tell me that you're shitting me," she said quietly.

"I'm telling you straight, sister," Ayesha reassured her. "There's going to be an ambush on the two convoys by a group that has as much reason to hate my father and the scum Hutter as much as we have. And they're armed and ready for a firefight. We're safe as long as we keep these assholes quiet."

"How the fuck—?"

"It doesn't matter now," Ayesha interrupted. "The only thing that matters is that we keep this wag rolling, and no one gets any notion that anything is wrong until we reach the meeting point. And then it'll be too late."

"It's risky," Claudette commented.

"So's anything," Ayesha returned. "What else can we do? If we break ranks and try to get this wag to run for it, they outnumber us in wags and firepower. All we can do is sit tight and wait."

"Okay, if that's the way it's got to be, then that's the way it will be." Claudette shrugged. "I just hope we can carry it off, babe."

Chapter Sixteen

It stood impassive and still under the burning heat of the rad-blasted sun, the sky a haze that shimmered above its topmost reaches. Formed of two groupings of rock that stood upright in the middle of the desert, with no other outcrops within sight, it was noble and awesome in its apparent ability to stand alone and unbowed against the elements.

The reddish-brown rocks were jagged and uneven, rising and falling in a series of peaks and troughs that seemed to mirror one another, with a channel in the middle that was surprisingly clear of rock falls. The fact that it stood alone meant that the elements had been equally harsh to each side of the outcrop, hence the similarity between the breaks and erosions along the top of the standing stones.

For that was what the two sides of jagged rock resembled. With their equal measures of wear and erosion, they looked uncannily as though they had been formed of individual stones that had been moved slowly and arduously across the empty desert by men, and then assembled into this pattern for a reason that could only be guessed. But once the men had vanished, the stones had become rocks, the very elements causing them to spread out and web together.

At each end of the outcrop there was a narrow channel, wide enough for two wags to fit side by side. This widened to about three times that width as the center of the small valley was reached. It was enough space for the trade to take place with both sides having room to move, but not enough to try any kind of maneuver. The rock on each side seemed too sheer for anyone to hide out or be strategically placed by one side seeking to gain advantage over the other. And the outcrop, standing solitary and magnificent as it did, fell almost exactly equidistant from the villes of Summerfield and Charity, meaning that neither side had to lose face by traveling a longer distance than the other to make the trade. A small thing in many ways, it was a matter of vital importance to both barons if they were to keep their prestige both in their own minds, and in the minds of their people.

The interior of the valley was smooth on this fine morning, the earth now dry and baked as the sun drew the moisture from it that had fallen during the chem storm. There was little sign of the churning mud pools and ridges that had been whipped up in the desert around the outcrop. The shape and position of the rocks had acted as a shield against the stronger winds, losing another layer of shale and rock on the outside as the chem-laden rain had lashed against it, but reducing the turmoil within to a minimum. Dean had been right in his assumption that the enclosed valley would throw up clouds of dust. The baking earth was nowhere near cracking, but already the layer of top-soil was so powdery and dry that any disturbance was likely to shake it loose and raise clouds of dust. But it was a fairly smooth and unpitted surface that would allow for a maximum of driving maneuverability.

As the only area for miles around with some kind of shade or moisture retained in the shadowy areas of the rocks, it harbored not only the small amounts of hardy plant life that could be seen in the surrounding area, but also acted as home to a small colony of insects, reptiles and mammals that were descended from meerkats and gophers, mutated into a scrawny yet defiant species that could scavenge and survive on very little, driven by instinct to defeat the odds and carry on.

But not today. As if some instinct for danger had told them as much, the scant wildlife that lived off the outcrop had dived for cover, retreating into their burrows and seeking security within the recesses of the rocks.

It was always quiet in and around the area, but this morning, as the sun hit the middle of the sky and the middle of the day, it became quieter still. There was a stillness and silence around the rocks that spoke of chilling and imminent death.

The silence was broken by a distant buzz, which grew in volume, deepened in tone, until it became a rumble. If any of the creatures that were now safely in hiding had cared to look, it would have seen a moving cloud of dust coming toward the rocks, with the outlines of a group of wags just about visible within the flying layers of dust and soil.

The Hellbenders were nearing their goal.

In the leading wag, Ryan and Krysty could see the distant speck on the horizon begin to grow and take shape as they got closer. Within a few minutes, they could see that the tall, thin outcrop formed a valley, with a narrow channel both in and out of the enclosed space.

"That's it?" Ryan questioned, although all he really needed was confirmation.

"That's it," Correll affirmed. He was driving the wag one-handed, his sinewy wrist strong enough to control the wag's steering over the rough ground, his knuckles white around the wheel. His other hand was caressing the box that was still cradled on his lap.

"You want to tell us what that's all about?" Krysty asked in a gentle voice. She had noticed that Correll had been staring down at the box more and more as they approached the rendezvous point, muttering under his breath in an intense manner, even though it was too quiet for her to work out exactly what he was saying. All she knew was that every time she looked at him, her sentient mane began to curl around her neck in a manner that even the thought of the impending firefight couldn't affect. She had the notion that Correll was being driven by an inner fire and flame that he would need to vent in order for them to understand why this firefight was taking place, and in order to make him more coherent during the battle ahead. Because of Doc, she had seen what madness could do, and the thought of that from someone directing a firefight wasn't something she wished to consider. The Hellbenders followed him loyally and to the letter. If he was to stay on the track of sanity, then it was best to probe this matter now.

"You know the basic story," Correll replied, his eyes darting from the track ahead to the box on his lap.

"Yeah, mebbe, but there's more to it than what you've told us so far, right?" she continued gently.

"Mebbe." Correll was silent for a second, but Krysty didn't respond. She wanted to let him tell the story in his own time. The Hellbenders in the wag stayed silent, not knowing quite how to react. Ryan, for his part, kept his own counsel. He figured that Krysty knew what she was doing, and that she would draw the secret of the box from Correll when the gaunt man was ready. He didn't have to wait long, for in the empty silence, Correll chose to begin his story.

"Thing is, friends, I told you something of what happened, but not all of it. Because there are some things that are hard to speak of, even when you want to explain. Some things that seem to stick in your throat, and no matter how hard you try to force them out, they just won't come. And they gather within you, festering like a poison in an infected wound, until there comes a time when you just cannot keep it in any longer. You have to force it out, break the skin and bleed the wound so that the pure blood can start to run free once more, and the healthiness can return to the wound. And that's what I'm trying to do now. That's what this is—for all of us except you and your friends—to our different levels. We all have those wounds.

I figure that mine are worse than anyone else's, but then that's because they're mine. Any one of us on this convoy could say the same thing.

"But if you knew why, if you understood the depths of degradation and despair, the very bottom of the pit that I feel that I've been staring up from for so long, this is my chance to clean the slate, to climb up the sides of that pit and get out where the air is fresh and sweet again. And if I buy the farm in the attempt? Well, what have I done but buy a way out of this misery and my own hell? Oblivion cannot be any more painful than what has been before."

He stopped, almost as though exhausted by the outburst, and Ryan cast his eye over Krysty. Her hair clung to her neck and shoulders in long tendrils, and his suspicion was confirmed. The man was raving, and on the verge of losing all control. If he did, then where would they stand when the firefight began?

The one-eyed man had rarely felt less in control of a situation than he did at this minute. His people were spread out over three wags in a convoy bound for a full-scale firefight with two other convoys, and at the helm was a madman. There had to be some way of pulling this together, if only he could communicate with J.B., Mildred and Doc, with Jak and Dean...and Danny, whose warnings were proving only too prophetic.

Before he had a chance to formulate any kind of plan, Correll had begun once more.

"See, I was head of sec in Charity, and I was real diligent. I did my job properly, not from any great sense of

loyalty or duty, but just because that's the way I'm made—
I couldn't do it any other way, it just wouldn't feel right.
And I was real careful. My people were good, because I
made damn sure they were. I wouldn't have any screwing
around that could reflect badly on me, or put anyone in
danger of Jourgensen's wrath, 'cause he was a mean bastard, and I just wanted to keep him happy and do the job.
If any of my people got in the shit, he'd have their tits or
balls in a vise. He was an evil asshole, and still is. But I
didn't know just how fucking evil until he thought I'd
done him wrong.

"See, there was a breach of sec when we were over-
seeing a trading convoy that passed through. The trader
tried to rip off Jourgensen by selling him some shit rat poison instead of jolt, and it's only because Jourgensen's personal drug taster took some and died puking out his own
intestines that we knew it was shit. Hell, looking back, I
wish it had been Jourgensen himself who tried it, greedy
asshole that he is. But no, he couldn't even oblige us on
that.

"I had the trader chased, but he slipped past the sec patrol pursuing him. Jourgensen was in a shit bad mood because he'd lost jack and face, and couldn't even get high
to make up for it. So he had the patrol chilled and called
me before him.

"I'd never fucked up before—I'd have long since been
chilled if that was the case, but even this time I knew that
I hadn't fucked up. Jourgensen left it nearly a day before
trying the merchandise. If the shithead had any sense at

all, he would have had his taster try it before handing over the jack. So it was too late for my men to pick up the trail and catch the prick who did it. Not their fault, not mine.

"But after they'd been chilled, I was told what a useless piece of shit I was, and how I was probably behind the plot to kill him. The crazy paranoid bastard had turned the whole thing into a conspiracy against him. And I was the one whose ass he wanted. Only he wasn't just going to chill me. Oh no, he was going to make me suffer first.

"I was beaten senseless—but well, I've got to give them that. It was my own men who did it, but I can't blame them. They were acting under orders, and you don't go against Baron Al. They beat me until I was in so much pain that I couldn't even think. Everything seemed to come to me from a long way away, as though in some kind of bad dream. But I wasn't allowed to lose consciousness, not at any point. They knew exactly the nerve points to jolt me back if I started to fall.

"I knew I was bound to be chilled, but I didn't give a fuck by then. Let it happen, release me from the pain. But he went too far—just that touch of fuckwit sadism that's sealed his fate. See, he wasn't content with it just being me. He had to bring Becky into it."

"Who was Becky?" Krysty asked as Correll lapsed once more into silence.

"She was my woman. Mebbe the only thing—person— I ever really cared about. I never liked people that much. That's why I was so good at my job—I could do it without getting involved, without caring. But Becky was different. She was the only thing I would have died for. Only that bastard Jourgensen didn't give me the chance.

"While I was lying there, sec men over me, too fucked up with pain to move, he had her brought in. They stripped her, and then he fucked her in front of me. And he had the others do it, too. That was bad enough for her, she was crying like I'd never heard, looking at me like she didn't know whether to feel bad for herself or for me, despite how much she was hurting. That chilled part of me more than any physical pain could.

"And then he got out the branding irons. He used them on the horses we have, to mark them as his own. Just a *J* mark beaten out of metal. He fired them up, and he did it himself. He branded each tit, then both cheeks on her ass. He made a line of them on her belly, and each time she screamed with the pain, and passed out, they'd bring her around with cold water and he'd start again. They spread her legs, and he branded her between the legs, burning the flesh and hair so that— Oh God, I can still smell it."

Correll was silent again for a few seconds. Ryan and Krysty left him alone, waiting for him to be ready to begin again as he stroked the box on his lap.

"And then it got to the point where she was near death, and he still wanted more. I swear the sick fuck had forgotten I was there by then, and he just wanted to please himself.

"They took her out into the yard at the back of his palace, and there was a stake hammered into the ground. Kindling had been piled around it, and they tied her to the stake, bundling the kindling around her feet and legs. Two of them held me up while I was made to watch. Becky was in no kind of state to fight against them—anyway, she was just one woman and there were so many of them. They tied her against the stake, then Jourgensen went up to her and fired up the kindling. That was when she started to scream. Yeah, she'd made noises before, but all the fight had been knocked out of her. But this was different. She was wide awake, totally conscious now, and knew she was going to buy the farm. And do it in a way that— Fuck it, I can't think of a worse way to go. The flames licked up her legs, and I swear I could see the flesh blistering as the heat got under her skin. The smell was horrible—sweet and strong, like roasting fat. I could see the flames traveling up her naked body, touching her and making her burn. I swear to anything that you can call a god that I could see her intestines roasting and burning away, I could see her bones start to show as the flesh and fat burned off them.

"I don't think she died until her guts spilled out and burned away. It must..."

He stopped, and paused for a few moments before continuing.

"Anyway, that asshole Al decided to save me for the next day. And that was his mistake. They left me alone, figuring that I couldn't move far enough and fast enough to be a danger. Wrong. I had enough willpower to get the hell out. I was head of sec, y'see. I knew where the wags were, how to hotwire one, when the sec patrols were due and who was on them. But first I had to do something. I went back to the fire and gathered together what was left of Becky. I took her with me and got the hell out. I didn't know where I was going, and I thought I was on my way to buy the farm...but on my own terms.

"But it didn't work out that way, did it? Fate will always decide. And it decided for me. It took me up that mountain to meet the end, but instead I found that old tech base. It was fate that then brought the others to me."

He looked down at the box.

"And it's fate that has finally brought us here, my love. Fate that has decreed we have a chance to be revenged. And if I buy the farm and join you, then so be it."

Chapter Seventeen

As the wags approached the outcrop, Correll picked up the radio transmitter in front of him and patched in to the other wags in the convoy, ordering them into the positions they had seen sketched on the map back at the redoubt. His voice was firm and clear, with no indication of the emotional catharsis he had been through just a few minutes before. Ryan and Krysty sat in the wag and observed in silence. There was no way they could communicate their concerns to each other, let alone to their comrades in the other wags. All they could do was sit tight and wait for that opening to occur.

"No sign of the trade convoys yet," Correll commented as he drove the leading wag through the gap in the outcrop and into what would soon be the arena for the final battle.

"Making good time, then," Ryan replied, keeping his voice level. Yet there was something about it that made Cy turn sharply, even if Correll didn't notice.

"What else?" the sec man asked.

Ryan shrugged. "Nothing. The desert was pretty bad in places, so much mud, dust and quicksand. Could have delayed us."

"Could have delayed them, too," Cy answered. He seemed to be reassured in some way, but there was a faint querulousness to his tone that suggested he still felt something wasn't quite right. He just couldn't define what that may be.

"If they've actually set off," Krysty pointed out. "We have no way of knowing this for sure."

"They will have," Correll said with a cast-iron certainty in his tone. "They've got no choice. It's this or a long, hard chill for both of them."

He drove his wag to the center of the dust bowl that was in front of the outcrop, then veered to the left, taking the wide load through a gap that was so narrow it almost scraped the paint from the side of the wag. As he took this path, the second wag, driven by J.B., went a little farther on and then took a right fork, finding its shelter behind another gap in the rock wall. Two wags followed each lead, and then the wags positioned themselves near the gaps, hidden from view but with an easy access to each end of the outcrop.

"That's their big mistake, Jourgensen and Hutter," Correll remarked to Ryan, although it seemed almost as though he were talking to himself. "They haven't done their research properly. They'll have their sec look out for something at each end, but they don't know about these channels. They won't know that we're hidden, waiting to circle around and take them out."

And it was true. Ryan looked out of the side window on the wag door. The gap in the outcrop was barely wide enough to pilot a wag through, but if taken with care it could be achieved. They were approximately halfway along the length of the arena, with the rock channel twisting in front of them and leading out at an oblique angle to the main track the trade wags would be taking. From the approach, that exit was well hidden, and it would be easy for the Hellbenders' wags to slip out and circle around to close off the entrances. In the heat of a firefight, these would be the only other avenues of escape, and Correll had plans to seal them off.

He picked up the handset and called J.B.

"You got the packages?"

"Yeah," J.B. replied simply.

Correll nodded to himself, satisfied with what was about to take place. "Okay, you and Jenny get them delivered. You got the remotes?"

"Yeah, and tested," J.B. answered. "The signals are fine, just got to prime 'em."

"Okay." Correll paused for a second, and Krysty felt a cold shiver run through her as she caught the gleam in his eyes. It was the culmination of his plans, and he was relishing every moment. "Let's do it," he said simply.

At this signal, the assembled Hellbenders sprang into action. J.B. and Jenny left their wag to plant plas-ex charges at the mouth of the rock channels, which they would detonate with remote detonators. J.B. jogged back to the entrance to the channel and began to climb the rocks, searching for handholds and testing them before supporting his weight and hauling himself up to a point where the rock had a deep crevice. He took the charge from a bag slung over his shoulder and punched in the code that would make it respond to the detonator he had in his pocket. The lights on the digital display of the small detonating device flashed the code back at him, then settled into one small, red, blinking light that affirmed the readiness of the device. This achieved, he secured its place in the crevice and scrambled back down.

While he did this, Jenny had sprinted across the length of the arena toward the opposite channel opening, and had started to climb, searching for hand- and footholds as she went. With a speed that wasn't surprising given her lithe build, she scaled the wall of the channel, finding a ledge on which to place her charge. It wasn't a crevice in the manner of the hiding place J.B. had found, so she had to secure the plas-ex in place with adhesive tape, hoping that this and the natural texture of the plas-ex would be enough to keep it in place until the charge was detonated. In truth, it was likely that even if the charge became dislodged and fell to the foot of the opening, it would still rip out enough rock to cause a fall and block the channel. She punched in the sec code as J.B. had done, checked that the single red light was flashing and then quickly descended, sprinting across the arena to return to her wag.

Meanwhile, the other preparations were taking place. Although the desert floor outside the outcrop was too disturbed by the chem storm, and too pitted and scarred to show any giveaway wag tracks, inside the arena itself the surface of the earth was relatively smooth and undisturbed, so any recent wag tracks would be all too visible. To this end, Correll had ordered that, on their arrival and secretion, some of his people would leave their wags and, using brushes they had brought with them from the redoubt, would clear the surface of any telltale wag tracks.

It was a risk. If the surface had been muddy and the weight of the wags had caused the tracks to be sunk into the earth beyond a certain depth, it would have proved difficult, if not impossible, to eradicate their traces. However, Correll had figured that the desert surface would have dried out and returned to its sunbaked hardness by the time their convoy had arrived, leaving just the disturbed top layer of sandy soil to be raked over by the brushes.

He was right. Led and directed by Rudi, ten of the Hellbenders set to with speed and alacrity to scour the surface of the arena, their ears bent toward the sound of distant wags and the rumble of heavy-duty wheels that would signal the imminent arrival of their quarry. The ten Hellbenders worked hard, and in a surprisingly short time had completed their task, working from the center out toward the sides of the arena, brushing and raking themselves clear back to the channel openings on each side, enabling them to return to their wags without leaving a sign of their passing.

Correll used the radio to confirm that each Hellbender had returned to his or her post.

"What now?" Krysty asked him.

The gaunt man fixed her with a stare that had the lust of battle mixed with a strange glow of almost infinite contentment.

"We wait," he said simply.

"THERE IT IS, Baron. I hope you're ready for this," Elias Tulk said softly as he piloted the leading wag toward the outcrop, which became larger with each passing minute, the narrow entrance framed by forbidding rocks that reached to the chem-clouded sky. Tulk added, after looking up at the sky, "Yeah, I really hope you are ready, 'cause it looks like it's headed for a sandstorm to me."

Tad Hutter gave Tulk a sideways glance that could have chilled him on the spot. "You being funny, boy?"

"Call it that if you want," Tulk answered, "but you just take a look up at that sky and tell me I'm wrong."

Hutter looked up at the sky through the windshield of the wag, and could immediately see that the chem clouds had returned to the previously hazy but clear atmosphere. They were scudding across the bloated red orb of the sun, and indicated that there were conflicting air pressures and zephyrs in among them.

"Fuck it, that's all we need," he murmured, annoyed both at the approaching storm and at the fact that Tulk had been proved right. If there was one thing of which Hutter was certain, it was that Tulk wouldn't live long when they returned to Summerfield.

"I figure that we're in for a sandstorm with it," Tulk continued, making a point of ignoring his baron's hostility. "With those kind of winds blowing up there, all it's gonna take is for one little sidewinder to come down and touch base, and it's gonna be a whole lot of fun. Let's hope we don't get it at the rendezvous, eh?" And he allowed himself a small grin at this.

They continued in silence, the outcrop looming larger. Tulk slowed his wag, wanting to take a good look at the approaching rendezvous point. It would seem that they were the first to arrive, as the shape of the arena within the outcrop allowed him to see virtually all angles—certainly enough angles to show any wags that were attempting to hide within. The arena was clear, and the far entrance was empty. He didn't know about the channels to the side of the arena, and a flutter of fear crossed his stomach. What if the Hellbenders hadn't showed? How the hell would he cope with a pissed-off Hutter after the trade? He didn't mind dying in a firefight or hand-to-hand combat, as long as Hutter bought the farm. But if he had to go back to Summerfield, he knew that his chilling would be painful and drawn out after the way he had treated the baron.

Mebbe Correll knew something he didn't, and everything was okay. He could only hope so. He spoke again, trying to keep the sudden wave of fear from his voice.

"Looks like we're the first here," he said simply.

Hutter grunted. "Take it to the entrance and then stop. We'll wait there—that way they can't encircle us."

"Okay," Tulk replied simply. It seemed to him that Hutter had momentarily forgotten their little conflict in his anxiety at making the trade. Which was okay...for now.

Tulk drove to the mouth of the arena and stopped the wag. Hutter shifted in his seat. "Come on, boy, we've got some orders to hand out," he muttered as he left the wag.

Tulk joined him, leaving the other sec men in the lead wag on lookout for the approach of the Charity convoy, which would be plainly visible through the opposing gap in the rocks.

Hutter moved back down the wags, ordering his men to keep alert. His basic plan was that they would begin to move into the outcrop at the same pace as the Charity convoy, beginning when Jourgensen's men hit the far entrance, so that both convoys could keep equal pace and distance.

"We don't move to hand anything over until I've spoke to Jourgensen. Then we unload our wags and place the goods in the center, between the two leading wags, while they lead the women out. When they're both in the center, then we swap and retreat, keeping our blasters on them."

"What do we do if this storm blows up?" Tulk asked.

Hutter gave him another chilling look. "We hope it doesn't," he replied.

INSIDE THE WAG containing the women who were the trade for Summerfield, Claudette kept her Uzi trained on the driver and shotgun sec, while Ayesha watched the women.

"How near are we?" Ayesha said shortly.

"How the fuck should I know?" the driver replied testily. "I can't see squat for all the dust in front of me. I'm just following the wag in front."

"Won't your daddy use the radio when we get near?" Claudette asked with a sneer.

"Don't give me shit with the attitude," Ayesha snapped. "You think if I had any feelings left for that cocksucking son of a gaudy whore I'd be doing this? No, I'd be going forth like the dutiful daughter and getting screwed by every man in Summerfield."

"Okay, I get it," Claudette replied reluctantly, "so I'll say it again without the sarcasm. Won't Baron Al have orders to give over the radio when we get near?"

"I'd guess so," Ayesha replied thoughtfully. "Is that what he's told you?" she directed toward the driver.

The two sec men stayed silent for a moment, considering whether they should answer, before the man riding shotgun said reluctantly, "He told us that we'd get a call from him when we were within ten minutes' drive. That way we'd be prepared when we get there."

"And you know what 'there' looks like?" Ayesha pressed.

"Yeah," the sec man replied without elaborating.

Claudette spared a glance at Ayesha; it was a glance filled with surprise. "You're shitting me," she whispered. "He never told you what was going to happen?"

Ayesha turned on Claudette angrily. "In case it's escaped your notice, I'm a piece of meat just like you, babe. I didn't get fuck all of a say in what happened to me, and I'm damn sure that under the circumstances there was no way my lovely father was going to tell me anything that was going on. You understand that now?"

"Yeah, I think I do," Claudette said quietly.

"Good, well, let's just get it together here, because we really need to get some kind of a plan together. You," she snapped at the sec man who was riding shotgun, and who had been turned uncomfortably toward them for some time, frightened to move in case he got blown to pieces, "what happens when we get to the rendezvous?"

"You get exchanged for the seed crops and the food supplies," the man replied simply.

Ayesha sighed heavily. "Don't be a stupe, or else I'll just get Claudette to blow you away, okay? I mean tell me exactly what happens, and mebbe you'll get out of here in one piece."

The sec man paused for a second, unsure as to whether he should say anything.

"Okay, I'll tell you. The plan is that we rendezvous at a bunch of rocks that form an enclosure, kinda like the field where we primed the wags. That means that we're covered on all sides, and there's only us and the guys from Summerfield in the middle, with no way of anyone sneaking around from the sides, 'cause there's only one exit at each end. So when we're there, we wait for them and then we get ourselves into the middle of the space, and we make the trade. If all goes well, and we get to do it, then you get led out in those shackles—" he inclined his head to the chains and cuffs that were spread on the floor of the wag "—and then we exchange you. They load you up, we load up the trade and we both back out slowly, keeping an eye on each other."

"You're not just handing over the wag?" Ayesha asked, a sudden wave of nausea riding up her throat.

"Hell, no," the sec man replied, "you think we'd hand over something as good as this? Anyway, they might think that it's booby-trapped. We'd suspect it of them, right?"

"Oh, shit," Ayesha said softly.

"What do you mean, 'oh shit'?" Claudette asked.

Ayesha looked at her. "I thought they'd just swap wags. I told the others that we'd hold this wag and stop these bastards blasting them as long as they left us alone. But what the fuck are we going to do if we have to leave the wag? Especially if we have to wear those stupe things," she added, indicating the shackles.

"Okay, girl, don't panic about it," Claudette said, a look crossing her face that showed she was deep in thought. A thought that was interrupted by Anita, who still—after all this time—hadn't stopped crying.

"I told you that it was useless. We're all just meat, and we're going to be used by those vile bastards."

"Will you shut the fuck up, you irritating bitch?" Claudette snapped, taking a step back and swinging the barrel of the Uzi so that it caught the heavy blonde full across the face, leaving her mouth a smear of blood and saliva, stunning her so much that she couldn't even squeal or cry anymore. Before the sec man had a chance to move, the iron-faced young woman had the blaster trained back on him.

"We're going to have to go through with it at least part of the way," Ayesha said softly. "No matter what the plan was, we're going to have to go out there with these shackles on."

"We can't do that," Claudette answered. "If we even make an effort to do that, then we're in the shit. We can't step out of here holding blasters, and these mothers will have to have some to make it look convincing, otherwise we bring the whole of the sec down on us."

"There has to be a way around this," Ayesha said, picking up the shackles and looking at them. On a close inspection, she could see that the cuffs could be left unlocked and uncoupled without it appearing too obvious. She looked at the other women. "Are you with us or against us?" she asked.

The majority of them agreed, glad of any opportunity to try to escape. Those who were initially unwilling reluctantly agreed when they saw they were outvoted. Even Anita grudgingly agreed between spitting out mouthfuls of blood and sobbing.

"Okay, here's what we do," Ayesha said. "We take the blasters and conceal them, leaving these assholes with one empty blaster that they can wave around. We go out with the shackles undone, and when it all goes down we head back for the wag and secure it. That sound good?"

"It sounds risky," Claudette stated, "but it's better than anything I've come up with, so it'll have to do."

"Ya know, babe, I don't think we're in any position to worry about it," Ayesha said. "We'll just have to roll with it."

Claudette shrugged, and was just about to comment when the voice of Baron Al crackled over the radio. "The rendezvous point is in sight. The Summerfield convoy is there, and it looks like we've got a dust storm brewing."

Chapter Eighteen

Correll looked up and sniffed the air. He was standing beside his wag, and had been there ever since the distant rumble of an approaching convoy had been detected. The rumble had gotten nearer and finally ground to a halt, the wag engines just ticking over as the Summerfield convoy stood inert at the entrance to the arena, waiting for the rival convoy to arrive. From the opposite direction, a different pitch of noise signaled the approach of the Charity convoy.

Ryan joined Correll and looked up at the skies.

"Storm," he said simply.

Correll nodded assent. "That'll be good. We may be determined, but we are outnumbered. Mebbe the confusion will even the odds for us."

Ryan agreed. "We know who we're attacking. They won't be sure what the hell is going on."

Correll allowed himself the ghost of a smile, which seemed oddly out of place on his gaunt countenance, and for one second gave the one-eyed man an insight into the man Correll may once have been.

But before it could go any further, Catherine came running up to Correll.

"Papa Joe, they're all in place. Should I send the lookouts up?"

Correll's face once again became grim and set as he nodded before turning and mounting the wag once more. Ryan, left standing, followed the small blonde as she ran back to the wag in which she had traveled. It was the one in which Dean, Jak, Doc and Danny had also journeyed. That meant that only J.B. and Mildred would be attacking from the other side, and be that much more isolated from their companions. But J.B. was more than just Ryan's trusted lieutenant. The two men had spent so long fighting together that in many ways they thought as one, as well as fought as one.

Ryan wondered who would be the lookout on that side of the divide. This side he figured was obvious.

Catherine reached her wag and climbed aboard, looking across to Jak. "Let's go," she said to him as she took the radio handset from Lonnie and rapped the one word— "Search"—before ceasing transmission.

The albino hunter rose from his seat with an effortless grace and took a portable handset from the blonde, who turned to him and said, "You know when?"

Jak assented. "At point exchange—most vulnerable."

"Right." She nodded. "Good luck."

Jak left the wag without another word, pausing only to clasp Dean's hand. The next time they saw each other, the firefight would well and truly commence.

Outside, in the narrow channel they were using as a hiding place, there was little space between the walls of rock and the sides of the wags, and Jak skipped down between them, away from Ryan as he stood watching. The albino hunter was searching for a good place to begin his climb. He found it just past the rear wag, where there was a small split in one of the rocks that gave him a good hand- and toehold. Hoisting himself up, Jak began to scale the rock, which rose for forty feet and was almost sheer.

The sandstone was soft and inclined to crumble, so the ascent was slower than the youth would have liked, each hold having to be tested for weight before he placed himself at its mercy. The quality of the rock was of concern to him. When he reached the summit of the rock, and was observing the trade-off below, he had to be careful that no stray gravel, rocks or pebbles be dislodged and alert the enemy below of his presence.

But he would worry about that when he reached the peak. Right now he was faced with the problem of the ascent, for the rock veered out slightly. He arched his back a few degrees to make the handhold, feeling the pull of the earth below. The extra effort made him break into a sweat, and the muscles in his arms and across his shoulders tensed and cramped at the extra strain. He was fortunate that the foothold was solid and deep, so that he could plant his combat boot firmly and take the strain in his calf and thighs.

One deep breath, one pull of his upper torso and it was done. He was over the worst and up to the summit.

The surface on top of the rock was uneven and jagged, and Jak was faced with the problem of trying to find a niche from which he could observe the happenings below without being himself easily spotted.

The rock was about four feet in thickness, more than enough for him to walk and climb comfortably along its length. He kept low, trying to adhere to a winding path along irregular dips in the top of the rock.

After a couple of yards, he found what he was looking for. The rock had a hollow carved out by erosion that formed a small observation post, the rock in front of the hollow enabling him to keep out of view, but also pro-viding—via a split down the middle of the face—a win-dow through which he could see the arena below. Jak settled himself into the hollow and looked through the gap, defining his field of vision. It was a wide area, and ob-scured only the very far ends of the arena.

He settled onto his haunches, beginning the wait, won-dering who his opposite number may be, and how he or she was faring.

ON THE FAR SIDE of the arena, in the opposite channel, the word from Catherine had come over the radio in J.B.'s wag. The Armorer turned to Jenny, who had previously in-dicated her willingness to tackle the task of lookout.

"Ready? he asked.

The woman shrugged. "As I'll ever be," she replied be-fore taking a handheld radio from Mildred and leaving the wag.

Like Jak, she had to scan the sheer rock wall for a suit-able place to begin her climb, and like the albino she was soon aware of the less than reliable nature of the rocks. She tested each hold thoroughly and hauled herself up the rock face. When she was about thirty feet up, she encountered a similar problem to Jak inasmuch as the rock seemed to curve out and over her. Unlike Jak, she didn't keep climbing, but paused for a second, casting a shrewd eye along the rock wall. If she could climb sideways for a few feet, there was a flatter part of the rock that would be easier to ascend, so she shuffled sideways, reaching out for holds until she was able to get past the outward curve and once more go upward for the last ten feet or so of the rock face.

When she reached the top, she turned and looked down along the length of the channel, and noticed something that Jak had missed during his ascent—the inward curve of the rock continued all the way along the length of the tunnel, suggesting that it acted as a tunnel for any storm forces that may hit the outcrop, the actual channel being caused by wind and sand erosion. She looked up to the gathering storm above and hoped that they would be able to leave the channel before the storm began to hit hard.

Like Jak, she was able to pick her way along the irregular pathway cut into the top of the rock and find herself a place to hide and observe.

Now they had only to wait for the trade-off to begin.

The lead wag from Charity stood at the entrance to the arena. Directly opposed was the lead wag from Summerfield. Both had their engines ticking over, both were waiting for the other to move first.

"Come on," Jenny whispered to herself as she watched them from her secured position. She looked up at the sky, and hoped they would move soon.

IN THE SUMMERFIELD WAG, Baron Tad Hutter was feeling much the same. So, too, was Elias Tulk, but for different reasons.

Hutter glanced up at the gathering sky and frowned. "That asshole Jourgensen better start moving soon, or else this storm is gonna make things impossible."

"Mebbe he's waiting for you to make the first move," Tulk said. "Mebbe you should, 'cause it sure looks as though he isn't gonna."

"Shit, I don't wanna give him any ground at all, but..." He indicated to Tulk to put the wag into gear and begin to edge into the arena.

ON THE FAR SIDE, Baron Al Jourgensen watched as the lead wag from the Summerfield convoy started to move into the arena.

"Okay, let's do it," he said simply, indicating for his own driver to begin.

The two convoys began to move slowly toward the center of the arena, each moving at a crawl to try to keep pace with the other, neither side willing to reach the middle before the other. The problem being, where was the middle of the arena? The lead wags in both convoys, stop-starting in a stuttering procession, reached a point where they were about thirty yards apart when Hutter signaled to Tulk to stop. As his wag shuddered to a halt, so Jourgensen signaled his driver to stop.

The two convoys now sat, facing each other, only thirty yards apart. They were both far enough into the arena for the rear wag in each train to be well within the boundaries of the openings in the outcrop. There was plenty of space behind each wag for the Hellbenders to pen them in before beginning their attack.

From their promontory positions, Jak and Jenny watched the wags proceed with mixed feelings. Jak was immobile, his red eyes fixed on the two trains, waiting patiently. Jenny, on the other hand, was less than patient, shifting uncomfortably on her perch and dividing her attention between the convoys and the sky. She was careful not to disturb or dislodge any of the rocks that surrounded the small perch she had made for herself, but nonetheless found it difficult to remain motionless. She felt itchy for action of some kind as the minutes ticked by and no one moved in any of the wags.

But that didn't mean that nothing was happening.

"GET THE WOMEN shackled and get them out in the open." Baron Al's voice crackled over the radio.

"This is it, then," Claudette said to Ayesha.

The baron's daughter nodded. "Let's get this done, then."

"You'll never get away with it, you do know that, don't you?" said the sec man who had been riding shotgun. "Even if this attack from your so-called allies happens, chances are that you'll all still buy the farm. Is that really what you want?" he added, directing this away from

Ayesha and Claudette and toward the other women, who had picked the shackles from the floor and were starting to put them on without closing the mechanism—even the bloodstained Anita, who had tried to clean herself up with water from the wag's supply rather than appear conspicuous. "Go through with it, keep your heads down, and all you'll get is shafted by the men of Summerfield until you make them some babies. Is that so bad?"

Ayesha shrugged. "Don't you get it yet, stupe? We don't want that. We don't want to be told what to do. We want to have lives where we aren't pieces of shit to be used and abused, and frankly we'd rather get chilled than go through with it. Your way we die a long slow death for sure. But we stick this out and fight, then mebbe we've got a chance of getting away. And that chance is worth more than you could ever give."

"That's a lot of words to prepare to buy the farm," he said quietly.

"Which is something you would have done a long time ago if not for the fact that we need you to lead us out, so as not to look suspicious," Claudette said harshly as she unloaded the Uzi. She tossed the empty blaster to him, and he caught it before it hit him full in the face. "You can take this, but remember that I've got a handblaster, and I can draw it real quick if I have to. Understand me?"

He nodded. "There should be two sec men with you. Otherwise Baron Al'll know something's wrong straight away. Davey should have been the other one," he added, with an indication of his head to where the chilled sec man was still slumped.

"How inconsiderate of me to end his miserable fucking life, then," Ayesha replied sarcastically. "The driver'll just have to take his place. Will my lovely father spot that? I think not." She explained, before the sec man had a chance to answer, "Because you all look alike to him. You're just the scum that do his dirty work. So get your fat ass over here," she said to the driver, signaling him to climb over the seats and join them in the rear of the wag.

"Why?" he asked, puzzled.

"Oh, a triple stupe, as well, eh?" Ayesha snapped. "You know as well as I do that the two guards wouldn't both get out of the front of the wag. Everyone else in the convoy will expect one man from the rear, with the women, and one from the front, where he was riding shotgun. You're replacing the boy from the rear is all. Now fucking move!" she yelled, gesturing with her knife.

The driver clambered over the seat and slid into the rear of the wag, passing near to Claudette, who gave him a warning kick—hard—to dissuade him from any idea he may have of trying to attack her. But he was just a driver, and had figured that this would be the easiest ride in the convoy. He was now pissed off and frightened. If any of the things Ayesha had said about the Hellbenders were true, there was little chance of him getting back to Charity in one piece. But every moment he could stay alive was still of the utmost importance to him, and so he complied with her request.

Ayesha gave him an empty blaster and joined Claudette in appearing to secure herself in the shackles. But she still had the knife in the palm of her hand; Claudette had a handblaster up the sleeve of her shirt, and some of the other women had the liberated blasters concealed about their bodies.

"Do it now," Ayesha snapped.

The sec man in the front of the wag slid out of his seat, opening the door of the wag and jumping out, running around to the back and opening up the rear of the wag. Gesturing with the empty Uzi, he beckoned for the apparently shackled women to get out of the wag. This they did, with Ayesha in the lead and Claudette somewhere in the middle, looking behind her all the way to keep an eye on the driver who was acting as second sec guard. When they were all clear of the back door, the rear guard closed the door to hide the chilled body within from the eyes of the sec wag behind them.

"Keep it hard," Ayesha whispered to the other women, aware of the eyes from all the sec wags that were now trained on them. There was an immense pressure on them to appear "normal" as they were seemingly led to their exchange.

"Same goes for you assholes, too," Claudette added to the sec guards in an undertone.

From the wags in front and behind, sec guards had appeared, climbing onto the roofs of their wags, and training their blasters on the opposing convoy. They didn't look down at the procession of women as they passed.

OVER IN THE OPPOSITE convoy, Hutter watched the women as they started to walk along the side of the convoy. He was almost visibly salivating as he caught sight of Ayesha. Tulk, seated beside him, could almost read his mind, and felt physically sick for a moment, until he considered the fate that was about to befall his baron.

"Ready the men," Hutter ordered, and Tulk gladly swung out of his seat and away from his loathed leader. He opened his door and jumped down from his wag, signaling to the other wags as he did so. Without the radio communications enjoyed by Jourgensen, Hutter had to rely on something as basic as one man sending out a signal. But at that moment, having witnessed the expression on the baron's face, Tulk was glad of that.

At his signal, the sec men from Summerfield took their places on the wags, some keeping watch on their opposing number, others mounting guard over the primitive flamethrowers erected over the seed crops and supplies.

FROM HIS POSITION on high, Jak watched the women being apparently led from the wag, and wondered what was going on. They were supposed to be in the wag that had brought them, and to secure it. He waited to see if Jenny would make a signal at this, suspecting that the Hellbenders wouldn't care about a promise made to Ayesha in return for her help. When no signal to attack came, he wasn't surprised.

Jak's dilemma now was what to do. Should he make the signal himself and precipitate the attack, or should he wait to see what Jenny would do before acting? He had a suspicion that she would leave it until the Summerfield sec were unloading their side of the trade, thus leaving everyone out in the open and much more vulnerable to attack and, much as he regretted what appeared to be selling Ayesha down the river, the hunter in him said that this course of action made much more sense.

And yet he was wrong in part. Jenny had only had part of her attention on the movement below; the movement above was more immediately disturbing. The clouds had started to move violently, and the wisps of breeze were snaking down to begin stirring the dust around her.

The change in air pressure made Jak look up, and he cursed softly to himself.

DOWN ON THE ARENA FLOOR, Claudette looked up as she felt breeze stir her plaits, and then down at the whirling eddies of dust that started to move around her feet. Her eyes met Ayesha's.

"They better fuckin' hurry," she murmured.

As the first load of seed crops were unloaded and the women readied themselves for the approach of the Summerfield sec, the dust began to rise from the floor of the arena to swirl around their lower legs.

"Shit!" cursed Jourgensen and Hutter, almost simultaneously.

Again almost simultaneously, Jenny and Jak yelled into their handsets, "Go!" before beginning a rapid descent to the wags below.

Chapter Nineteen

The wind began to howl through the jagged gaps at the top of the rocks and swept through the entrances at each end of the arena, conflicting currents meeting in the center and lifting great whirling eddies of dust and grit that stung the eyes and coruscated the skin. The noise from the beginning storm was enough to drown out the sound of the wags hidden in the channels at each side as they gunned their engines into life and began to roll through the narrow rock tunnels to circle out of the exits, turn and make their initial attack.

J.B. waited until Jenny had slid down the rock and into the wag, breathless and already covered in a thin film of dust from the atmosphere outside.

"You okay?" Mildred asked her as the woman settled in her seat and coughed violently.

Jenny nodded. "Yeah, just about. That's a wicked dust storm blowing up out there, and I figure the worst of it may just blow through these holes, so we should get out as soon as possible."

"Get this thing going, John," Mildred affirmed.

"Already there," J.B. muttered through clenched teeth as he moved the wag forward.

It was going to be a delicate balance between speed and

getting out of the channel in one piece. Already the storm had increased in intensity to such a degree that the sand and grit that had been churned up was hitting the windshield of the wag with a loud, clattering rain that threatened to pit the toughened sec glass that had been fitted on the preDark vehicle. But that wasn't what worried J.B. The problem was that the rain was so dark and consistent that he couldn't see where he was going. Funneled into the channel from the outside, the wind, sand and grit were forming a visibility barrier that was preventing him from really putting his foot down on the accelerator and getting the hell out of the tunnel. If he took the narrow passage too fast, he was running the risk of driving the wag straight into the rock and not only damaging the wag itself and risking vulnerability in the firefight to come, but also jamming the vehicle across the channel and blocking the wags behind from making progress.

Sweat stood out on his forehead as he concentrated on keeping the vehicle straight, trying to define the darker shapes of the rock walls through the opaque mist of dust. He ground his teeth, keeping a foot poised on the brake to apply it the second it was necessary, while keeping pressure constant on the accelerator.

"Chill, John," Mildred muttered, "you're doing fine." But even as she said it she was aware, as was the Armorer, that the Hellbenders in the wag were impatient, their body language telling of the tension waiting to be unleashed.

PERHAPS THEY WOULD have been less so if they had realized that Correll was encountering exactly the same problem trying to negotiate his way out of the opposing tunnel.

The gaunt man had already started moving his wag before Jak was down and into the wag driven by Lonnie.

"What's hurry?" Jak said phlegmatically as he regained his seat.

"I guess Papa Joe wants to get out of there before that storm gets too much," Lonnie replied as he, too, set his wag in motion.

"All very well, but we can't risk too much speed in these conditions, not if we want to get out in one piece," Danny pointed out.

"You saying you don't want to fight? After all this time, and when you finally get the chance?" Catherine posed aggressively. The small blonde was hyped up and agitated, moving on her seat in such a manner as to suggest that Danny would be the first to be chilled if he said a word out of place.

For Dean and Jak, this attitude just brought home the problems the companions faced if they hoped to get out of this alive.

Doc, however, had a few words that he hoped would calm the feisty blonde until the right time for action.

"My dear girl, we all want to come out of this little contretemps without being chilled. And we want a chance to actually face the enemy. All young Danny was doing was pointing out the folly of more haste, less speed. It was not a reflection on his, or indeed our, courage."

Catherine looked at Doc, suddenly still in her seat. She

carried with her a puzzled expression that told the others she had no idea what he was talking about, but at least it had opened the tap on her pent-up aggression, her confusion dissipating it.

Dean tried not to smile. A second later, even this was forgotten.

"Shit!" Lonnie yelled. "Rockfall!"

He dipped and swerved the heavy wag as the boulders started to fall from above. The howling gale had dislodged more than just shale and loose gravel. Larger rocks and stones from the top of the rock wall had begun to tumble into the narrow channel, clattering onto the roofs and hoods of the wags, hitting the ground in front of them and causing the drivers to take evasive action.

"Let us hope it leaves us enough space to negotiate this obstacle course and get out of here," Doc muttered.

Lonnie swung the wheel to try to dodge the obstacles, ignoring the loud bangs and crashes on the roof, hoping that they wouldn't hit the windshield and shatter it.

"Great, we'll be fucked before we even get out of here," Catherine murmured with disdain.

"Have some faith in our pilot," Doc returned.

"Thanks," Lonnie gritted, "but I'm not that sure that I have that much faith in the bastard storm."

IN THE LEAD WAG, Correll was also cursing the sudden rockfalls.

"Fate could not do this to us—not when we have come

so far, my love," he yelled, addressing the box that still sat on his lap as he drove.

He swerved his wag in and out of the falling rocks— those that he could see through the sudden dust storm that whipped against the windshield, obscuring his view of the track ahead.

Ryan looked over at Krysty, whose hair was clinging to her scalp and neck as if it were trying to envelop her, the tendrils of Titian red curled around her pale flesh.

"Hang on," the one-eyed man muttered through clenched teeth. "We get through this, the rest of it is going to be easy."

She spared him a smile. "Or easier, at any rate," she murmured.

"Nuking hell, but the fates are on our side after all!" Correll exclaimed with a triumphant shout. "We're out."

Looking through the windshield, Ryan could see that the violence of the storm appeared to have abated a little, as there was now sky and light visible through the particles of dust, dirt and rock that swirled in the air. They were clear of the tunnel, and Ryan braced himself as Correll put his foot down and took the wag out into the empty desert with a sudden burst of speed before swinging the wheel with an incredible force, turning the wag at a tight angle so that it almost lifted onto two wheels. He felt the force of the turn fling them all across the wag, heard the screech of the wag's brakes as it complained in its very structure about the gravity-defying feats that were demanded of it.

"Fireblast! I hope the other drivers are as good as you— otherwise we'll lose wags like this," he shouted at Correll.

The gaunt man turned his head for a second and gave a ghoulish grin: "They can do it—I just hope J.B. is up to it."

THE ARMORER WAS ASKING himself the same thing at almost the same moment. There hadn't been the rockfalls to contend with in their channel, the upper level of the rock being a little more secure, but the storm had clouds of the dust and dirt whipped up and flung them against the windshield, blinding J.B. He kept his speed up and steady, but knew that the exit to this channel was narrow—much more so than the exit that Correll and the drivers on the other side of the outcrop would have to contend with. He squinted and cursed to himself as he tried to see where the channel narrowed and the exit gap occurred.

"Dark night, I can think of better ways to start an assault," he gritted.

"If you get us through this in one piece, I wouldn't give a shit if you sat back and let the rest of us get on with it," Jenny said, "'cause you sure as hell would have done more than enough."

"I might hold you to that—if I get us through," J.B. muttered, swinging the wheel as a looming dark shape, coming up suddenly out of the rain of dust, proclaimed that he had sighted one wall of the channel.

He stomped on the brake to skid the vehicle to the left, catching sight of the other wall, and the slightly lighter gap between that proclaimed he had found the exit gap. Cursing softly, unwilling even to waste energy or concentration on talking aloud, J.B. headed straight for the light, and put his foot down, ignoring the dust that rattled against the windshield.

"Sweet mother, you've done it!" Mildred exclaimed as the wag came out of the channel and into the lighter air of the desert. It was suddenly easier to see, and J.B. was able to get his bearings.

The Armorer knew that there was little time to waste. The sound of wags roaring out of the enclosed channels and into the desert at either end of the outcrop would be enough to make the two trade convoys aware of an attack, and every second lost in turning and heading back into the arena to take up battle would be a second that the two sets of sec could prepare a defense. Every second counted, and no time could be wasted on turning the wags.

So J.B. leaned heavily on the wheel and executed exactly the same kind of torturous metal-bending turn that Correll was executing at that same moment. His wag complained heavily, the wheels seeming slow in their ability to respond to his efforts at the wheel.

"Turn us over now and I'll never forgive you, John," Mildred murmured to herself as the wag tilted alarmingly, throwing them across the interior.

"Trust me," the Armorer replied, almost to himself, as the wag righted itself and was facing the right direction— heading straight back into the arena. Through the lighter desert rain, he could see that the wags in front of him were still facing the wrong way to meet an attack, and the sec men still out of position, facing toward him but with the air of those frozen in sudden surprise.

"I always do, John," Mildred added, checking her Czech-manufactured ZKR target pistol. A handblaster wouldn't be useful in the first attack, as they would be using the machine blasters mounted in the side of the wag to attack, but at some point, she had the feeling, it may just descend to hand-to-hand combat, in which case she wanted to be ready.

At least, far more in readiness than either of the convoys they would be attacking.

"SHIT! GRAB THE GIRLS and let's get under cover," Baron Tad Hutter yelled at his sec men as the storm started to blow up. He jumped down from the wag and ran toward the seemingly shackled girls until he was halted by a voice that sounded loud and strong above the howl of the wind.

"Just hold your ass still right there unless you want to have it blown off!"

Unwilling as he was to appear to heed such terms in his position as baron, Hutter's instinct for self-preservation made him pull up sharply. He looked up to see Baron Al Jourgensen standing at the door of his own wag, a Sharps rifle in his hands, raised and trained on Hutter.

"Don't be a stupe," Hutter snapped. "Look at the storm. We need to get this done with as soon as possible!"

"Then tell your sec men to hurry up with the unloading," Jourgensen snapped back.

"Be reasonable."

"Be reasonable nothing—you fulfill your side of the bargain, and we'll fulfill ours as soon as you've got everything unloaded."

"But—"

The catch on the Sharps clicked, audible to Hutter even above the howl of the storm.

"Don't argue, Tad. You're not in any position to start handing out orders, okay?"

Hutter held his hands aloft. "Okay, Al, you've got all the cards right now, but we'll see." He turned slowly so that he faced his men. "You heard the man, start—"

He was cut short in bemusement by the sight that met him. It would appear to him that his men had, in fact, given up the unloading altogether, as they seemed to be facing completely in the opposite direction to the central exchange point.

It was then, as he looked at them, that he became aware of an undertone to the storm that had been bothering him for a few minutes without him being able to put a name to what it was. There was a growling sound that had nothing to do with the rush of wind and debris through the arena formed by the outcrop. It was the sound of wag engines being pushed to the limit. And as he looked past his immobile and stunned sec force, he could see three wags turning tightly and coming toward his men, headed directly for the entrance to the outcrop. Furious, he turned back to scream at Jourgensen.

"You bastard! You've set us up!"

But the words died on his lips. He could see beyond Baron Al that a similar situation was occurring at the rear of the Charity convoy. Jourgensen's eyes met those of Hutter across the dust storm wastes, each ready to accuse the other but stopped dead by the bewilderment on the other's face.

"You?" Jourgensen yelled.

Hutter shook his head. "Ambush," he screamed. "Get back, for fuck's sake, get into defensive positions," he yelled at his men as he turned and headed back to the lead wag on the Summerfield convoy.

Jourgensen, too, had decided that the best course of action was to ignore his opposing baron and concentrate on the menace that was now threatening. There would be time enough for Summerfield after this was sorted out. He slipped back into his wag, and picked up the handset, yelling, "Defensive now—watch the rear, turn the wags."

In the confusion, seed crops and supplies were left scattered across the center of the arena as the sec men headed back to the safety of their wags and the machine blasters and mounted flamethrowers, which would now prove to be of use in a way that Hutter couldn't have predicted.

Which actions also left the women, seemingly shackled together and guarded by two sec men, standing in the middle of the arena, with nothing to do and nowhere to go.

Which wasn't quite the case.

Ayesha and Claudette had both recognized the sound of the wags beneath the storm, and had been looking out for them. Now that the only sec man paying them any attention were those with empty blasters, it was the time to act.

"Okay, let's try and head back to the wag," Ayesha screamed above the noise of the storm.

"Good move," Claudette yelled back, her plaits whipping around her head in the howling storm. "At least we can get a defensive position better there than out here in the open."

"What about the sec men?" one of the women asked. "Won't they think it's suspicious if we go back to the wag?"

"Not if these stupes take us back," Claudette replied, indicating the two sec men who had been acting as their unwilling cover.

"You've got to be joking," the sec man with the empty Uzi said with venom, throwing his useless blaster down to the desert floor and turning to run. "Baron!" he yelled, but was cut short by a burst of blasterfire from Claudette, who figured that all pretense was now blown and that they had been forced into the open. Before he had the chance to advance more than a few yards, the words were chilled on his lips as blood flooded into his lungs and bubbled up his throat from the immense internal injuries he received as a result of Claudette's Uzi slugs hitting home.

The sec driver turned to Ayesha, all his nerves now, ironically, quelled by a terror greater than any he had ever known before.

"You bitch, this is all your doing, " he yelled, flinging himself toward her.

The girl stepped back, slipping off her shackles and bringing the knife up so that it was blade upward in her palm. As he lunged, she stepped calmly to one side and slashed at him, catching him across the side of his face. As he stumbled and fell, his hand came up to his face, leaving his ribs open at the side. She slashed under the rib cage, the razor-honed blade cutting through his clothes and scoring through flesh, fat and muscle. He howled in pain and doubled up on the floor of the arena, no longer an immediate threat.

"Drop the shackles and run like hell," Claudette yelled, hanging back to marshal the women along to the wag while Ayesha dealt with the driver. When the girl joined her, Claudette looked around to see that Anita was the only one of the women who hadn't run directly to the wag. In the confusion, no shots had been fired on them, and frankly it was unlikely that it had even been noticed that they were unshackled—until Anita had chosen to draw attention to this.

The blowsy blonde was hammering on the window of Baron Al's wag, screaming at him to let her in and save her, and she would do anything for him, and she wasn't to blame, it was his good-for-nothing daughter who had sold them down the river to something called the Hellbenders.

In a torrent of words that emerged as an almost incoherent jumble, the blonde had managed to spill the whole plot to Baron Al in a pathetic attempt to save her skin. The irony being that, in among the noise and confusion, and the fact that the window of his wag was firmly wound to shut out the dust, all the baron could see was a red-eyed, swollen-faced woman screaming at him. He looked at her in complete incomprehension.

"Bitch," Claudette muttered, "I've been wanting to do this for hours." She raised her blaster.

It was quick, but far from painless. She put two slugs into the woman's knees, and Anita crashed to the ground with an ear-piercing yell of agony. The next two shots were into her shoulders, making it impossible for her to do anything but lie there, immobile, wailing in pain and confusion.

Claudette and Ayesha made their way hurriedly back to the wag, Claudette pausing briefly to put a slug into Anita's guts, blood spreading across the blonde's dirty white blouse, her face contorted in pain.

Her death was quickened by a final slug that was put through her open, mewling mouth, blowing her head apart. Claudette then stopped to spare the astounded baron a wink before making her way back to the safety of the wag.

As she bounded in and slammed the doors, she said breathlessly, "I hope you can drive one of these things, girl, 'cause I sure as shit can't."

Chapter Twenty

"Man the guns!" Correll yelled. "We've got them chilled and buried—they can't get out!" He whooped joyously as he brought the wag out of its dangerous skid-cum-turn, and the two airborne wheels hit the desert floor with a bone-jarring thud. He slammed the wag into the highest gear and ground his foot into the metal floor, hunching over the wheel as much as the metal box on his lap would allow him.

Ryan, Krysty and the other Hellbenders in the lead wag slid from their seats, balance still a little uncertain from the erratic passage of the wag, and positioned themselves behind the machine blasters that were mounted inside the wag, with the barrels protruding through engineered holes in the sides. Because these had been made and mounted before skydark, they were the latest in military sec tech from before the nukecaust, and had cameras and infrared mounts that relayed a view of the outside world, and the target area, to whoever was seated at the end of the mount.

Ryan settled his good orb against the sight, adjusting to the slight variation in quality between the image on the small eye screen and the reality around him. The age of the equipment was beginning to tell, even though Correll's people had maintained all the wags as best they could, and the image that settled on his retina was slightly flat and two-dimensional, with a faded quality that wouldn't help anyone to differentiate between wags and clouds of dust in the chaos outside. The broken digital image pixilated the outside world into little more than a series of shadows. But those shadows were enough.

"We're closing," Correll yelled. "Get ready to blast the bastards!"

Ryan shifted forward in his seat, his eye jammed up against the sight, the stock of the blaster hard against the cords of muscle on his shoulder. The rear wag of the Charity convoy came into view, and he was aware of moving shadows along the roof. Above the roar of the wag engine, a chatter of blasterfire could just about be discerned, and there was the high-pitched scream of tortured metal as the shells from the Charity sec men's blasters hit the outside of the armored wag and ricocheted off. Before he had the chance to squeeze the trigger and pick off some of the shadows, Correll had piloted the wag past at speed, and they were headed for the lead. It was obvious that Correll wanted the lead wag and the life of Baron Al Jourgensen, the man he had referred to as "Red, the son of a gaudy whore." Behind them, he heard the throatier roar of a machine blaster from the next wag, as it attempted to take out the wag that had fired on them.

Beside Ryan, Krysty squeezed off a few shots to test her machine blaster, aiming at shadows that moved across the top of a wag they passed. The heavy-caliber slugs tore into the shadows, leaving red tracers in their wake, some of the shadows disappearing into the sandstorm around as the red lines ripped through them, throwing them off the wag.

"Lead wag coming up," Correll yelled over his shoulder without glancing behind him, making sure that the personnel of his wag were aware of his priority.

BEHIND HIS CONVOY LEADER, Lonnie pushed his wag to the max, keeping hard on Correll as they roared through the narrow gap that formed the entrance to the arena. It was narrow, and filled with the swirling dust thrown up by the storm, but it was nothing compared to the channel they had just left. In the wake left by the leading wag, Lonnie charted a course into the arena with ease.

"Heads up, we're about to hit it," he rapped out sharply as the crew behind him took up positions.

This wag was also a preDark military vehicle, but hadn't been designed as an armored wag in the same way as the one piloted by the Hellbenders' leader. This was an armored personnel carrier in which the Hellbenders had cut holes large enough for heavy-duty blasters to be placed. The work would have taken a long time, as the armoring of the wag was strong, but then the group had been waiting for a long time, and this was the reward for their patience. The holes were small, but large enough for the barrel of a blaster and also for the sight to gain some view of the area around the barrel. It was a small circumference, but with wags in front and behind, the important thing was to focus on what you could see, and leave the rest to your compatriots.

It was none too secure to try to sight carefully, as the seats in the wag hadn't been made with the idea of trying to fire from the sides. They were made purely for transport, and so were facing the wrong way, and at the wrong angles for the crew with the blasters to sit and sight their targets comfortably. Instead, Jak, Dean and Catherine were lined up down one side of the vehicle, balancing and trying to compensate for the erratic motion of the wag as it rode roughshod over the even rougher terrain. The blasters down this side of the vehicle were all AK-47s, the Kalashnikovs grouped together as part of the overall plan to allow for a smoother transition of ammo when needed. In the same way, the far side of the wag, where Danny, Doc and the other crew stood idle, waiting for the wag to turn on the return run before they sighted and began their assault, were all equipped with Heckler & Kochs, the pool of ammo for these blasters being grouped on their side.

In this sense, the planning had been superb; however, there had been no way that anyone could have allowed for the sandstorm that was now raging outside. The clouds of dust raised by the motion of the wags would have made things difficult enough, but the roughly hacked holes for the blaster barrels and sights, although tight as they could have been made, still allowed a little room for the howling wind outside to drive sand through the gaps and into the interior of the wag. It wasn't much, but for those who stood by the blasters, trying to get a sight on the enemy, it was enough.

"Hot pipe! This'll take my eyeball out before I have a chance to pick off anyone out there," Dean shouted as he took his eye away from the sight to try to clear it of the stinging grit that was misting his vision.

"Aim for dark, fire quick, then clean eyes," Jak snapped, ignoring the stinging in his own fiery red eyes in order to pull cleanly on the trigger of the AK-47 and take out some of the sec firing at them, slamming a couple of slugs into the side of a wag, whose armoring and protection was minimal, for good measure.

"White boy's right," Catherine said between shots of her own. "Ignore the pain. It's much more satisfying to see those bastards go down," she added with a grin as one of her shots took out a sec man, his head splitting like a ripe melon, visible even through the dust storm. The blood and brain from his exploding skull was absorbed into the swirling dust around as his body slumped, the impact of the slug absorbed almost totally above neck level—where there was nothing now left to indicate he had ever had a head.

The grin on the blonde's face turned to a grimace of pain as a flurry of shots from the opposing sec ripped along the side of the wag. The vast majority of the shells ricocheted harmlessly off the wag's armor, but Catherine had drawn the short straw when it came to luck, and was about to become the first casualty among the Hellbenders.

Two slugs from the sec men squeezed through the gap around the barrel and sight of the AK-47, and if she hadn't turned to reply to Jak's comments, they may have just wounded her in the upper arm or missed altogether. But that fraction that she moved to speak, pushing her head away from and higher than the sight on her blaster put her in direct line for the shots that had squeezed through.

The first one caught her on the cheekbone, freezing the grimace for an awful second as it ripped the flesh away from her face, exposing the bone and teeth of the jaw, before the bone seemed to splinter and powder in front of them. It seemed as though everything were happening in slow-motion as her head jerked upward slightly, the second slug hitting home at her temple, ripping flesh and hair from her head. Her green eyes seemed for one fraction of a second to register the most intense pain and surprise, pleading for a reason why this had happened by such a fluke, before the light went from the eyes, followed by the viscous fluid of the eyeball itself as it exploded under the pressure of the blow.

Just as her shot had made the opposing sec man's head explode like a melon, so the two shots that had squeezed through the gap in the armoring reduced her head to pulp in a matter of a second or two and extinguished the life of the belligerent and feisty blonde.

"Oh, for fuck's sake," Lonnie said, looking over his shoulder as her body was thrown across the wag and landed in Danny's lap, making the youngster puke. "When Rudi finds out, he'll go shit mad—he'll probably take 'em out on his own. And don't stop firing just because of that," he added as Jak and Dean returned their attention to their blasters and started to loose shots once more at the trade convoy.

One thing was certain, though—the sudden, freakish

and unexpected chilling of one of their own people had
brought home to everyone in the wag that they were outnumbered at least two-to-one by those on the outside of
the Hellbenders' caravan, and that every life lost, especially in such a stupe manner, was more of a blow to them
than to the men of either Charity or Summerfield.

"WHAT DO YOU MEAN, you can't drive one of these?"
Claudette yelled at Ayesha. "Didn't your daddy ever give
you a wag as a present, like your brothers?"

Inside the wag that had carried the women into the
arena, the noise from outside was drowned by the argument within. With the chilled body of the sec man still in
the corner, and now bereft of both sec shotgun and driver,
as well as the traitorous Anita, the women were huddled
in the rear while Ayesha and Claudette stood face-to-face.

"Of course he didn't, you stupe," Ayesha yelled back.
"I'm a girl, not a boy. Shit, you worked at the palace, or
so you say—you know what he was like. Girls are for
fucking, and boys get the toys."

A look clouded across Claudette's face suddenly, as
though the argument was suddenly forgotten.

"Yeah, you're right," she said quietly. "My ma always
said that Red was like that."

Ayesha's anger suddenly dissipated as she heard her father referred to in that manner. There were few people left
alive who referred to Baron Al Jourgensen as "Red"—she
had no knowledge of this being one of the ways in which
Danny and the rest of the Hellbenders knew the baron

from Correll's ranting—and a cold shiver ran down her spine as she suddenly realized something.

"Your mother?"

Claudette nodded briefly. "Yeah, she ended up slit from pussy to throat in a gaudy house by some drunk asshole, but before that she'd been one of his regular sluts before he got bored. That's how come I'm here. And she told me how he got the name of Red, and how come people don't use it anymore unless they want to die."

"Red like the blood of the women when he finished them," Ayesha said in a small voice. "That what happened to your mother?"

Claudette shrugged. "Mebbe. If not him, then some wiseass who was working for him or wanted to be him and knew who my ma was. She always said there were only so many sluts, and every man gets around to them sooner or later. Don't think she meant to kill them, though."

"So you're my sister," Ayesha said quietly.

"Yeah, me and mebbe half the women under twenty in this wag." Claudette laughed harshly. "Don't get stupe on me about it—it still don't change the fact that you can't drive this stupe wag. Can anyone here?" she asked in a louder voice, addressing the rest of the women. There was a general agreement that Ayesha was right—women in Charity weren't given the power to do these things, and none of them had any driving experience.

"Boy, that's us well and truly fucked," Claudette said, rubbing her face, "more than if we'd let those assholes from Summerfield get their paws on us."

"Mebbe not," Ayesha said, her face determined and set as she went past Claudette and climbed over and into the front of the wag, ignoring the blasterfire that was erupting all around and could easily come through the windshield, toughened glass though it was. "Come and ride shotgun—you've got just about the only blaster we've got," she added to her newly discovered sister.

"What the rad-pocked, scum-sucking, sticky-fucking hell are you doing, girl?" Claudette spit out as she slipped over the seat and joined Ayesha.

"Look, I might not know exactly how to drive one of these things right, but I must know something. I've sat next to sec men driving, to my brothers, to my asshole father. I've seen these stupe things being driven all my life. It can't be that hard to work it out."

"Hell of a time to start learning," Claudette said with a smile.

Ayesha laughed. "Never better, babe."

J.B. WAS FAR from happy. He could see that Correll's strategy was already falling to pieces, and he and Mildred were a long way from where they wanted to be—at the side of Ryan and the rest of their companions. The only way to get out of this—if there was any way at all—was to be back-to-back with people they could trust. At least that way they had a chance, with people they knew they could rely upon.

Not like here. Not like now.

The Armorer straightened his wag and headed toward the gap between the rocks that formed the entrance to the arena.

Ahead of him he could see the Summerfield convoy from the rear, getting nearer as he closed on them. The front of the convoy was lost in the swirl of the dust storm, but he could see sec men chasing back to their wags, and those who were already mounted turn around, blasters at the ready. He could also see the sec men who were standing guard on the top of the supply wags, with the homemade flamethrowers. They bore little resemblance to anything else the Armorer had ever seen, but he recognized the danger with an unerring instinct.

"Get into position and hold on," he yelled, "this is going to be a little tricky."

J.B. rarely overstated anything, and this was one of those occasions—for, almost as he spoke, the sec man on the flamethrower nearest the approaching wag swung the contraption toward the oncoming Hellbenders' vehicle and attempted to open up with a jet of flame.

"Dark night," the Armorer cursed softly at the sight that confronted him as the sec man opened up the pressure on the flamethrower and attempted to ignite it. The rickety and ramshackle weapon spluttered twice as the sec man attempted to ignite the flame and then exploded on top of the wag, throwing up a ball of flame and a dense cloud of oily smoke that made it even harder to see in the arena as the wag beneath also went up, a dull *whump,* resounding around the rock walls as the sides of the vehicle flew outward...just as J.B. piloted his wag into range.

The Armorer threw the wheel of his vehicle, swinging it as far to the left of the arena as he dared, hoping that the majority of the debris would avoid damaging their wag. The vehicle shook as lumps of metal thudded into it, driving it toward the rock and making him swing the wheel back to try to compensate.

"Sweet Lord, will you look at that," Mildred whispered as the sec men on the exploding wag were thrown into the air and across the arena, one of them thudding against the wag with a force equal to that of some of the metal debris. Their clothes and skin were covered in the flaming fuel that was used to power the flamethrower, and they described arcs of flame in the air, cutting through the dust and poor light to show where they landed.

"Heads up—more ahead," J.B. yelled, mindful that the explosion may yet have distracted his crew from the wags ahead.

It was a good point. The sec men on the two wags in front of the one that had exploded had thrown themselves onto the roof of each of their wags, and were now scrambling to their feet with only one idea in mind—to meet the oncoming assault head-on.

J.B. righted the course of his wag, and the Hellbenders and Mildred armed the blasters, ready to start firing as soon as the flame and smoke cleared and they could get a sighting.

Unfortunately for them, the next Summerfield wag in line was able to fire first. The flamethrower crew was raised just above the smoke that was still pouring from the ruined wag, and so was able to sight the Hellbenders' wag first. Swinging around the flamethrower, and not even thinking about the fact that one before had exploded, the sec man in charge of the contraption fired it up and ignited the flame.

A great yellow-and-red gout of flame roared from the barrel of the flamethrower, scorching the side of J.B.'s wag and heating up the interior so that the blasters on the inside became almost too hot to touch.

"Shit!" Jenny yelled as the rapidly heating metal burned the palms of her hands, "what the fuck are they doing?"

"Take him out, Millie," J.B. yelled.

Mildred acted quickly, yet seemingly with little fuss. She slipped her arms out of her jacket and used the sleeves to pad and insulate her hands against the heat. She moved the floor-mounted blaster until the sight caught the top of the wag, and kept her head just a fraction away from the blaster sight, so that she could feel the heat drying out her eyeball and scorching her eyebrow, yet it didn't actually touch or burn her skin.

Mildred had always been a crack shot. A short burst of fire from the drum-mounted machine blaster shattered the fuel tank for the flamethrower and also ripped a line of holes through the flesh of the sec man standing by it, throwing him backward off the roof of the wag as the fuel ignited and shot a line of fire along the feed line of the flamethrower, exploding it from its mounting on the roof of the wag.

But it wasn't just the flamethrowers that were causing problems. Although they were the most immediate danger, there were sec men both in the wags and also climbing onto the roofs of the wags armed with Uzis, Heckler & Kochs, and also AK-47s. They were starting to fire, not just at the wag driven by J.B., but also at all the Hellbenders' wags that followed the Armorer. Heavy-duty blasterfire thudded into the armored and reinforced sides of the wags as the Hellbenders used their mounted blasters to return the fire.

It was here that they had the advantage. There may be less of them in terms of wags and manpower, but they knew from their recce and spy reports that the wags from each ville weren't entirely armored. The wag stock of each ville was low, and the very nature of some of the trade to be exchanged would make the use of an armored wag impossible for a quick turnaround. So it was that the Hellbenders could, in theory, take advantage of surprise to cut down wag and man numbers if they hit hard and fast.

It was then that both Baron Al Jourgensen and Baron Tad Hutter changed their own agendas and made the entire matter a whole lot more complicated.

Chapter Twenty-One

"Tulk! What the fuck is going on?" Hutter raged.

Elias Tulk spared himself a small smile as he sat at the wheel of the static wag. "I don't know, Baron. We appear to be under attack of some kind." He giggled. His mind was filled with thoughts of revenge, and in part he no longer cared if Hutter guessed the part he played.

Hutter fixed his sec chief with a long hard stare, for a moment forgetting the battle that was raging outside. "This is something to do with you, you son of a gaudy slut," he hissed, "and I'll find out when we get back home."

"If..." Tulk interjected.

Hutter said nothing for a moment that seemed to stretch to forever. The inside of the wag was like a calm eye of the storm that—both in terms of nature and of a fire-fight—swirled and raged around them.

"We will get back," he said finally, and in a menacingly quiet tone. "And what's more, we'll take the women with us. Screw the rest of this. We're going to grab them and get the fuck out of here."

"How am I going to relay orders to the rest of the crew, then?" Tulk pointed out the carnage outside.

Hutter looked behind him at the two sec men who were manning the wag with himself and Tulk. They had their attention seemingly fixed on the outside, flinching at the slugs that hit the armor plating and toughened glass, starring it, but the baron knew that they had been listening intently to the discussion in the front of the wag.

"There's four of us. In case it escaped your notice, those sluts don't have any sec with them, and Baron Al and his boys are occupied with the assholes attacking them from the other direction. We just break ranks here, ram into the middle of the convoy, scattering everyone in their surprise, grab the girls and get the fuck out."

Tulk grinned wryly. "And that's a plan?"

Hutter was serious. "Got anything better to do, Elias?"

BARON AL "Red" Jourgensen was seeing the color of his nickname—which hadn't been used by anyone except Correll in many a year, both in terms of his temper, and in the blood that was flowing into the earth outside as both sides counted casualties against the sudden assault group.

"What the motherfucking hell is going down here?" he demanded of no one in particular. "That shithead Hutter thinks he can sell us down the river like this?"

"Don't think it's him, Baron," replied the sec man who had been driving the leading wag. "He's getting the attack as much as we are."

Jourgensen shot a look over his shoulder at the men who were manning the blasters behind him. They were rattling off bursts of machine blasterfire at the Hellbenders'

wags as they passed, but were trying to conserve ammo
and shoot on sight, their visibility impaired by the storm
and the dust raised by the circling wags.

"How we doing?" he snapped.

One of the sec men took his eye away from the blaster
sight for a moment to answer. "Can't see a thing out there,
Baron. I dunno if we're hitting anything or even what it
is we're aiming at half the time."

Baron Al nodded. "Right. We need those crops, so
we're gonna take 'em." He picked up the handset of the
radio. "Listen up," he yelled, "all wags head to the opposite camp and try to take the trade. Then get out as fast as
you can."

"You think anyone actually heard that?" his driver said
as slugs from the Hellbenders' blasters whined and ricocheted off the armored wag.

"Dunno." Baron Al shrugged. "But at least we've tried.
Now hit the fucking gas!"

Ayesha heard the message from her father on the radio
as she tried to hot-wire the wag with all the women who
were the trade from Charity. The sec driver had taken the
ignition key with him, possibly as some kind of private
token of his own security, or just from habit. As he was
now lying chilled in the center of the arena bloodbath,
there was no way that either Ayesha or Claudette was
going to risk getting it back again.

Claudette, seated beside the girl, also heard the message. "Lovely man," she muttered. "No mention of us in
there."

"Did you expect anything else?" Ayesha said through gritted teeth as she stripped, then joined the wires. "Please work this time, you stupe bastard," she added to the machinery. With a cough and a splutter, the wag's engine came to life. "Shit, I thought that'd never happen," she added with relief, then, "let's get ourselves out of here and wait for the dust to settle."

"In this storm?" Claudette grinned.

Ayesha didn't grace the poor joke with an answer. Instead, she stared ahead of her at the chaos framed by the windshield as she tried to put the wag into gear. With a squeal and grind that was painful, and made all the women inside the wag wince, the wag ground into gear. Swinging on the wheel, Ayesha pulled it out of the convoy.

Straight into the line of the approaching wag.

THE HELLBENDERS, led by Correll, had completed four or five circuits of the convoy, and the firefight was starting to get monotonous. In the wag driven by the gaunt man, Ryan and Krysty exchanged glances that spoke volumes, and both knew that their thoughts were being echoed by Jak, Dean and Doc in the wag behind, and by J.B. and Mildred in the opposing convoy. Any attempt at strategy had gone out of the window, and after the initial gains made by the Hellbenders when they had been able to pick off sec men who hadn't been able to make it back to secured or armored wags, the firefight had degenerated into the assault party driving around and around taking shots at whatever they could see through the storm, while sporadic fire returned at them suggested that the sec men from Charity were now all safely inside wags that offered them some protection from the fire.

It couldn't go on like this. Sooner or later, ammo or fuel would run out, and then it would descend into hand-to-hand combat. Ryan knew that his people were more than capable of holding their own, but they would be outnumbered, and if it came to a situation where blood lust held sway, he knew that they couldn't guarantee that the Hellbenders would recognize them when it came to face-to-face combat in a sandstorm.

Glancing across at Correll, Ryan could see that whatever shreds of sanity and reason had kept the man going for so long had now all been cast to the winds of the storm. The Hellbenders' leader was staring maniacally ahead through the windshield, hunched over the metal box on his lap, stroking it and muttering to it as he piloted the wag in a continuing circle, occasionally whooping as he saw some blasterfire hit home.

"Not good, lover," Krysty whispered to the one-eyed man, noticing the direction of his glance. "I figure he's gone totally. Problem is, how do we get out of this?"

Ryan spared the woman a look. Her hair was coiled tightly to her head and neck, reflecting the way she felt about the conflict and the manner in which it was proceeding rapidly to stalemate.

"Fireblast! There's nothing we can do while we're stuck in here."

It was at this point that fate took a hand.

Ayesha pulled the wag out, stamping on the accelerator to get the vehicle out of its confinement quickly, while the wheel was still at full spin and the tires bit into the swirling earth, turning the wag out of the space it occupied in the stationary convoy. The wags had been stopped and parked up close to one another, and she braced herself as the wing of the wag caught the rear of the wag in front with a squeal and a shower of sparks as metal ground on metal, slowing the progress of the wag with the women, and making Ayesha bite so hard on her lip with concentration that the salty taste of blood flooded her mouth.

The noise of grating, grinding metal was such that it seemed to the occupants of the wag to completely overtake the other sounds from outside, filling the wag with an eardrum-bursting noise that made it hard to think.

And then, suddenly, the wing of the wag had passed beyond the rear of the vehicle it had been pushing against, that vehicle now pushed to one side, the occupants thrown across the interior and abandoning their blasters.

"Shit!" Ayesha cursed as the wag, suddenly released from the restraints of the metal bulk in front of it, shot out across the gap between the convoy and the wall of the rock arena. She stamped on the brake, making the vehicle skid on the uneven and loose surface, the suddenly locked tires searching for purchase on the shifting sands of the desert floor. The wag skidded in a circle, and she righted it in time to be facing the entrance at the rear of the Charity convoy. The only problem with this being that the path to the entrance was blocked by the circling wags of the Hellbenders' convoy, with Correll in the lead, approaching at speed through the dust of the storm and conflict.

"Aw, fuck," Claudette muttered. To get this far, this close to getting away, and then to get chilled by the very people who were supposed to be on your side... The dark-skinned girl watched openmouthed and wide-eyed as the lead wag closed on theirs, seeing through the grime and dust an equally surprised gaunt face as the driver jammed on his brakes and went into a skid, attempting to pilot his wag into the narrow space between the women's wag and the convoy that still stood in the arena.

Ayesha mirrored the actions of Correll, swinging the wheel of her wag and risking crushing the wag against the rock wall.

The two wags swung violently away from each other, like two magnetic poles that repel, but it was too little, too late. The front wings of both wags locked together in a squeal of metal, the opposing forces of each powerful wag engine forcing the metal into ridiculous shapes, pushing at each other so that the steering wheels in each cab failed to respond to the drivers.

Ayesha found herself thrown across the wheel, the hard plastic jarring and bruising her chest and stomach, knocking the air from her and leaving her dazed and confused. She shook her head to try to clear it, and felt the need to violently vomit as a result, a need that was increased when she looked around to ask Claudette how she was, and found the dark-skinned girl staring at her from one life-less eye, the other impaled with a long sliver of toughened glass from the windshield that had been worked loose from its frame by the twisting, distorting effects of the impact and had driven through her left eye and into the brain, lobotomizing her so that she died blissfully unaware of the pain it had caused her.

Ayesha puked over the dead girl, then heaved and spit out the bile that tasted raw in her mouth. She looked over the back seat. Some of the women were unconscious from the impact, but most were still able to move.

"I dunno," Ayesha muttered, "we'll just have to try and get out of the battlefield and wait for the result."

"Some good you've been," moaned one of the women, picking herself up.

Ayesha boiled inside. She'd tried, as hard as she could, and all she had was this?

"Fuck it, look after yourselves, then," she spit before opening the wag door on her side of the cab and sliding out into the sandstorm.

Outside, the Hellbenders were pouring out of their wags, their circling assault action having been halted by the crash between Correll and Ayesha. The leader of the Hellbenders was one of the first to hit the desert floor, having given orders over the radio for his people to disperse and begin the fight on the outside. Correll grasped a Heckler & Koch in one hand, and in the other he had a long-bladed saber that was of tooled steel and had been taken from the redoubt. Coming face-to-face with him, Ayesha stopped dead in her tracks, taken aback by the wild-eyed, gaunt man, and also by the fact that he had a long metal box strapped to his chest. Whatever was in it, it wasn't just being used as armor, and Ayesha practically shrunk beneath his gaze.

Jak, Dean and Danny were out of the second wag quickly, and the bespectacled youth led the way through the crowd of wild-eyed fighters to where the crash had occurred.

Correll was looming over Ayesha through the dust and smoke. She was sure that he would cut her down where she stood, especially as she was the daughter of Baron Al Jourgensen, his sworn foe. In the heat of those eyes, all bargains would be forgotten.

And yet he looked at her with eyes that suddenly cleared from their fires of fury, and just for a second registered an infinite tenderness.

"Poor child," he murmured before brushing past her with a wild yell and heading for the front of the convoy, where Baron Al's wag was just moving off.

"Ayesha!" Danny yelled, coming upon her out of the dust and grasping her. "You're okay!"

"Just," she replied, "and it won't stay that way unless we find some way of getting away from this slaughterhouse."

"This way," Jak said, "find wag."

"Yeah, good idea," Dean agreed. "Where the hell is everyone?"

"I, my dear boy, have finally got here," Doc said, coming up to them, "but of the others..."

Dean and Jak looked around them. It was almost impossible to see in the swirling dust and smoke of the battlefield what was going on. Ryan and Krysty had to be in among it, and from the sounds of blasterfire and close combat, it seemed that mere yards away the sec men from Charity had emerged from their wags to take up hand-to-hand combat with the Hellbenders. They were forced to, as the sudden static nature of the other vehicles had left them with no target large or visible enough to fire at from inside the safety of the wags.

Suddenly, Dean caught sight of Krysty's Titian flame of hair moving freely in the breeze as the woman encountered a sec man from Charity. As she moved nearer, they could see that the sec man had mistaken her for one of the more docile women from the wag, and was trying to trap her with a view to carrying her off. He had a Glock handblaster and a skinning knife, which he used to thrust at her, driving her backward. What he failed to realize was that she was leading him on, goading him into more confident, harder thrusts with the knife, nearly puncturing her skin. And then his confidence got the better of him, and he made his big mistake. He grinned with a leer and thrust the knife to try to rip the shoulder of her coat, to expose her bare flesh. But Krysty stepped under the blow and struck at his vulnerable side, striking below the heart with the heel of her hand. As the jarring blow turned the triumphant leer to a look of astonished agony, she drew back her arm and delivered a straight-fingered blow to his throat that ruptured the tissue within. He began to choke, and as he sank to the ground she raised one leg and delivered a chilling blow with the silvered toe of her boot, striking him at the joint of the jaw, just below the temple. The trauma to the brain finished off whatever life the sec man still had within him.

"Nice to know you haven't lost your touch," the one-eyed warrior commented as he emerged from the dust and smoke, the Steyr in one hand and his panga in the other. "I don't know who's chilling who out there, and I don't think they do, either. My bet is we should get the hell out and regroup on the outside of the rocks, try and see what the hell is actually happening in here."

"We could take one of the wags at the rear," Dean suggested. "They've all gone blood-chill crazy out here, and I figure we should just shoot whoever gets in the way— can't trust any of them not to chill us."

Ryan agreed. "Only problem is, how do we let J.B. and Mildred know what the hell is going on?"

"HOW THE HELL are we supposed to know what's going on here?" the Armorer asked Jenny as the wag spun yet again in the increasingly dense mix of smoke and dust that rose on the arena.

"And how the hell am I supposed to know?" the woman snapped back.

"It's your operation, not ours," Mildred replied with a bite in her tone. "And what was that about abandoning the wags because they've crashed?" she added, referring to the garbled command from Correll that had emerged from the static and confusion of the radio.

"Shit, how do I know? It must be something that happened back there."

"How about making it happen here?" the Armorer suggested, sighting the wag driven by Tulk and bearing Baron Tad Hutter begin to move out into the middle of the arena.

"What?"

"He's moving, and we can't keep going in circles forever," J.B. said sharply. "So brace yourselves."

With which the Armorer put his foot down hard to the floor of the wag and shot toward the moving wag. Tulk had moved forward cautiously, trying to sight the assault convoy as it came around again, and this had given J.B. the slight edge that he needed. As the baron's wag moved outward, J.B. drove straight at it, flinging his wag to one side at the last moment so that it caught the baron's wag with a broadside that made it skid in a circle, the front wing badly dented and bent in so that it trapped the front wheel and prevented it from rotating.

Behind the Armorer, the other Hellbenders' wags skidded to a halt in order to avoid crashing into the leading vehicle, and the doors opened to discharge a crew hell-bent on revenge.

"My God, John, you could have given us a little more warning that that," Mildred gasped, the air driven from her by the impact.

"Had to be done," the Armorer replied tersely. "Hutter was trying to get over to the other side."

"Why the hell would he do that?"

"My guess is he wants to grab the women in the confusion—shit, looks like Jourgensen had a similar idea— get the fuck out!" the Armorer yelled as another wag appeared in the center of the arena through the mist and smoke.

J.B. grabbed Mildred and pulled her through the door of the wag, diving for cover and carrying her with him as Jourgensen's wag pulled up too late to avoid a collision with the two wags that had already crashed into the middle of the arena.

"Tell me this isn't going to get worse," Mildred said as she saw Correll charging after the crashed wag, yelling at the top of his lungs.

"Dark night, I could tell you but I'd probably be lying," the Armorer replied. "Come on, let's see if we can get over to the other side. Ryan and Krysty were with Correll, so chances are they're still over there somewhere," he said, raising the M-4000 in order to cut a path through any firefight they may chance on. Mildred had her Czech-made ZKR to hand. It was hardly ideal conditions for a sharp-shooting target blaster such as the ZKR, but any handblaster would be effective in the close conditions.

Baron Al climbed from the wreck of his wag, still stunned by the impact of the crash, to come face-to-face with Tad Hutter, who had clambered from the wreckage of his own wag, leaving Tulk long chilled and impaled on the remains of the steering column, the dark metal protruding out of his back where the impact had driven it through his chest after the steering wheel had sheered off. He had died with the certain knowledge that his hated baron couldn't get out of the conflict alive.

"Jourgensen, what the fuck are you playing at?" Hutter yelled, leveling his blaster.

Baron Al looked at him with surprise, as though he couldn't quite believe what he was seeing or hearing.

"Me?" he said blandly.

"Asshole," Hutter muttered as he raised the blaster.

"No! Leave him—he's mine!" came a yell from behind Jourgensen that made both barons look around in surprise.

Correll was charging across the open space, oblivious of the carnage around and the blaster shots that strayed across his path. He had his saber raised, and was upon the startled Jourgensen before he had a chance to move.

"We've waited so long for this, you pox-riddled bastard, but at last you'll pay," he screamed, long strings of saliva hanging from his jaws as he set to the baron with a vengeance, the saber chopping through Jourgensen's flesh and bone, scoring nerves and gouging out muscle so that great gouts of blood flooded from his body. Jourgensen, still not fully alert and now aware only of his own defenselessness, realized too late what was happening to him, and went down under the frenzied attack.

Hutter raised his blaster to chill the mad dog and also to put Jourgensen out of his misery, but his sole attempt at charity for the baron of Charity was stopped by two streams of blasterfire that came his way from Jenny's and Rudi's Uzis. They'd heard their leader cry out and wanted him to achieve his revenge without interruption.

But in their single-minded desire, they had neglected

to watch their backs, and so found themselves open to blasterfire from those few sec men who had decided that they should keep a watch on their baron.

Jenny and Rudi weren't the only ones to leave themselves open in this manner. Correll was now in a world of his own, the chaos and carnage around him meaning nothing, failing to register in his addled brain. For Joseph Correll, the Hellbenders and the whole assault and ambush on the trade convoy between Summerfield and Charity was as of naught. The only thing that mattered was that Baron Al "Red" Jourgensen was now beneath his blade, the chilled corpse of the baron nothing more than a mess of offal as the saber hacked him into ever smaller pieces. Correll raised his head to the skies, clouded as they were with smoke, sand and the smell of destruction, and laughed long and loud. He looked over to where some of Jourgensen's sec men had emerged from the mists.

He knew what was to happen, but it no longer mattered. There was nothing now left for him to live for. His raison d'être was fulfilled. He turned to the sec men and raised the saber aloft triumphantly, laughing wildly and welcoming the hail of blasterfire that ripped into him. The metal box on his chest gave way under the hail of fire as it ripped into his exposed head and limbs, the stress on the primitive welding making it give way beneath the onslaught.

Correll stayed on his feet—kept partly upright by the force of the bullets ripping into him—long enough for the box to fall open, and its contents to finally be revealed.

The charred and semimummified remains of Correll's wife tumbled from the box and fell on the mutilated remains of her tormentor...followed closely by Correll's lifeless corpse.

The real battle was over. Now it was just a question of who would get out alive.

Chapter Twenty-Two

Dean, Jak and Danny backtracked through the sandstorm and smoke, each with his blaster at the ready, in search of a wag that could be used to get them out of the arena. Doc followed, bringing Ayesha with him. But the one-eyed man held back.

"What is it, lover?" Krysty asked him.

"J.B. and Millie," Ryan replied simply. "We need to find them. They won't know where we are."

"They might if they saw Correll," Krysty replied. "They knew he was in our wag, and they'd probably guess which direction to take."

"That's a lot of mebbes," Ryan said grimly. "I've got to try and find them."

"In this? We could wander forever and still not find them," Krysty told him.

"We?" Ryan queried, then grinned when he saw the expression on her face. "Okay, let's do it."

While Ryan and Krysty set off to try to find J.B. and Mildred, the other five in the group were making their way toward the rear of the convoy in search of a wag they could use.

"Shit, I'll be glad when we can get the hell out of here," Danny whispered to Dean.

Jak heard him and grinned with a vulpine relish. "No one get in our way," he said simply, a leaf-bladed knife appearing in his hand. "Get close, chill quick and quiet— no one guess where we are."

"You don't know how much I hope so," Danny murmured fervently.

The party of five had been lucky so far. The main hand-to-hand was taking part toward the middle of the desert floor, where the Hellbenders had rushed to take on the sec men as they emerged from their wags. So getting back as far as the rear of the convoy was a matter of keeping eyes and ears open and staying close to the wall. Jak, Dean and Doc knew their respective strengths and fighting skills, but Ayesha and Danny were still unknown quantities, so they didn't want to risk conflict unless it was absolutely necessary.

The last wag in the Charity convoy was nothing more than a personnel carrier, closed in with welded sheet metal and a few slots cut in the side for blasters to be pushed through. The slots were empty, and there were four people engaged in hand-to-hand combat around the vehicle, with as many corpses between them. Forced up close by the poor visibility, these three men and one woman were fighting full-on, handblasters trying to get into a position where they could get a clear shot.

Jak looked at Dean. "You take those two," he murmured, indicating a woman and man—one of whom Dean recognized as a Hellbender—up close to the wag. "And I take them," he added, indicating two men who were careering across the desert floor, locked in a deadly embrace, the only outcome of which could be one of them buying the farm.

Both of them would, if Jak had anything to do with it. Before his words had even died on the air, the albino hunter had slipped across the desert floor, through a cloud of dust and was up behind the grappling men. Even in the dull light, the leaf-bladed knife was an arc of gleaming steel as it cut through the air and then through flesh and artery. Jak had timed his movements precisely, so that the edge of the knife sliced the carotid artery of the man whose back was to him, catching him as he turned.

The knife caught the second man on the downstroke, as he stared at Jak in wide-eyed, openmouthed surprise. It was his last expression, as the knife swathed patterns in the dust and sliced open his throat, his life draining from his eyes as blood drained from his open throat.

The entire chilling had taken only a few seconds, in which time Dean had slipped through the smoke and approached the other fighting couple. He had the Hi-Power in his hand, and although it was risky to fire, in case the blaster noise attracted other combatants who may be near, two well-placed slugs should see the job done. The two combatants were so engrossed in their own personal struggle that they didn't notice the younger Cawdor approach them stealthily. Dean loosed two shots at less than three yards. Both were aimed for the head of each fighter, and in less than a second both struck home. The two combatants hit the desert floor unaware of how they had been chilled.

Jak turned and beckoned Doc, Danny and Ayesha forward. As they joined the pair, Jak and Dean were checking that the wag was empty. There was a corpse in the front, which Jak pulled out and discarded on the desert floor.

Dean turned with a puzzled expression. "Where have Krysty and Dad got to?"

THE ONE-EYED MAN and the red-haired beauty were, in fact, making their way toward the center of the arena in search of J.B. and Mildred. Given the degree of cover afforded by the sandstorm and the smoke that filled the area, it was easy to avoid hand-to-hand combat as long as you kept a sharp lookout for any warring factions. Ryan and Krysty found it easy to dodge around the skirmishes, and kept a sharp view for J.B. and Mildred.

The Armorer and Mildred were following much the same pattern. They had figured that Ryan and Krysty were likely to be in the direction that Correll had emerged from, so they were battling their way through the sand and smoke to try to locate their comrades, dodging the skirmishes that were taking place. The fighting was now localized, of necessity because of the conditions, and it was relatively easy to skip through the troubled patches and conserve ammo.

Nonetheless, when the two couples nearly ran into each other coming out of a bank of swirling sand, all four had their blasters raised lest trouble was in the offing.

"Dark night, thought we'd never find you," J.B. said laconically.

"Yeah. What took you so long?" Ryan replied with a wry smile, born of the harsh conditions, then added quickly, "the others are back this way securing a wag. Let's go."

The four companions made their way back across the battlefield, sticking to the outer edge of the arena to make quicker progress and avoid conflict. By the time they arrived at the wag, Jak had gotten the machine going, and the engine was ticking over.

"John Barrymore, my dear doctor," Doc enthused, "we had some doubt over whether we would see you again."

"It'll take more than this for you to be rid of me, you old buzzard," Mildred replied as the four piled into the wag.

"Go, Jak," Ryan snapped as he closed the doors.

The albino hunter wasted no time. Putting the wag into reverse, he roared back toward the entrance to the arena and away from the other wags in the convoy. In the dismal light of the storm, he was unwilling to risk reversing the wag all the way through the entrance and perhaps crashing it, so he put the vehicle into a skid and turned it so that he could hit the entrance head-on and get out of the war zone.

As they broke through the almost solid wall of sand that was swirling at the entrance, where the storm was being forced through the restricted gap, the air suddenly became clearer, vision less impaired.

"Where you want me to stop?" Jak asked.

"I don't," Ryan replied.

"But I thought—" Krysty began, before Ryan interrupted her.

"Yeah, we were gonna regroup and evaluate, but that's all changed. That coldheart hell in there is just gonna sort itself out in its own time. We need to head back to the redoubt, see what happens then."

"Then I drive," Jak said simply, increasing his speed as they pulled away from the arena of chilling and headed back for the Hellbenders' deserted base.

The redoubt was eerily quiet when they reached base. They parked the wag, showered wearily and prepared food and drink in a subdued manner, hardly speaking. It was only when they were seated in the now all too empty meeting room that Ayesha spoke.

"Do you think any of the others will get back?"

Ryan shook his head. "I doubt it. They were ready to fight to the chilling, like their leader. Correll was that fanatical, and he instilled that into all of them. Even if a few of them survive the slaughterhouse, I doubt if they'll have the strength left to get back, even if they get any of the wags going."

"But we owe it to them to wait," Krysty added.

They left it for two days, using the time to rest and recuperate. Ryan and J.B. scoured the redoubt for any armory materials that had been left behind, of which there were few; Mildred and Krysty had better luck with the med lab supplies; while Doc and Jak squabbled good-naturedly over the self-heat and food and drink supplies.

Dean, meanwhile, joined Danny and Ayesha in starting to explore the old tech that was in the redoubt. From the few things the young men had been able to teach each other, Ayesha was able to add a little from what she had picked up watching her father. It didn't take any of them much further on, and Dean soon lost heart about being able to crack the secrets of the CD-ROM in their possession, but it was a step in the right direction.

Dean also noticed something developing between Danny and Ayesha that made what happened a few days later completely unsurprising.

As they ate, Ryan said, "I figure it's pretty clear that no one's coming back. And I also figure our chance of getting any of that old tech is pretty much gone, as well. There isn't enough here for all of us to survive, so I reckon we get a good night's rest, get it together in the morning, then jump through the mat-trans."

"That should be interesting to see," Danny remarked, Dean having made him familiar with the machine.

"That suggests you're not coming with us," the one-eyed man said.

Danny shook his head, then looked at Ayesha. "No, there's a lot here for us to find out, then mebbe we'll try a jump and see what happens, or mebbe just go back to Charity and see if we can get at the rest of the old tech. But, seeing as you'll be gone and there'll be food and water to spare, mebbe we'll just stay here for a while, out of harm's way," he finished.

"Shame. I'll kinda miss you," Dean said simply.

Ayesha looked at the companions. "I guess we'll miss you, too. But this is something we need to do for ourselves."

"Parting is such sweet sorrow. You know, that's a phrase I recall from somewhere, but it eludes me somewhat," Doc said as he took Ayesha's hand and kissed it. "No matter—the origin is unimportant when the sentiment remains constant."

"You are one weird old guy, but I do like you," Ayesha replied with a soft smile.

The companions were gathered in the mat-trans unit to enter the chamber and jump, ready for whatever fate may throw at them next. They turned and entered the chamber, having made their goodbyes. Dean was the last to enter, and as he did he stopped and turned to Danny.

"Remember, as soon as the mechanism locks then the comp starts charting the course. Never been able to stand outside and see it, but if you watch, it may teach you something. And mebbe one day we'll cross and you'll be able to tell me," he said.

"Bet on it," Danny said with a tinge of regret in his voice.

Dean's last view of Danny and Ayesha was as he closed the door. He could tell that they were already poring over the comp console, watching intently for the mechanism to grid into action.

Dean seated himself, with some regret, on the chamber floor and watched as the white, curling mist began to rise from the circular disks inset into the chamber's floor and ceiling, and he and his companions stood poised on the verge of another leap into the unknown.